D0349881

The Man with the President's Mind

TED ALLBEURY

Simon and Schuster   New York

COPYRIGHT © 1978 BY TED ALLBEURY
ALL RIGHTS RESERVED
INCLUDING THE RIGHT OF REPRODUCTION
IN WHOLE OR IN PART IN ANY FORM
PUBLISHED BY SIMON AND SCHUSTER
A DIVISION OF GULF & WESTERN CORPORATION
SIMON & SCHUSTER BUILDING
ROCKEFELLER CENTER
1230 AVENUE OF THE AMERICAS
NEW YORK, NEW YORK 10020

"AS TIME GOES BY"
© 1931 WARNER BROS. INC.
ALL RIGHTS RESERVED
USED BY PERMISSION

DESIGNED BY ELIZABETH WOLL
MANUFACTURED IN THE UNITED STATES OF AMERICA

1   2   3   4   5   6   7   8   9   10

LIBRARY OF CONGRESS CATALOGING IN PUBLICATION DATA

ALLBEURY, TED.
   THE MAN WITH THE PRESIDENT'S MIND.

   I. TITLE.
PZ4.A415MAN   [PR6051.L52]   823'.9'14   77-15494
ISBN 0-671-22908-7

To my son David
and his pretty wife, Pauline

The final lesson of the Cuban missile crisis is the importance of placing ourselves in the other country's shoes. During the crisis President Kennedy spent more time trying to determine the effect of a particular course of action on Khrushchev or the Russians than on any other phase of what he was doing.

—FROM *13 Days,* BY ROBERT F. KENNEDY

. . . you will have noticed that I have not mentioned Berlin at all. That place is no more than a geographical definition to me . . . pure theater that may be safely left to the Russians.

—RADIO MESSAGE FROM GENERAL EISENHOWER TO FIELD MARSHAL MONTGOMERY, MARCH 31, 1945

The forces of peace and progress now have a visibly increased preponderance and may be in a position to lay down the direction of international politics.

—ANDREI GROMYKO, FOREIGN MINISTER OF THE SOVIET UNION, IN *Kommunist,* SEPTEMBER 1975

War does not have a rational beginning, and we must be aware that the Soviet Union is developing forces to win.

—U.S. AIR FORCE GENERAL GEORGE S. BROWN, CHAIRMAN OF THE JOINT CHIEFS OF STAFF, FEBRUARY 1976

	U.S.	U.S.S.R.
Armed forces	2,084,350	4,412,000
Tanks	10,000	42,000
Strategic missiles	1,710	2,378
Mega tonnage	4,000	10,000
Strategic aircraft	463	135
Tactical aircraft	8,500	6,100
Major combat ships	182	226
Aircraft carriers	14	1
Missile submarines	41	73
Attack submarines	73	253

—*Newsweek,* March 1, 1976

chapter
1

There was a threat of rain from the heavy clouds lying still and ominous on the other side of the river, but the forecast had said the rain would hold off until midevening.

They had watched him hurry down the narrow steps and open the door of the black 1970 Buick, and they had followed, two cars behind, as he passed the Veterans Administration Building, heading due east. They had lost him at the lights near the Pension Building but picked him up again on Indiana Avenue. Then Pennsylvania Avenue, Fourteenth Street and U.S. 1 to the other side of the Potomac.

The man in the Buick was taking things very steadily, but the heavy Friday-night traffic gave them good enough cover. By the time they turned off at Twentieth Street the flow of vehicles was thinning out, but as they hit the Arlington Ridge Road a military convoy broke up the traffic flow. On Mount Vernon Avenue the black Buick pulled into the parking lot of a diner. They were just short of Hume.

Murphy took the station wagon down to the next intersection, drove around the block and went back up the highway. He pulled into the diner area and parked in the second row of cars, directly behind the Buick.

They sat there smoking and waiting, and it was almost twenty minutes before he came out. He was with another man, and the two of them strolled across the parking lot talking and laughing. The other man was Ustenko from the Soviet Embassy. Ostensibly assistant press officer, actually a captain in the KGB.

As they stood there talking, a man trotted out of the diner, heading in their direction. He was wearing a white apron, and a paper fluttered in his hand. He pointed at the paper, talking to Ustenko, who laughed and took out his wallet and gave him a bill. Then, as the man in the apron turned to go, the man from the Buick suddenly put both hands to his chest. His face was distorted as if he were in pain. His legs gave, and he fell forward, his hands still clutching his chest as he lay on his side. One leg slowly bent up to his chest, straightened again, and then he was still.

The man at the wheel stubbed out his cigarette.

"What d'you make of that?"

"Could be a knife wound, or a heart attack. You wanna go and look?"

"No. Let's see what happens. You recognized Ustenko?"

"Sure, look—the little guy in the apron's heading back for the diner. Probably going to phone for an ambulance."

"Is Ustenko off limits over here?"

"You betcha."

As they watched, Ustenko bent down and touched the man on the ground. Then he stood up, looked around slowly and carefully and walked to the black Buick. He tried to open the trunk, but it was locked. He hesitated for a moment, then walked quickly down the line of parked cars to a white Volkswagen. They heard the engine start up and then the car swept past them in the darkness, turning left as it got to the road.

Only minutes later they heard the siren and saw the flashing light of the ambulance as it turned into the parking lot. The man in the apron ran out waving as the ambulance stopped alongside the prone figure on the tarmac. A doctor in a white coverall jumped down, stethoscope swinging, and they saw him bend down over the man on the ground.

"Let's see what he's got to say."

"You go, Murphy, I'll keep watch here. You never know, there may be others we haven't seen yet."

Murphy had strolled over to the little group, and as he got there the doctor stood up and looked at the man from the diner.

"He's dead."

Murphy held out his card. "Murphy, doc, CIA. What was the cause of death?"

The young doctor stared as if hypnotized at the ID card, aware of the lines of text and "CIA" in large yellow letters overlaying the print. His head came back up to look at Murphy's face. "It's not possible to say. Looks like a cardiac arrest, but there'll have to be a postmortem." He turned to the man in the apron. "Did you see it happen?"

"Sure—he put his hands like this on his chest and fell down."

"What's your name, mister?" Murphy looked amiable enough, but customers who die on the premises are no good for any restaurant and the little man said, "Is nothing to do with me, I just run the diner."

"What's your name?"

"Busoni, Emilio Busoni."

"What did this guy eat?"

"He eat nothing. Just a coffee. His friend eat a— Say, where is his friend?"

"He's gone, Mr. Busoni, don't worry about him. Did they sit at a table or at the counter?"

"They just stood. Drinking coffee, and the other guy had a beef sandwich special."

"Anything pass between them, papers, a package, anything like that?"

"I don't think so. But I can't be sure." He shrugged. "I don't watch the customers, I'm too busy, mister."

Murphy turned to the doctor. "Where will you take him now?"

"He'll have to go to the morgue in Arlington. That's regulations."

"OK. I'll travel with him. We'll want an autopsy."

Murphy strolled back to the station wagon, and Peters rolled down the window.

"He's dead. Looks like a heart attack. I'll go back in the

11

meat wagon and you take over the Buick. Get the lab boys on it and don't let anybody else near it. See you back at Langley in about a couple of hours."

The sign on the desk said "J. Shapiro" and the man behind it was leaning forward, rocking slowly and gently as he looked at the two men on the other side.

"I don't see the point, Murphy. The lab has been over the car. You've seen their report. There's a special report on the contents of the trunk and you've seen that too. Zilch. And the postmortem confirms that the kid died from natural causes."

The thick gray eyebrows went up in interrogation and the mouth was pursed to emphasize that his time was being wasted.

"There must be some explanation, Joe."

"Of course there is. There's an explanation for everything. But this particular explanation doesn't concern you and me. You've got a coupla dozen tapes covering a day's broadcasts from three or four radio stations. You've got a bundle of newspapers from around the country. So what? Forensic has been over them with microscopes, magic potions, infrared, quartz and Christ knows what. Ciphers has been over everything for codes. National Security has had a go at them, and the conclusions are the same. Just some tapes and some newspapers. Nothing more. The chief printer at each newspaper has checked 'em. The radio companies have checked the tapes. They've even checked the recordings against the record tapes they hold for the FCC. Identical except for the actual tape base used. So what d'you want?" He looked from one to the other, his face portraying sweet reasonableness but his shoulders indicating impatience.

Murphy wasn't ready to give up yet, despite the signs of irritation.

"What was on the tapes?"

"Like I said, a whole day's programming. News, music—all the usual crap. Listen to them yourself."

"And the stations?"

"WABC New York, KNX Los Angeles, WRC Washington and KMOX St. Louis."

"And the newspapers?"

"Here's the list. Read it yourself." Shapiro pushed across a single sheet of paper, and Murphy read it carefully. The list said:

Abilene Reporter
Seattle Post-Intelligencer
Chicago Tribune
Calgary Herald
Edmonton Journal
Austin Citizen
Los Angeles Times
Burlington Free Press
New York Times
Christian Science Monitor

Murphy shifted uncomfortably in his chair. "Maybe we should strip the kid's room down to the bone."

"Oh for God's sake, Murphy. There was nothing there."

Shapiro shuffled through the papers and held one up, reading it carefully. Then he shook his head. "A few clothes, a Jap radio set—the technical boys checked it and it hasn't been modified, not even repaired. Sells for ten-fifty all over the country. Half a dozen soft-porn photographs. Ninety dollars fourteen cents in cash. A plastic kit, half finished, of a 747. That's it." He let the paper drop to his desk to mark its unimportance.

"Maybe just a couple of weeks, Joe. It's just a hunch."

Shapiro shook his head. "No way. We've got too much to do that's for real. Let's not waste time." And he stood up to end the interview.

Peters was the diplomat. "Maybe we could look through the reports in our own time, Joe." Shapiro smiled as he came around his desk. "OK. You're entitled. Anyway, it gave us an excuse to chuck out Ustenko. They didn't like that."

While he was talking he had leaned forward with his arms on the wooden lectern, and his face turned slightly sideways to avoid a shaft of late-afternoon sunlight that swept over

the tiers of students to illuminate the far side of the black-
board. Now that he had finished he stood up, shading his
eyes with his hand as he waited for their questions.

He was a handsome man, in his early fifties, and his optional general-psychiatry lectures tended to pull a preponderance of female students. There was one girl who had been
coming for two months and always asked a question. He'd
checked and found that she was a third-year engineering
student, but her questions showed that she was capable of
making penetrating judgments that always held a tinge of
criticism to cover her apparent devotion. She had waited on
this occasion, so that her question was the second.

"Does Professor Levin see a conflict between the reflex-
ology of Pavlov and the views of Vygotski?"

He put his hands casually on his hips and smiled in her
general direction. "There have always been conflicts of
theory in all the sciences, but in the example you give there
is least conflict of all. Vygotski established the 'cultural-
historical' view. It was this ability to stand back from con-
temporary research and assess the future effects of current
thinking that made Lenin's *Philosophical Notebooks* so important in influencing the early Five-Year Plans."

There had been the usual questions on Belinsky and
Dobrojubov and then he had escaped. There was a bundle
of mail in his locker, and a couple of phonograph records
that he had requested from the university record library. He
had waited almost three months for the new Ashkenazy, and
the Scott Joplin LP was an open sign of privilege.

He walked slowly to the canteen and joined the line. It
was fifteen minutes before he sat down at one of the long
tables. As he spooned out the yoghurt he read his mail. There
were invitations to seminars at Göttingen and Cornell Universities in the autumn, three scientific journals that he
subscribed to, an appointment with a doctor he had never
heard of for a health checkup, and a letter from his opposite number, the head of the psychology faculty at Moscow
University.

The final envelope was obviously feminine. Pale lilac, and
faintly perfumed as he tore it open. But the letter inside was
brief and official. He would attend another meeting in three

14

days' time. It came from the State Committee for Coordination of Scientific Research Work of the Council of Ministers of the USSR. The address was 11 Gorky Street, Moscow. That was the address he had had to go to for the interviews.

With subconscious caution he looked up from the pile of letters and checked to see if anyone was observing him. But nobody was even looking his way. They had said that the next interview would be the last.

No sound, no music, had ever affected him like this before, and he had almost forgotten for those minutes the purpose of his visit.

Across to the right was the orchestra, and the smiling conductor who faced the audience. A mass of shouting, whistling, applauding young people. And as the cheering grew louder the conductor turned again to face the orchestra, and, as his arms lifted, the fantastic music started again. The first time he had listened carelessly as the strings fought their battle with the tympani, mounting in scale and crescendo until the cymbal clash. Then it started, the soft magnificent melody that made him think of tsars on white horses slow-marching along the Nevsky Prospekt with the Imperial Cavalry spread out behind. And the voices as the crowd sang, the words confused against the orchestra; they sang as if it were a national anthem, and even in ignorance he was moved.

And now they sang it again, louder and clearer this time, the orchestra subdued; and he could just make out the words ". . . mother of the free, God who made thee mighty make thee mightier yet . . ."

He lifted the glasses and focused them on the girl. She was beautiful, there was no doubt about that, but in that sea of open mouths hers was closed. She didn't sing. And he could see the sparkle of tears that ran down her cheeks, and as he watched she brushed the back of her hand across her full soft mouth.

As the cheers seemed to shake the hall he looked across at Yerin, who was leaning forward with his elbows on the edge of the box. Yerin's face was impassive, and if he was affected by the music, or the response of the audience, he didn't show it.

It was the last night of the Proms, and they sat through to the end before he and the other embassy guests gathered up their things and walked down to the cars that were already waiting for them at the entrance to the Albert Hall.

Yerin suggested that the two of them walk. It was not far to the embassy in the private, tree-lined road alongside Hyde Park, And it was Yerin who broke the silence.

"What do you think?"

"The girl, you mean?"

"Of course."

"She's very beautiful. How long has she been a member?"

"Two years, maybe a little more. Haven't you seen the dossier?"

"Yes. I saw it in Moscow, but I don't remember all the details." He smiled at Yerin. "We've been busy on other things, you know."

Yerin nodded, without returning the smile. "How long has this operation been going on?"

"Just over a month."

"And they feel it is useful?"

"The orders were direct from the Presidium, comrade."

And they lapsed into silence as they approached the police sergeant, who nodded to them as they passed.

Ivan Slanski sat in the elegant room at the embassy, a decanter of whisky and a glass on the small circular table alongside his chair, the red-covered dossier closed on his lap.

He had only two days to make up his mind about the girl. Levin had picked her out himself from the photographs, and he could well understand why. Even in black and white her face was startlingly beautiful. The calm high brow, the fine eyebrows that emphasized the heavy-lidded eyes, the finely chiseled nose, and the big mouth with the heavy indentation on the upper lip, all contributed to a sensuality that was diluted only by the humanity of the dimples that touched the fine smile-lines that bracketed her lips.

There was a photograph of the girl in a bikini, the long black hair in strands across her cheeks so that you could see

16

the line of her slender neck as it swept to the square shoulders, where the shadow from her collarbones led the eye to the full breasts that seemed too heavy for the straining white halter to contain. The firm curved belly, the rounded hips that flowed into the long shapely legs, and the narrow white briefs that barely captured her sex.

He had heard the tape of her talk on "The Organization of Fine Gail and Fianna Fail and their effect on the Trade Unions in the Republic of Ireland." If you ignored the words it was undoubtedly a bedroom voice, a brown-eyed voice that would touch hearts and loins even when it was meant to touch minds.

Clodagh Maria Kevan could have been Italian or Spanish if it were not for her name, and the history of Ireland gives evidence enough to explain those Irish men and women whose beauty and bearing still bespeak those shipwrecked genes that once foundered on her western coast. At twenty-four, the girl's turbulent spirit had found a haven in the Communist Party. And this was the thing that prejudiced Slanski against her.

There are a hundred reasons why people join the Communist parties in Europe, and the reasons range from cold calm analysis to neurotic emotion. And the recruits of emotion are themselves full of conflicting motivations. There are the old warhorses of the Communist-oriented signposts: the Spanish Civil War, the Sword of Stalingrad, the twenty million Russian dead of World War II, "Lara's Theme" from *Zhivago*, Olga Korbut, Moscow Dynamo, Tchaikovsky's Piano Concerto in B Flat Major, and unrequited love.

Weaving a thread through many of the symptoms is one peculiar skein. The lifeline of the law-abiding in revolt. A man or woman whose life is largely law-abiding sometimes experiences the sharp edge of authority. An injustice from police or law court, school or employer, commerce or church can fan frustration into flaming hate for those who were previously respected the most. A lust to strike back can easily be assuaged inside a political party whose express purpose is to destroy those very institutions. Like the desperate pointing finger of the suicide note, the clandestine member of the party can find relief with like-minded souls and when

17

the day of the revolution dawns, who will be the masters then?

It is much easier to love a country that you have never seen, that is two thousand miles away, and that asks nothing but your faith. The rationalizations are easy, and if you can't think of them others can.

The dialectic of emotion is as potent as the dialectic of materialism.

Clodagh Kevan had been brought up in one of those rambling mansions that litter County Kerry and County Cork. But that life had ended when she was twelve, the day they had brought home her father's body, on the rough lath gate, still in its mudstained hunting jacket. His head askew and one hand trailing on the stairs as they staggered upstairs to his bedroom.

Then there were the years with her mother in the two big rooms on the top floor of the Georgian house in Dublin owned by her mother's brother. She had witnessed daily the deterioration of the pretty woman who played the part of a poverty-stricken Zelda Fitzgerald. There was little pretense, and the young girl saw the indifference of the men who supplied the whisky and left the crumpled notes on the mantlepiece. Long afterward she had seen their pictures and their names in the newspapers. Lawyers now, and artists, minister of this and that, poets and shopkeepers, politicians and company directors. Two or three had had the courage to attend her mother's funeral. By then the girl was at university, paid for by her uncle.

It was at the end of her second year that she had first slept with a man. He was a lecturer in the history faculty and both parties had deemed it an excellent arrangement. There had been some affection and enjoyment in the liaison, and although it wasn't in the contract, she was assured of her degree. And she had learned the power she commanded with her pretty face and exciting body. From time to time she used that power, sometimes with affection, never with love.

She had joined the Communist Party during a postgraduate year at the London School of Economics, and the local officials in Croydon had recognized immediately the value of her education and intelligence. She had attended only one open meeting. An old hand had given a hearts-and-flowers explanation of the Soviet reasoning behind the Helsinki détente conference, and at question time the pretty girl had ripped his analysis apart in a diatribe that quoted Presidium pronouncements and demonstrated an appreciation of Soviet policy over the previous five years. The case she made for détente was established with a chain of logical syllogisms that were irrefutable. There was silence as she sat down, because most members present couldn't make out whether she was for it or against it. But one man knew, and he was not going to let this sharp talent be compromised by carrying a membership card.

Clodagh Kevan had been invited to sit in on meetings at the stately home in Buckinghamshire where policy was discussed for hours on end. She argued with icy logic the case for the Soviet Union's withdrawing from the United Nations. The visitor from Moscow had smiled and asked her to make the case *against* withdrawal. And she had done just that.

But party life was not all meetings and policy discussions, and the girl was a bit too much of a good thing. The breathtaking beauty was enough, or just the dialectic, but the two together made for a richer diet than even the enthusiasts could digest, and the girl had slowly turned to other interests.

Slanski was worried about the twelve-year-old bit. There was going to be a payoff sometime for that period of parental indifference. And there was the strange attitude to sex. In no way could she be classified as promiscuous, but there was a readiness to make herself sexually available as a reward for compliance. There was the report of the comrade from King Street who had been working with her one evening on a report in the "safe" house in Kensington. By midnight he had had enough of the tables and charts illustrating comparative earning power and suggested that they complete the report the next day. When her words had failed to persuade him to finish the work she had calmly offered to satisfy him sexually. And there was the man named Jephcott, a party member of only six months, who worked for the Ministry of Defence and was besotted with the girl. He brought her

19

highly classified documents the way a dog brings a bone. He constantly proposed marriage and was insatiable in their brief sexual encounters.

However, bearing in mind the role they had in mind for her, even the negative factors could be advantageous. He would have to decide after the interview.

chapter
2

It had started that autumn evening way back in 1962 when the radio message from Moscow had ordered the Soviet missile ships to turn back from their Cuban destination. The lessons that had been learned in Moscow and Washington should have been the same. But they weren't.

Khrushchev had been on a visit to Bulgaria when he dreamed up the plan for nuclear warheads in Cuba. There had been a handful of hawks who went along with him, but the Red Army commanders had given it the coldest of receptions. So Nikita K. had bulldozed the Central Committee into reluctant agreement, and when it had fallen apart there were enough Politburo signatures on minutes of meetings to allow him to escape the normal fate of failed Soviet premiers and shufflle off into retirement.

The Planning and Analysis Directorate of the KGB had carried out its routine evaluation of the Cuban affair, and its report had gone through the usual channels without comment. When, in 1972, the KGB moved its operational functions to the big new complex out on the Moscow ring road, the report got a routine reread. That was the start of Operation 471.

There had been two veins of gold in the Directorate's routine sludge, but it had taken the perception of Ivan Slanski to recognize them.

The report contained the first-ever reference to "the intelligence of intention." And had recorded the evaluation team's opinion that in the coming decade it was going to be more important to know what the reaction of the Soviet Union's enemies, the United States and China, would be to Soviet world plans, rather than the "hard" intelligence of weapons and strike power. It recommended a shift of resources and effort to a new penetration of the decision-making apparatus in Washington and Peking. And from this recommendation flowed their analysis of Kennedy's role in the Cuban debacle. And they underlined what should have been obvious. For all the checks and balances of Congress, the Senate, the Pentagon and the machinery of state, when it came to war-like action, in the United States it was one man who decided. The President.

Operation 471 had put together a small expert team that had monitored continuously all those factors of personality, background, health and intelligence that could affect the decision-making of the four American Presidents from 1972 onward. And after President Langham's election they were ordered to start Phase 2 of Operation 471: a man was to be recruited who would be the analog of the U.S. President.

Ivan Slanski had been promoted to full colonel in the KGB. He was forty-three, tall, slim, with a rather sad sallow face. From Moscow University he had gone to the Ministry of Culture, and from there his languages had edged him into the Novosti Press Agency, which he had served in the United States and Ireland as a journalist. He had been brought back to Moscow on the direct instruction of the KGB and had been employed in Directorate S of the First Chief Directorate. Directorate S is responsible for the selection, training and deployment of KGB agents who operate abroad, and the United States was Slanski's special province. Although he had been outstandingly successful in running two groups of illegals, one in New York and the other in Washington, he was essentially an administrator. His analysis of situations was extraordinarily accurate, both about people and about events, and he had that special gift, an ability to anticipate, an eye for a trend.

He had set up Operation 471 in a suite of rooms on the top floor of one of Moscow's more modern hotels, the National. With the hotel's constant flow of visitors, it provided perfect cover. The massive array of aerials on the flat roof above pointed westward to the various capitals of Europe and was invisible from any part of the city.

Although it was barely three o'clock in the afternoon it was dark, and Slanski stood at one of the windows, his hand holding the curtain aside as he looked out. In the far distance he could see the lights of a train as it pulled out of the Savelovsky station. And farther east the red light flashed continuously from the top of the TV tower block. The thick snow looked gray, with double black ribbons where the traffic had cleared the main roads. And from the look of the heavy sky there was more snow on the way. As he turned away from the window there was a knock on the door, and it opened for a man in a fur hat and a heavy winter coat.

Panov nodded to Slanski and shook his coat and hat before hanging them on the old-fashioned clothes-rack. He walked across to the table, rubbing his hands. He looked over at Slanski. "Any whisky around, Ivan?"

Slanski waved to the array of bottles, glasses and fruit on the wooden sideboard. He half smiled. "Help yourself."

Boris Panov, a KGB major, was the oldest member of the control team on Operation 471, and the toughest. His stocky body with its barrel chest and his red raw face were an accurate picture of the man. Brought up in an orphanage, he had joined the Red Army, and, as with many others, the war had established him. After the war his six years with the GRU, the Red Army's own intelligence service, had shown him to have all those qualities of resourcefulness and cunning that the service demanded. His total commitment to the Army made him naturally aloof from politics, and his transfer to Operation 471 had given the team a formidable advocate for military aggression as the solution to most political problems. He was an expert on American military tactics and Pentagon thinking, and he had been made responsible for setting up the Phase 2 operational headquarters at Kiev.

He sat down opposite Slanski at the long table, the whisky

and a glass in front of him. Loosening his collar button, he leaned back and looked across at Slanski.

"Well, it's ready, comrade."

"Everything?"

"The building work is done, the staff is already down there, and we've trained a special security unit to guard the installation. The service for the tapes and newspapers is behind schedule—you'd better kick their asses in Washington."

"We didn't put a high priority on it at this stage."

"The unit down there is being run in, they can't establish methods or techniques if the stuff isn't available. There are technical problems we need to solve."

"Like what?"

"The radio programs have to be rerun off the original tapes to get them onto the big Revox spools, and because of the difference between the voltage when they're recorded and when they're played back we are having to use a variable transformer."

"What about the TV programs?"

"We've bought completely new equipment. We're standardized on Sony at both ends now."

"What about the people who have been doing the conversion work?"

Panov half smiled. "They'll be going as a team to a special project. No problems there."

"What if they talk?"

"They won't. Forget it. Just leave it to me."

Slanski opened his mouth as if he were going to ask another question, thought better of it and was silent for a few seconds. Panov looked back at him as if challenging him to pursue the point. When Panov reached for his glass Slanski spoke.

"We had the final instructions from the Presidium subcommittee today."

Panov looked up, his eyebrows raised quizzically. "And?"

"And we have to make the choice in the next three days."

"Well, the hard work has been done, thank God."

Slanski leaned forward, his arms on the table, his hands flat on the table. "Do you think this is going to work, Boris?"

Panov's big hand unbuttoned his tunic and eased his belt.

"The basic thinking is fine, comrade. A lot depends on the man we choose, and his ability to absorb the material he gets. But, after all, he's only one checkpoint. Everything else will go on as usual. Most of the time our decisions will be taken off all the normal data. But I can remember the Cuban time. The strategy, the objectives, were all worked out, but the Americans discovered what was going on four days too early, and we were caught napping. For ten days everybody was sitting there trying to work out what Kennedy's reaction would be if we did this or that. Khrushchev listened to anybody who'd ever met Kennedy. As you well know, from the original evaluation, most of the hard military guesses we had were right on target, but in the end those bastards chipped away at us until it was just Kennedy versus Khrushchev. Twice Khrushchev made clumsy moves, and in the end he had no choice but to back down. He didn't *know* enough to do otherwise.

"When you set up this operation it meant that we were in a position to know a hell of a lot more about the American President, and in Phase Two we shall have another piece of insurance. Just imagine the situation we shall certainly arrive at. We only need traditional troops and weapons to take what we want—provided the Americans don't use nuclear tactical weapons. Do we give them a sign that if *they* use nuclear toys we'll carry out Khrushchev's old threat and bury them? Or does that put Congress behind him? The High Command will say their say, the Presidium will give its views, and they won't agree. Then we shall have our man. *He* can say. It's not a crystal-ball operation, it's a man who has the President's mind. Put at its very lowest I'd rather have that man than not have him. He'll be more accurate than a team of experts, that's for sure. Even if he's wrong we shall be no worse off. And if we think he's wrong we can ignore him. We shall have done everything we can to get the right answer."

Slanski smiled. "You'd make a wonderful uncle, Boris."

Panov half smiled as he stood up.

Marshal of the Red Army Chuikov, after forty years in the Red Army, was oblivious to the snow that slanted between him and his companion, and his bright-blue eyes were intent on the other man's face as he spoke. Andropov, head of the KGB, was aware of the wetness that ran from his hat down both sides of his neck and the clammy feel of wet trousers against his legs. But he listened intently to what Chuikov was saying.

"It's not Panov who worries me, my friend, it's Slanski. He's brainy all right, but he strikes me as a weak man. And that could be dangerous."

"In what way, Marshal?"

Chuikov put his head on one side, and the alert cockerel's eyes had all that peasant shrewdness that had brought him success.

"You choose a man—this professor fellow, or some other—and you set him up to think like the President of the United States. You give him Panov as his hawk adviser. You give him Slanski as his soft-pedal man. So it's two out of three who will be seeing everything from an American point of view."

"But they will all be doing that—even Panov."

Chuikov clicked his teeth with impatience. "You don't understand, comrade. Panov is a military man. He won't be dealing in all this psychological bullshit. Just military facts. The other two are civilians, there will be no restraints on their thinking. If they don't think like Americans we're wasting our time. But if they do think like Americans where does that begin and end? That's what I ask you."

"It will be up to the Presidium to accept or ignore the advice we get from Operation 471. It can always be negative."

Chuikov's gloved finger poked at Andropov's chest. "You wait and see, my boy. I was in the Kremlin for twelve days while the Cuban affair was on, and any bastard who had even said hello to Kennedy was treated as if he were a damned oracle. And the same could happen this time. But this time it wouldn't be turning back a handful of merchant ships. You can't turn back ICBMs when you've pressed the button, my friend."

"So what do you suggest, Marshal?"

"I don't suggest anything, Andropov. It's your people's

idea, and the Presidium has given you your orders. All I say is watch these people very carefully."

Chuikov's raw red face was a reflection of a lifetime's experience of top-level maneuverings, and Andropov was already aware that with Operation 471 he was walking on very thin ice. He wasn't even sure now that the Red Army was not playing a separate game of its own. Maybe Chuikov and others had already picked out Operation 471 as a tool for their own plans or a sacrificial goat if something didn't work out. Maybe it was less of an exercise than the Presidium had indicated. Maybe his guess about Berlin was only part of the story. When his eyes went back to Chuikov's face he saw the crinkled knowingness at the corners of his eyes and he turned, stamping his feet.

"I shall be very careful, Marshal, you can be sure of that."

chapter
3

On the day that Langham became the new President of the United States, detailed instructions had gone to the KGB residents at the embassies in Washington, London and Mexico City to provide maximum cooperation to the specialist teams that were already on their way from Moscow.

The team instructions were to obtain every possible piece of information concerning Theodore "Teddy" Langham. His parents, childhood, education, medical record, hobbies, girl friends, sporting interests, finances, business interests, psychological makeup; his cronies, his vices and virtues.

There were hundreds of journalists, writers and broadcasters covering much of the same ground. They provided fifty percent of the routine material for comparatively little cost, and their simultaneous activities provided ideal cover for the KGB teams.

At the end of six weeks there were 521 six-by-four-inch fiches of microfilm in Moscow. They weighed four pounds nine ounces and held just over 140,000 documents, reports, magazine and newspaper cuttings, photographs, medical certificates, school reports and all the paper sludge that records a man's life in a high-technology nation.

Slanski had sat in front of the visual display unit looking at a couple of hundred key documents. Deciphering the

scrawls of country doctors, high-school teachers, commanding officers and a whole raft of politicians and businessmen.
The data-preparation section in the new headquarters building had card-punched every single detail, cross-referencing
sources and documents, grading reliability. At 25,000 cards
an hour the team had taken a week, with an extra day for
edits. The ocean of information had been transferred to
mag-tape as a data base split into thirty-one categories.

Teddy Langham was fifty-two. An alumnus of the University of Texas, born in Wichita Falls on October 24, 1928.
He had never completely lost his Texas drawl and he had
never tried to. The words he used were more important than
the accent, and they had more of the ring of Harvard Business School than of the wide-open spaces. The GOP had
reckoned that at long last they had found their John F. Kennedy. And Teddy Langham meshed easily with one and all.
He didn't get into the water with them, but he knew what
made them tick.

It had been a strange campaign, a novel campaign, because it was Langham's view that the American public was
tired of the party jamborees. His appeal had almost been
over the heads of the professional politicians, direct to the
people. And to the horror of his professionals he had publicly praised the virtues of his opponent.

The polls indicated a landslide, but there were solid
doubts from the old China hands who did the wheeling and
dealing. But for the first time they had a candidate who
appealed not only to the traditional Republican voter but
also to that influential middle mass of the working popula-
tion. When the creative people, the writers, the film stars
and the music men got on the bandwagon it looked like a
foregone conclusion. But Langham had known that the
months between nomination and the November election
would see a drawing back from the almost unknown new
boy in favor of the professional politician put up by the
Democrats. The electorate was sick of the professionals, but
wondered if maybe Harry Truman hadn't been a one-of-a-
kind President. Langham had nodded and smiled at the advice he constantly got from his campaign staff and had
carried on the only way he knew. He had only one advan-

tage over the professionals—he understood ordinary people.

When Teddy Langham had set himself up in Houston as a management consultant he had netted five thousand dollars in the first year. And he learned a lesson. You can talk Harvard Business School talk only to fellow alumni. The small businessmen were spellbound by the words and they could grasp the thread of the theory, but it was impossible for them to apply the thinking to their own small and medium-sized companies. Their businesses were not just dollar-making machines, they were a way of life. They were good at their jobs and they just wanted to be better. They didn't even want to be Standard Oil or Du Ponts. In the second year he had made fifty thousand and he had learned a lot about small and medium-sized businesses and their owners and workers.

Gradually his business management turned to arbitration, and he had learned another lesson. If you said the truth out loud, and eschewed the rituals of negotiation, you could settle most strikes in a day. In the third year he was earning as much from unions as from employers. He was frequently described as a business psychiatrist, but it was far from the truth. He was just an experienced, sensible, honest man. And he was never sure whether this was a strength or a weakness, but he spent little time analyzing the problem. He had slid into politics almost without noticing.

When it was all over there had been no landslide, just a reasonable workable majority, and there were very few who recognized that Langham had done it again. He had won the day, but the professionals had not been exposed. He had attributed the victory to them. When the electorate had gone into the voting booths, old party strings, to both pockets and hearts, had drawn votes back to traditional patterns. As Khrushchev himself had once said, "Success has a thousand fathers; failure is an orphan."

The team that had worked on establishing the criteria for choosing the Russian counterpart to Langham had given the computer section fifty basic requirements to search for, and from this briefing over a thousand cards had come up for consideration. When this number had been reduced to just over four hundred they had written in the requirement of fluent English, and the list had been reduced to seventy-four. To have visited the United States at least once reduced the list to thirty. One of these had died, and the remaining twenty-nine dossiers had been handed over to Slanski and Panov with the proviso that the Presidium would play a part in the selection when the list had been brought down to three candidates.

The fact that Langham had served for one year in the United States Army in Korea had finally eliminated nineteen of the remaining candidates and brought the list down to ten. It was reckoned that the attitude to any warlike situation of a man who had served in the armed forces could be influenced by that service. It could have generated a revulsion for war, or even a tendency to patriotic belligerence. One way or another it could play a part in a go/no-go situation.

But it was Slanski who had put his finger on the controlling criterion, and that had put the spotlight straight onto Levin, who was already in the top quartile from the evaluation of the final ten. It had been easy enough to make his case to Panov, but it had not been easy to formulate the proposition in inoffensive terms to lay before the Presidium. The problem that Slanski had seen was the conflict between party reliability and the need for the facsimile President to think as an American would think. To think as Langham would think. The rigid education and indoctrination that surrounded all Soviet citizens who achieved even minor status in the regime inevitably led to a thought pattern that automatically rejected anything but the Soviet official position on even the most minor conflicts of interest.

In the event, the Presidium committee had absorbed the rationale without demur, and Levin had gone to the top of the list.

As a psychiatrist, Levin was in a special position. He was used to analyzing human motivations and inhibitions, and he was concerned with their politics or nationality only in the few cases where it affected their mental health. And in the Soviet Union there were enough differences between Russians, Georgians, Uzbekistanis, Armenians and all the rest for a leading psychiatrist to recognize that nationality was only environment writ large.

Slanski and Panov had interviewed Levin twice; they had talked of a special assignment, but had not given any indication of its nature. At the first interview he had been openly defensive, answering their probing questions with no more than a yes or no whenever it was possible. When they asked for his views on a wide variety of problems the answer always reflected the party line.

At the second interview he seemed to have sensed that neither his status nor his reliability was being questioned and the competitiveness of a successful man began to show through. By the end of the second hour they had chatted easily about the latest idiosyncracy of Plisetskaya at the Bolshoi, and the theme of Hemingway's *A Moveable Feast*. There had been no attempt to disguise the fact that his interrogators were both KGB; neither was it emphasized. An oblique criticism of the organization of the psychology faculty at Moscow that showed that they knew about the internal tensions there was rewarded with a smile and a dry comment that was both witty and noncommittal.

It was Slanski who had asked him what he felt about the Americans. Levin shrugged and smiled. "I met mainly academics and students. I barely left the university buildings."

"But your general reaction?"

Levin shook his head as if denying any firm views. "They're human, I guess."

"It's been said that the Americans are much like us. Do you agree?"

Levin drew on his cigarette and leaned across to tap the ash into the glass ashtray. Then he looked up at both of them. "A fallacy. The usual bases for that argument are that both nations are children lovers, technologically ambitious, admirers of large-scale enterprises, sport-loving and the rest of the current jargon."

"And you don't agree?"

Levin shook his head vigorously, stretching out his legs as he sometimes did at tutorials when he was collecting his thoughts. He looked at the two of them, no longer on the

32

defensive but the lecturer now, with two bright students waiting for the words of wisdom.

"These so-called affinities are just a ragbag of undistributed middles in a handful of broken-backed syllogisms. Americans like children, Russians like children; therefore all Americans are like all Russians. But Jews like children. Italians like children. They say we are alike because we admire technological advance. So does every crackpot African country. What is the first thing they want? An international airport and a nuclear reactor. These likenesses are all newspaper talk. Ridiculous."

Slanski nodded. "You see no real similarities, then?"

Levin smiled. "Now you're putting words into my mouth, comrade. Of course there are similarities, just as there are between us and tribes in the South American jungles. It's environment that makes the difference. Genes are only potential. Environment is what forms the stone. The essential difference is discipline. *Our* resources, *our* people, are combined to achieve certain objectives. The Americans are not. They struggle one against the other."

The talk had gone on for another hour and Levin had been thanked and told that he might be asked back for another talk. Or maybe not.

After Levin had gone Slanski had poured out whisky for both of them, and they had moved over to the big armchairs by the fire. As Slanski swirled the whisky around in his glass he said, "Let's talk about the negative factors, Panov. My first negative point is that Levin is an academic. Langham has long experience in business."

Panov shrugged. "Not relevant, Ivan. When we are making our moves, Langham's business experience won't help him or hinder him in his reaction. A number of the American articles on Langham mentioned that he had been offered an academic post at Harvard and that he had given it serious consideration. I'd say that's no problem. What worries me is the girls."

Slanski smiled, "You're a prude, Panov."

Panov shifted in his chair and leaned back, looking at Slanski. "Do you rate screwing at least nine different girls in three years as normal?"

"Oh, for God's sake. These girl students throw themselves at the teaching staff. And he's a handsome man. It's bound to happen. He's a widower. No harm done."

"I'm not talking about harm, my friend. I'm thinking of him being shut up for six months, seven months even, without a woman. A horny bastard like that could be a problem."

Slanski leaned forward and put his glass on the table. "We can provide him with women. No problem."

"Never. Apart from the security risk, haven't you read that part of the reports? All these relationships are personal. Bunches of flowers, seats at the Bolshoi. He falls in love with 'em. I've seen these kinds of men in action. *They* are the prudes. They see a pretty face and a pair of big tits and they're off. They want to screw her, but they can't just do it like that. Oh no, it has to be romantic. Love. Romeo and Juliet. Poetry readings in Gorky Park. They're all the same."

Slanski lay back in his chair, his face upturned, his eyes closed as he thought. "Maybe we find him somebody, one girl. Something really gorgeous. They all last about four months, maybe she could be like Scheherezade and go the six months."

"She can't be Russian, Slanski, she would talk. She'd be aware of what was going on."

"So would a foreigner."

"Not so readily, and anyway she'll have no contact outside as a Russian girl would."

"Finding the girl won't be a problem."

"Are you going to find him a Jewess?"

"Why a Jewess?"

"His name is Levin. He's a Yid."

Slanski's eyes half closed against the crudity. "You haven't read the notes very carefully, comrade. He's not a Jew. And neither of his parents was a Jew."

Panov smiled as he slowly swirled the whisky in his glass, and he was still smiling as he looked up when Slanski spoke again.

"And when it's over?"

"Get rid of her."

"Maybe."

Slanski stood up slowly and stretched his arms. He turned

to look down at Panov: "It looks to me as though Levin will be our man."

Andrei Ivanovich Levin was born on August 7, 1928. In Russia that year was the start of the first of the Five-Year Plans. In the United States Walt Disney showed the first Mickey Mouse cartoon, and in London D. H. Lawrence's novel *Lady Chatterley's Lover* was published.

His father, a well-known physician, had been shot in the second wave of Stalin's murderous purges. His mother had spent six months in jail. Meanwhile the young Levin had been sent to a state orphanage on the outskirts of Leningrad. He had seen his mother once, when he was eleven. He learned afterward that this concession was made because the authorities had informed her that her husband had been executed "in error." There had been another Ivan Levin in Moscow, a surgeon and a Jew.

Andrei Levin had graduated from Moscow University with the recommendation that he be transferred to the faculty of experimental psychology at Leningrad. His paper on "The Psychological Effects of Male Hormones on the Female Psyche" and his "Study of the Neurochemistry of Aggression" had brought him quickly to the notice of his superiors and his opposite numbers in overseas universities. He had served two years on the North Korean battlefront, through to the armistice in 1956. He had devised interrogation techniques for use on American prisoners of war that had subsequently become standard, and he had been appointed professor of applied psychiatry on his return to Leningrad. He had published a pamphlet on "The Psychology of Master Chess," and this had been published not only in *Nature* but in a weekend edition of *Pravda*. And one of his fan letters had been from a pretty twenty-two-year-old blond student named Galina Malenkova. They had been married in the autumn of 1958, and she had died the following summer giving birth to their child. A girl.

The baby had been cared for in the infant orphanage at Smolensk, and he had closed his mind to both the child and its mother. It seemed like some strange dreamlike aberration in his life. His Viennese predecessor had used another word for dreams of this kind, but even after Levin had published the work that really established him in the eyes of his foreign contemporaries he had never noticed the connection. Levin, and a team of students, had researched the effects of the war on memory. They had found that many witnesses of savage tragedy had been able to expunge the nightmares from their minds. But in so doing they appeared to have wiped out a whole data base of other contemporaneous memory at the same time. You could force yourself to forget, but you could not limit by will how much you would forget. His paper "The Suppression of Trauma and Its Effect on the Unconscious" had been published in most countries.

This led to a number of invitations to talk at overseas seminars and conferences, and he had been granted permission to attend a number of these. He had paid several visits to the United States, one to London and two to France and Italy. He had even played a part in a bungled attempt at détente with the Chinese, by being allowed to attend, but not speak publicly, at a conference in Peking.

There was talk of his being appointed as head of all psychological and psychiatric research at Moscow University, but it hadn't happened. He suspected that his sex life had been an inhibiting factor. There was nothing extraordinary about it, no abnormality, and he guessed that if he had stayed in the Army it would barely have made the record. But the sight of a pretty face and a well-filled sweater could all too easily divert him, and girl students with ambition were only too eager to comply. The professor's bunch of red roses in a girl's locker was as well known an opening gambit as P–K4. But like a good many such Romeos he was not good at ending the relationships smoothly. He was strictly a one-girl man, but the endings tended to be a bit messy.

The Presidium committee had considered the final report from Slanski and had given their approval. Andrei Levin was to be the man.

chapter
4

Before starting the final interview with Levin, Slanski and Panov had met in the small room at 11 Gorky Street.

"What if he refuses, Panov?"

Panov looked up from pouring himself a whisky and then looked back at the decanter as he put back the glass stopper. He was silent as he walked back to one of the chairs that were spaced around the low circular table. He took a sip before he spoke.

"Then we tell him it's an order, my friend."

"That would be useless."

The big aggressive head came up quickly. "It's a fact, Ivan. We haven't implemented this operation to be told by some damned intellectual that he doesn't want to play."

"An unwilling man, a resentful man, would be a disaster. Presidents don't get elected against their will. He wouldn't be typical. And apart from that he wouldn't absorb the mountain of stuff that we shall be pushing across his desk. And he could play games with us and we would never know."

"So we keep testing him right up to the time when it matters."

"We shall do that anyway."

"So what is it you're saying?"

"I want him to understand that he's the key figure in a

vital operation. That he's the head of a team in an operation that's vital to the state."

"But he's not. You're in charge of the operation."

"That's the point I'm making, Boris. I want you to relax a bit, not be so damned military."

"That's what I'm in this operation for, comrade. I *am* damned military. And this whole thing is part of a military operation."

"He's not the kind of man who will respond to a military atmosphere. All I ask is that you look as if you're on his side, supporting him."

Panov leaned back smiling. "Don't worry, Andrei. I won't rock your boat."

"Shall we get him in?"

"Fine. Let's get started."

Slanski had spent no time on chitchat. He outlined Levin's role in the operation while the other two sat in silence. When he had finished he reached for his glass.

"And you've been chosen, Comrade Professor, to head this operation."

"How in hell did you choose me?"

"Scientifically. It's taken months to assemble the data, and a lot of computer time."

"How do you know you're right?"

"We don't. But we're as near right as research can get us, and for the rest we rely on you."

"In what way am I like the American?"

"You can see the selection records in due course. You'll find them extensive and very detailed."

"Do I look like Langham?"

"No. But looks are irrelevant. It's your thinking that we want. And your ability to absorb the facts that we'll give you, and react as you feel Langham would react."

"What if I fail? What if I'm wrong?"

"Then nothing will be lost. All the usual intelligence sources will be used and all the usual military and political apparatus will function. Our main role will be as a checkpoint on what the President's own reactions and instincts are. Others can evaluate what advice he gets, and what pressures he is under from the Pentagon, or Congress, or the Department of State, but our contribution is solely about that one man. The President. What is he thinking that he doesn't even tell his closest advisers?"

"What about my work at the university?"

"It will be in abeyance until you get back."

"And the operation is based in Moscow?"

"No, Andrei, we shall all be down in Kiev. Do you know Kiev?"

"Not well. I've been to university meetings there a few times, and a couple of holidays. But that was some years back."

"Well, we shall be outside the town. There was a documentary-film studio there that has been converted for us."

"You will be there, and Comrade Panov?"

"Yes, we shall both be there as part of your staff. There will be a signals group, a secretariat, an archive section and a small staff of researchers."

Levin shifted in his armchair, not uneasily, but to look across at Slanski. "Can I think about this?"

Slanski looked back at Levin without speaking, and when he felt that his silence had made his point he said, "Tell me what you need to think about, Andrei."

Levin shrugged. "I'm an academic, not particularly politically inclined. I'm not sure that I can do what you want successfully."

"That's our responsibility. You haven't put yourself forward, you have been carefully chosen by others. And that includes the Presidium itself."

Levin half smiled. "I'm flattered."

"You'll get every possible support from a highly skilled team."

Levin realized that, in fact, he had no choice. Whatever his objections they would have effective answers. When Slanski had introduced the Presidium as part of his array of persuasion, that had made refusal impossible. Or dangerous. There would be no promotion at Leningrad or anywhere else if he refused, and it would not be long before his papers went unpublished and his work was criticized. He looked over at Slanski.

"When do we start, comrade?"

Slanski shrugged, smiling. "We have started, Andrei. It's comrade no longer—but mister."

"How long will it take?"

"Six or seven months, maybe a little longer. We have notified the university that you have been assigned to a research project. You will still receive your pay from them and also from us. And you will have no expenses."

"And when it is over?"

"You will be suitably upgraded. That will not be a problem."

"When do we leave Moscow for Kiev?"

"In two days' time. There is your general briefing about Langham. Documents for you to see and absorb. We have arranged a suite for you at the National. I'll take you there now."

And it was in the suite at the National, when he was alone with Levin, that Slanski had raised the question of the girl.

"You know that you will not be allowed out of the operational headquarters."

Levin looked surprised. "Why is that? I have friends in Kiev."

"For security reasons. You could be recognized. People would speculate. It has the highest security grading."

"But surely we could contrive some cover story. Special research, as you said."

"Andrei, when we arrive in Kiev you will cease to have any part in Russian life. You will never speak Russian. You will hear no Russian radio or TV, read no Russian newspapers. Not even eat Russian food. You will live as an American. The news broadcasts will all be American. When you switch on a radio or a TV you will get American programs. Real ones, genuine ones. And you will read American newspapers and magazines."

"How can that be?"

Slanski smiled. "Tapes, videotapes, and the newspapers—they will be the real thing. The only difference will be that we'll be two days behind the rest of the world. We hope to improve on the time lag, but at the moment that's the best we can do."

Levin was silent, and Slanski gave him time to absorb the realities of what he had said.

"There's one other thing, Andrei."

He waited until Levin looked up at him.

"You'll know that we have obviously checked very carefully and in great detail on your background?"

Levin shrugged. "Of course."

Slanski reached for his briefcase and took out a brown folder. He held it toward Levin but not quite within his reach.

"I'd like to do a little test, if you don't mind."

Levin laughed. "My own much used words."

"Tell me which one you prefer."

And he pushed the folder so that Levin could take it.

There were photographs of seven girls. Portraits, and shots that showed their bodies in bikinis or swimsuits, and in one case the girl was naked. Levin looked through them twice, not hurrying; a test was a test, and should not be hurried unless speed was one of the criteria. Finally he didn't hesitate and he handed a photograph to Slanski. It was a photograph of Clodagh Maria Kevan.

The plane had followed the highway as far as Bryansk, and then they had met snow, the thick flakes building up against the square windows until the shuddering of the fuselage cleared them momentarily. But the snow stopped as they approached Kiev. The sky was pale blue with streaks of pink on the horizon. The forest of beeches and oaks to the north of the town seemed to spread for miles in every direction. Somewhere in that forest was the place that was going to be his home for the next six months. As Levin took a deep breath the plane sank lower and they were following the Dnieper. There were barges on the river, and across the town he could see the tower of St. Sophia and then the massive bulk of the Supreme Soviet of the Ukraine. They turned, the plane banking steeply, across the outer ring road, and then they flew alongside the railway, past the central station, and suddenly the small houses flashed under the wings, the runway met the landing gear and there were lights blinking on the control tower as they rolled to a stop.

Levin had been accompanied only by Panov, and the stocky major took his bags as they walked across to the big black Zil. Levin closed his eyes from the stinging cold of the wind and put up his gloved hand so that he could see where he was walking.

The driver saluted Panov and carefully arranged the bright red rugs across their legs. Their route did not take them back into the town. The dirt road followed the ditches that marked the boundary of a collective, passing sheds and barns until they came to a cluster of farm workers' cottages. Then it was an empty landscape on both sides, the long plowed furrows white with a sprinkling of snow on their windward slopes as far as the eye could see. They would stay like that until the wheat and barley thrust up pale-green shoots late in the spring. Even this far south it had to be early sowing and late harvesting.

The car swung left and the dark line of the forest marked the end of the farmland, and as it grew nearer Levin could see the giant oaks and beeches, their branches bare of leaves; the only green was of ivy and mistletoe that clung to the massive trunks and spread up into the lower branches.

Two miles inside the forest they came to a wooden guard house, and an officer came out to check their papers. Levin no longer held any means of identification, and Panov handed out a typewritten paper with two photographs stapled in the center. The young officer glanced briefly at Levin, stepped back and saluted. The long white-and-red-barred gate swung slowly open, and the road was paved now.

A mile or so later there was a blaze of light in the trees and the car swung to the right, and ahead of them was a wooden wall, eight or nine feet high, painted with the brown and green splotches of standard camouflage. Another guard-house was alongside the two great gates. Levin could see the guard commander talking into the phone. After he had hung up there was silence except for the hum of the car heater. Levin guessed they must be calling someone even more senior, and for the first time he realized that he was at the center of all this elaborate security. This was no academic exercise, it was for real, and he shivered; with anticipation rather than fear. He had left the security of offices and lecture rooms for the realities of machine guns, crack troops in their best uniforms and a lot of people, probably hundreds of people, deployed to make possible a plan that was surely about tanks, divisions, squadrons, tactical missiles and God knows what.

The officer who came wore Red Army insignia and the flashes of one of the Kazakhstani regiments. He asked for no papers but opened the car door and looked at them both for several minutes, his olive face smooth and bland, his brown eyes cold and hard above his high cheeks as he looked them over without reaction and in silence. Then he stepped back, swung to the door, and waved toward the guardroom. The big gates swung open, and for a moment Levin was reminded of the music of Moussorgski's *Pictures at an Exhibition* and the magnificent section "The Great Gate at Kiev." Another wide gate swung open in front of them and then there was the massive structure of the old film studio.

The car stopped, and when the driver came to open the door Levin stepped out. The earth crackled frozen beneath his feet as he turned to look at the building. It was perhaps thirty feet high, like an airfield hangar, corrugated iron, painted a brilliant white, and from all sides searchlights were trained on it so that the rime of frost sparkled and coruscated over all its surface as if it were the setting for some exotic opera.

An officer took Levin's bags and they walked toward a wooden door protected by an old-fashioned porch. Panov stood to one side as Levin walked through into the brightly lit interior. A long wide corridor split the building into two unequal parts. To the right and left were white walls with plaster decorations, gilded white ribbons and leaves intertwined. Huge windows and chandeliers and a red carpet that ran the whole length of the building, as far as he could see. The contrast with the outside was stunning, and as he stood there Panov gently edged him forward to where the officer stood at an open door.

It was a bedroom as ornate as the corridor. A big double bed with a carved headboard, a dark-green carpet. French-style furniture—dressing table, bergère suite—and along one wall a white wide shelf with modern hi-fi and shelves of records and tapes. A small Sony TV was on a round table. Along the adjoining wall was an array of male cosmetics, electric razor and small leather cases.

As if he were an important guest at a hotel, the officer showed him the adjoining room, with its long teak table and high-backed chairs, and his eye went to the digital clocks on the far wall, their red diodes switching their square characters as they marked the seconds. Under the left-hand clock it said "WASHINGTON" and under the right-hand clock it said "MOSCOW."

As they went into the next room he recognized it from the newspaper photographs. It was a replica of the White House's Oval Office. Even the flag was there, its stars and stripes brilliant in the strong light, and over to the right of the desk was another flag.

He and Panov ate at the table in the big bedroom, and after Panov had gone he put back his head in the soft leather chair and closed his eyes. His head ached, he could see the snow on the Ilyushin's windows, the black mass of the forest, the Asian face of the officer of the guard, and the blood pounded at his temples as he tried to control his thoughts. He slept in the chair for two hours, and when he awoke he stumbled, indifferent to his surroundings, into the big bed, shedding his clothes as he went. And, for some reason, as he sank into the oily waves of sleep it went through his mind that his daughter must be twenty-one now. Older than some of the girls he slept with.

Slanski had had no real problem with the girl. Driving with her in the embassy car to Heathrow Airport, he saw her looking out the window as they went over the Chiswick overpass.

"Will you miss any of this?"

She turned her head to look at him and he was aware of the green eyes and the full sensuous mouth.

She shook her head. "The outskirts of hell must look like this."

He smiled. "The outskirts of Moscow too."

She turned to look at him again. "You're an unusual man, Comrade Slanski. Particularly for a Russian."

44

"In what way?"

"All the Russians I have met are so defensive about conditions in the Soviet Union. Everything is fine, or if it isn't it will be next year. But you speak as if there is no need to convince me."

He leaned back and looked at her face. "You are unusually intelligent, Miss Kevan. That's not flattery, you must already know it. Tomorrow you will see for yourself. Moscow has plenty of this." He waved his hand toward the gaunt factories and the sodden clay where water lay in pools beside the bulldozers. "And I want you to rely on what I say. In the future."

The girl touched the soft fur to her lips for a moment. "And you took it for granted that I would do as you ask."

"By no means. I *felt* it was possible. I *hoped* it was probable."

She turned to him quickly. "And why did you choose me?"

"I didn't choose you. It was not my choice to make. As I told you, the man concerned chose you."

They were silent to the airport roundabout, and he put his hand lightly on her arm.

"It's still not too late if you wish to change your mind."

She shook her head without looking at him. "Oh no. It interests me. It interests me."

And he left it at that.

They waited in the VIP lounge until the Moscow flight was called, and he was aware of the envious looks that came his way. Neither of them had noticed the drab Hillman Minx that had followed them from the safe house in Kensington.

For two days Levin had filled his hours in meetings with Panov and the specialists. He had been given intelligence reports based on the information which the KGB expected to be available to the President of the United States. The reports covered only the NATO area and the Balkans. He saw minute-by-minute reports of the previous day's schedule of the President, and a précis of the American press.

The computer terminal linked to Dzerdzhinski Square in Moscow gave rapid answers to the various queries he raised, and on the big wall map in the conference room an army captain marked up hourly the order of battle of all Allied troops in Europe and their Soviet counterparts. The position shown for the Allies' deployment was eighty-nine percent accurate. The Soviet positions were four months out of date.

A doctor from the research unit at Irkutsk went over Langham's medical history with Levin, and a currently serving member of the Washington embassy staff went over with him a written report on the operation and organization of the White House.

The third day had been meeting after meeting. A KGB man working as one of the Washington representatives for *Izvestia* had gone over the family history and business career of the President, and a senior officer from the First Directorate Special Service Unit had covered Langham's political career with a list of six books for background reading on the organization of the two political parties.

In the evening he had been shown a special film that had been stripped together, showing Langham in various activities over the past twenty years. Although he was tired he had asked for it to be run through a second time. It was a mixture of network material, newsreel shots, private film and Republican Party records, and it went from flickering black-and-white home movies to highly professional color. Levin never took his eyes from the screen. This was the man he was supposed to be. Physically they were not much alike, the American's hair was still dark and the only gray was at his temples; they were much the same height and build, but the President had bright-blue penetrating eyes that dominated his whole face. The drawl was much like John F. Kennedy's, although the accent was different.

After the second showing they had projected a ten-minute film on Texas. There were slow panning shots of Wichita Falls, shots of the frame house where the President was born and where his parents still lived, ending with aerial shots of Dallas, Fort Worth and Austin. And then he had had enough. When he told them that the first meeting would be at eight the next morning he realized for the first time since he had arrived that it was he who gave the instructions.

He went back into the Oval Office to collect extra cigarettes and his lighter, and as he stood by the desk he realized that he felt at home. He was no longer the new boy. This was his office and his operation. He looked at the other flag, and held it out to read the legend. It was the flag of the American Legion. On the right-hand wall there were portraits of former Presidents. Kennedy, Johnson, Roosevelt and a face that he didn't recognize.

At the back of the desk were the big windows, but they had no view; neither did the smaller windows set in the wall. They were of frosted glass, and behind them there were lights that operated from a panel in the control room. The lights were bright or dull according to the weather and the time of day in Washington. The lighting control was programmed each day from the Washington weather statistics. It was evening now, but there was still some simulated sunshine that cast long shadows across the floor and over the desk.

He wondered, as he looked around the big room, if Slanski and Panov felt the same vibrations of power that he felt. As if the room itself by some strange osmosis were not in Kiev but in Washington, and the reports and paraphernalia were the real thing.

Panov, he sensed, was not affected by the surroundings. The stocky soldier seemed to have an encyclopedic knowledge of the United States armed forces. Talking about divisional commanders as if they were old friends from West Point or Annapolis. Aware of their strengths and shortcomings, their chances of promotion and the notes in personnel files that might consign them to dead ends on the periphery of the defense machine. But he was not much given to imagination in other areas. A man who could belch during a Schubert trio as Panov had done at lunchtime was not going to be touched by the shape of a room or a couple of flags. Panov's small eyes looked at him sometimes as if he doubted his suitability for the operation. But Panov looked at Slanski in much the same way.

Slanski was easier to understand. Essentially friendly, maybe not moved by the outward trappings of the setup, but excited by the thinking behind it. Maybe because it was his own. Levin had learned a lot from their one game of chess. The analytical self-control that mounted Slanski's pieces to control the central squares, the elation at the power invested in his attacking forces, the plotting that could work out the permutations for two moves ahead. And the visible shock at a countermove in the middle game that tore his one-sided attack to pieces. The readiness to lay his king on its side in resignation. Slanski, like many creative people, would crack rather than bend, under pressure.

They were an interesting combination and it would be amusing to use Slanski against the monolithic Panov. There would be a rivalry there, he guessed, before the operation was over. He had the feeling that Panov would be the survivor, like some giant stone head on Easter Island.

On a small table alongside the big desk was a pile of magazines, and he pulled up the massive black leather chair and reached for the stack. He put six or seven of the magazines on the desk in front of him and slowly leafed through them. There were *Newsweek* and *Time,* and he lit a cigarette and leaned back as he read a piece on the Soviet Union. He smiled at the misconceptions but was slightly surprised at the favorable comments on the Soviet medical system. He spent a long time on *Scientific American* and reached, without looking, for the next magazine. It was a copy of *Playboy.* On the cover was a pretty young blonde. She was quite naked, astride a shiny Japanese motorcycle, and you didn't need to be a professor of psychology to recognize the symbolism of the shiny black saddle that reared up between her legs. As he turned the pages he was amazed. The girls were young, and so pretty, and they smiled into the camera as if they were unaware of the lens's observation of the excitement between their casually spread thighs. And among the thrusting, bouncing breasts and the long shapely legs was an article about the KGB. He read it with contempt and turned back to the pictures. He wondered if the photographer was allowed to enjoy the girls when the work was done. They had told him that a girl would be arranged for him. He pushed the copy of *Playboy* to the bottom of the pile of magazines and stretched his arms as he stood up.

The conference room was empty as he passed through to his bedroom. He saw that it was midnight, Moscow time. As he entered his room he stood and adjusted his watch to Washington time.

He walked over to the hi-fi and bent down to look at the rows of cassettes. He took one out and slid it into the recorder and pressed down the key. The music came up as he moved the volume sliders; it was Errol Garner playing "Manhattan."

It was when he was reaching for the whisky bottle that he saw the girl. She was sitting in the bergère armchair, her long legs crossed and a magazine on her knee. She was looking up at him and smiling. And she was breathtakingly beautiful.

"Good evening, Professor. I hope I didn't startle you."

And without waiting for a reply she leaned over the side of the chair and reached for a long cardboard box. She lifted it up and held it out to him.

"A little something," she said, "from me to you."

His fingers untied the knots and he eased off the white ribbon. He took off the lid and pulled aside a layer of tissue paper. And as he looked the smile came, and when he looked at the girl and saw that she was smiling, too, he threw back his head and laughed. He looked back at the girl and said, "The bastards have been talking already."

He lifted out the bunch of red roses and put them on the bed. He stood hands on hips, smiling at her. "I'll ring the bell and get them to find a vase."

And for the first time his eyes went to her breasts and he saw her amused smile as he looked back at her face, and he asked her too quickly, trying to hide the embarrassment, "How was your journey?"

"They gave me two days in Moscow. That broke up the journey and gave me time to get used to this terrible cold."

She smiled back at him as he looked at her sitting there. She was wearing a black dress and there was white fox fur in a line around the hem and along the robelike fold that slanted across her legs to her shoulder. Her face was still rosy from the cold outside, and her eyes sparkled. She was even more beautiful than the photographs, and they hadn't shown those green eyes or the air of self-confidence. This wasn't going to be just a girl to sleep with.

"It must seem very strange to you—all this?" And he waved one arm at the room.

The green eyes looked at his face and she said softly. "A lot of things will be strange for both of us."

He felt awkward as he stood there, not quite knowing what to do. Not embarrassed, but at a loss for a small way to please her, to make her at home.

He drew up one of the chairs and sat facing her. He reached out and took her hand. Her fingers laced in his and she smiled as his thumb smoothed the back of her slim hand.

"Let me play you some music and we'll drink some champagne to celebrate."

He stood up right away without checking her face for a reaction, and walked over to the hi-fi and the shelves of cassettes. He reached up and took down one of the plastic containers and turned to smile at her as he slid the cassette into the deck. "This is really music for a sunny morning, not late at night." And he turned to press the controls of the machine. She smiled as she heard the perky opening bars of the Fifth Brandenburg and watched as he bent to open the small refrigerator.

A moment later she was touching her glass to his, smiling. "How do you say it in Russian?"

"*Na zdrovya.*"

"So I say it to you—to us. *Na zdrovya.*"

He leaned back in his chair, his tension receding, and he looked at her face over the top of his glass as he sipped the champagne. The pert nose was as fine-carved as if it were marble, its shadow touching the deep cleft to her lip. And her lips were soft and wide and full, not quite closed, and her teeth were just visible when the dimples came as she smiled. She was almost too beautiful to make love to, but the shadow between her full breasts canceled these thoughts so surely that for a moment he closed his eyes. With his eyes still closed he said, "You're very, very beautiful."

When she didn't reply he opened his eyes slowly and saw that she was leaning forward toward him, her eyes on his face.

"Andrei Levin, professor of applied psychology, you are

working too hard to help me. Let us relax. I am your willing guest."

Levin put down his glass on the round table and offered her a cigarette. When she shook her head he lit a cigarette for himself and walked over to the hi-fi and switched off the deck.

"Did you have people you left behind in England?"

"None."

"No relatives?"

"No."

"Boy friends?"

"Men, yes, but not boy friends."

"People you liked?"

She put her head on one side, her lips faintly pouting, as she frowned in thought. "I'm not really a liker, Andrei, more an admirer."

"And what do you admire?"

She leaned back comfortably in the chair, her long slim fingers smoothing the wood of the arm sensuously, her face turned toward the pink light beside her. She looked back at his face before she spoke.

"Minds, open minds, wide-ranging minds. The ability to be creative in human terms, not just theories."

He was moved and pleased that she didn't wait for his approval. She stood up and stretched her arms. "Can I look to see what music you've got?"

"Of course. It wasn't my choosing, but it covers a wide range. There's quite a lot of American jazz."

She stood looking at the rows and columns of cassettes, and from time to time she took one down until she had a small pile of six or seven. He walked over and stood beside her and picked up her choices one by one.

"Do you know any of them, Andrei?"

"The Oscar Peterson, yes. I went to his concert when he was here. The Django Reinhardt I know, but none of the others."

She turned. "Right. Go and sit down and I'll give you a little concert." She suddenly looked at her watch and then back at his face. "It's so very late. I forgot. Are you too tired?"

"Of course not. Give me a concert."

They sat listening to the lush warm music in silence and when it was over she was smiling.

"So who wrote that, Professor?"

"It could be Russian, but I've never heard it. Maybe English—something by Elgar?"

She shook her head. "It's by an American, Samuel Barber."

"And what's it called?"

"'Adagio for Strings.' It was originally for a string quartet, but nowadays it's always played by a full orchestra."

"It doesn't sound American, not even now that you've told me."

The green eyes were alight with the pleasure of her small victory. "And now a little song from me to you. Sung by an Irishman—John McCormack."

She reached over and changed the cassettes, sitting back as the piano accompaniment started and the thin honey voice crooned the golden notes. Levin sat enchanted as the words and music faded ". . . and each picture of the past in its circle I see—this little silver ring that once you gave to me."

"Is it an Irish song?"

"No. It's a French song by a man named Chaminade. It's a favorite of mine. I can remember hearing my father singing it to my mother."

"What was he like, your father?"

She shook her head. "I don't remember him really, Andrei. People told me that he was feckless and gay. All dogs and horses and pretty ladies. My mother loved him very much. He died when I was very young."

He shivered for a second time with tiredness, and she stood up. "It's time to go to bed, Andrei. It's nearly three o'clock."

He put his hands on her shoulders, and the gooseberry-green eyes were so near his that they were out of focus. He was aware of the warm softness of her body against his as his mouth found hers. When he moved his head back from hers to look at her face he knew that she must be well aware of his desire for her. And she smiled up at him and said softly, "You want me, yes?"

He nodded. He knew that part of the reason for the talking

had been to put off this moment. From the moment he first saw her he had wanted her. Urgently. But that was when she was just a beautiful girl and a superb body. The talk had made her a person, and now his lust fought with liking and affection. Like him, she had no supporting troops of family or friends, and some instinct made him feel that she would accept him sexually immediately, but that afterward he would be just another man. Already he wanted to mean more than that to this girl.

His hands slid down to her smooth hips and for a moment he drew her against his body so that his desire was obvious. Then he kissed her gently.

"Let us just sleep tonight."

Levin took off his tie and unbuttoned his shirt and walked over to the hi-fi and changed the cassettes. Only when he was naked did he press the start button and walk over to the bed and slide in between the sheet and the flowered duvet. The big chords of the Rachmaninov No. 2 started as the girl walked from the bathroom. Her long black hair was down below her shoulders, and she was naked, a white toweling bathrobe trailing from her right hand.

When she slid in beside him he could feel the warmth of her body, and for a moment he wished that she were just another girl student who would satisfy his lust without real involvement. But it was only for a moment and as he leaned forward to kiss her his hand reached over to extinguish the light, and in the darkness he said, "*Da zaftra.*"

"What does that mean?" she whispered.

"See you tomorrow."

Her hand touched his face as she kissed his mouth.

He lay wide awake, listening to the music as the concerto drew to a close. Then there was the click as the automatic stop functioned, and the room became silent and still. He heard the faint ringing of a telephone far away, and as the silence deepened he could hear the distant chatter of a teleprinter. He closed his eyes against the faint noise and the first stab of pain behind his eyes. It had been nearly twenty hours since he had last slept. He was exhausted, but the distant noises seemed to combine with his lust to keep him awake. He could hear the girl's deep breathing, but there was no way of telling if she were asleep. And he remembered the white body, the full breasts trembling as she walked, and the long shapely legs.

Without thinking he sighed, deeply, and turning his head on the pillow he could see the faint glow of the signal light on the hi-fi. Despite the warning swish of the sheet he jumped when her hand touched his chest, but it was trigger enough to his lust, and their mouths met eagerly. And then it was a frenzy of soft flesh in his hands and an excitement that matched his own. It was an hour before they slept, but sleep came easily in a slow warm vortex like the heavy waves of the sea.

The next morning when he woke, the bed beside him was empty. He reached over to the chair and lifted the toweling robe and draped it around his shoulders. As he stood up slowly he slid his arms into the sleeves and tied the belt. He looked around the room and then walked over to the TV and switched it on. The picture came up quickly, and the colors gradually resolved the image. It showed workmen in the street, and a woman stopped to speak to them. She wanted to know how to get to Carnegie Hall. The workman grinned and said she'd have to practice a lot, and then the image dissolved to a can of beer. He leaned forward to switch off the set and saw the girl beside him. She was wearing a white dress with a fringe around the skirt. She wore neither shoes nor stockings, and her toes wriggled in the deep pile of the carpet. She was smiling as she looked at him.

"Did they sell you on Colt Forty-five?"

"I couldn't understand it. What has beer got to do with Carnegie Hall?"

She laughed and her hand rested gently on his arm. "Nothing, Professor. It's a kind of propaganda. It says strong men like this beer, men who dig up streets are strong men, and they have a wonderful way with old ladies, so if you'd like to be seen as a strong man drink this beer."

He looked at her quizzically. "Do you drink beer?"

"No. And I don't dig up streets and I don't like most old ladies."

He laughed. "Where have you been this morning?"

"Exploring."

"Where?"

"In the two offices. They've made a good job of it, haven't they?"

"I haven't really absorbed it all yet. Let's go and look."

She slid her arm in his as they walked through the operations room to the big office, and they stood in the doorway looking at the room.

Everything had been cleaned overnight. The ashtrays sparkled, the magazines were in a neat pile and the date on the desk calender had been changed. And there was a pile of papers in the center of the big desk.

She looked at his face. "Does it seem real?"

"Yes, it seems real enough. It's just that *I* don't feel real."

He walked slowly over to the desk and pulled out the black leather chair and leaned over to look at the pile of papers. He moved the papers as he read the titles of reports and the headings of background notes. He read the titles out loud as he moved them from the main pile.

" 'Pentagon Scientific Committee Appreciation of Soviet Solid Fuel for Gorky Missile.' 'Order of Battle Updating of Warsaw Pact Forces in East Germany.' 'Analysis from US Treasury of Soviet Trade Indebtedness to EEC Countries.' 'Surveillance Report on Soviet Embassy Staff in Washington.' 'Report from National Security Agency on Soviet Diplomatic Code Number 47/4.' 'Notes on Interrogation of Soviet Defector Vassili Godov.' " He looked up at the girl. "And so it goes on—the gossip of government."

He pressed the phone button and lifted the receiver. "Who is that? . . . *Dobre den.* . . ." He smiled. "OK—good morning. I'd like coffee—for two. Yes, in the office."

He hung up smiling and walked around to where the girl was sitting in one of the chairs in front of the desk. He took the other seat, facing her. As he sat down he looked at her face.

"You're very beautiful, Clodagh."

She put her head on one side, smiling. "Thank you, kind sir."

"Can I ask you something?"

"Mr. President, I am yours to command."

"Why did you come here? How did they persuade you?"

The girl leaned back in her chair, and despite his interest in her answer his eyes went involuntarily to the long shapely legs. He looked back at her face as her hand pushed a swatch of the long black hair over her shoulder.

"What did they tell you about me?"

"About your background in Ireland. That you were a party member in England. A first-class mind. And I saw a photograph of you. That's about all."

She was silent for a moment before she spoke. "They told me about you, your background, your career, and they told me that you were concerned with a secret project that was vital to the interests of the Soviet Union and the Communist world, that you would be cut off from the world for many months and that it was considered necessary for you to have a companion, a girl." She paused. "And they showed *me* a photograph, too."

She watched his hand stretch out to his desk and close over his cigarette lighter. She watched as he lit a cigarette. His fingers were long, like an artist's or a surgeon's, and even his casual movements were graceful. His face was handsome, but his eyes were extraordinary. They were the eyes of a judge, a father, a listener, an observer—a lover. And as she watched the smoke curl slowly toward the ceiling from the slim fingers she knew that she would be more than a mistress, more than a lover, to this man.

"And the bed business. Do you find that objectionable?"

Her smile was slow and friendly as she shook her head. She said softly, "No. I find it male and normal."

"It does not *have* to be."

She stood up. "You must dress, Mr. President." She looked at the clocks on the wall. "It's nine o'clock in Washington and they say the President's an early riser."

His hand reached out as he stood up and gently cupped one of her breasts. For a moment she smiled up at him as his fingers explored and then she gently took his hand away and walked back toward the bedroom. He felt a moment's relief at her gesture. She was willing but not complaisant, and somehow that made it more tolerable. He wondered if she was wise enough to know that. He surmised that she was.

56

chapter
5

It was one of the neat sterile offices in the new building at
New Scotland Yard. There was a reproduction of the Karsh
photograph of Churchill on the wall. Otherwise the walls
were bare, except for a printed appeal to switch off the lights
when leaving the room. The desk was a standard typist's
desk. A layer of teak laminate and three drawers. On the
desk was a pad of pale-yellow paper with a Ministry of Defence crest, and a jam jar stuffed with pencils and ballpoints.
There were two phones side by side. One had a scrambler
box alongside it. There were no windows, and two strip
lights were slung across the full width of the ceiling. The
floor was of cork tiles with some kind of varnish that had
worn away in a rough circle where the visitor's chair faced
the table.

The man behind the desk was young and inclined to fat.
Although he looked in his early thirties he was almost completely bald except for a thin blond fuzz that circled his head
like a monk's tonsure. He wore a blazer with gilt buttons and
a Royal Artillery tie. He wasn't entitled to wear it, but it gave
him the appearance of being a simple, honest ex-soldier.

He stood up as the young man was shown into the office
by a uniformed police constable. He held out his hand.

"My name's Clayton. Commander Clayton. Take a seat."
And he waved to the standard-issue chair in front of the desk.

When the other man had made himself comfortable Clayton reached for his pad and sorted out a pencil from the jam jar. "Now let's get the basics down. How do you spell your name?"

"Jephcott. J-E-P-H-C-O-T-T."

"Christian names?"

"Martin James."

"And your address?"

"Flat Two-A, Adam and Eve Mews."

"That's Kensington, isn't it?"

"Yes."

Clayton put down his pencil and pushed the pad away. The standard, rather overemphatic Special Branch indication that notes were not being taken. Just a confidential chat. Except for the tape recorder in the bottom drawer.

"I understand you've made an official request to see an officer of Special Branch. Is that correct?"

"Yes. I asked my section head to arrange it."

"That's Mr. Paynter, isn't it?"

"Yes."

"Tell me what it's all about."

"Is this in confidence? Just you and me?"

Clayton launched himself into the standard response that Special Branch used. "Well, a lot depends on what it's all about, Mr. Jephcott. But your interests will certainly be borne in mind. You have signed the Official Secrets Act declaration, haven't you?"

Jephcott nodded, and Clayton registered that this routine reminder that was merely intended to change the subject produced a positive reaction from Jephcott. He had folded his arms across his chest in that standard giveaway defensive gesture of self-protection.

Clayton did nothing to break the silence, and it was several minutes before Jephcott shifted in his chair and leaned forward.

"It's about a kidnapping—by the Russians."

"I see. Who do you think was kidnapped?"

"A girl."

"What's her name?"

"Clodagh. Clodagh Kevan."

"Tell me about it. When did it happen?"

"Two weeks ago. The twelfth."

"And how did you get to hear about it?"

"I didn't hear about it. I saw it."

"Go on."

"She was taken in a car to Heathrow and put on a plane to Moscow."

"Where was she taken from?"

"The safe house in Kensington."

Clayton kept very still as he spoke. "What safe house is this?"

"The one the party uses. It's a flat over the supermarket."

"Safeways?"

"Yes." Jephcott nodded.

"You know Miss Kevan, do you?"

"Yes, very well. We were going to be married."

"Was she a member of the Communist Party?"

"Yes."

"And you?"

"More or less."

Clayton ignored the evasion. "Why do you say she was taken by the Russians?"

"It was one of their cars. From the embassy."

"Can you give me a description?"

"Maroon Jaguar. UPP 332 L. It's still there at the embassy garage."

"Was anyone with Miss Kevan when she left?"

"Yes—a man. I don't know who he was."

"Was the girl under any kind of restraint?"

"Not that I could see."

"Did she appear drugged or unsteady, anything like that?"

"I didn't see her all that much."

Clayton leaned forward, his arms on the table top. "You say you were going to be married. Was a date fixed for this?"

"Nothing definite."

"Had you quarreled at all?"

"No, we never quarreled."

"What makes you think she went against her will?"

"She wouldn't have gone without telling me."

"When did you last see her, apart from the twelfth?"

"The first of the month."

Clayton looked up sharply. He regretted it immediately. "What happened? What did you do?"

"We had a meal and went back to my place and had sex."

Clayton's hand reached out and fiddled with the pencils in the jar. There was something odd here. They never volunteered the sex bit, it had to be squeezed out of them. And Jephcott hadn't seen her for nearly two weeks. He turned slowly to look at Jephcott and noticed the flushed cheeks and the defiant mouth.

"What did she look like, Martin? Was she pretty?"

"I've got a photo." And Jephcott reached into his inside pocket and pulled out a wallet. He leaned forward and put a photograph on the desk, but Clayton ignored it, his eyes still on Jephcott's face.

"I'd rather you tell me. Was she pretty?"

"More than pretty. She was beautiful. Like a film star."

"How often did you have sex with her?"

"About once a fortnight. Roughly."

"Was she on the Pill?"

Jephcott shrugged. "I've no idea."

"And when you had sex on these occasions, how long did it take?"

"She'd let me do it all night."

Clayton leaned back again in his chair. "Did you have any rivals that you know of?"

"I don't think so. No."

"Have you asked any of the others about her? Asked where she is?"

"I've asked two or three, but nobody knew anything."

"Did you tell them your thoughts about kidnapping?"

"No."

"Why not?"

"I don't know."

"I'd like you to come with me to another office and look at some photographs to see if you can identify the man."

"OK."

Clayton sat on the long bench watching the men who hung up their hats and coats, shaking out umbrellas and even using umbrella spikes to ease off shiny galoshes. The members of the Travellers were not the kind to be caught by the winter's first flurry of snow.

He saw his host walk in, look toward him and nod a greeting as a club servant helped him out of his coat. Michael Andrews was one of those big-faced men who always looked as if they were just back from climbing a mountain or administering justice in some farflung outpost of the empire. In fact, like a good many top Intelligence people, he was an Oxford man, onetime lecturer at Magdalen in European history, whose massive frame provided good cover for an ascetic spirit. He would get his "K" next year if protocol was served.

He dabbed with a tissue at his face, wet from the snow, and walked over to Clayton, taking his arm and leading him up the wide staircase.

"We'll use one of the private rooms. But I must be gone in twenty minutes. Got to pick up Maggie and change for a reception at the Soviet Embassy. They probably want an up-to-date picture for my KGB file." He roared with laughter as he stamped his feet on the thick carpet.

"Here we are. They should have put the drinks in. Yes, they have. Pour me a whisky, young Clayton, and tell me what the trouble is."

"It's a little man who came to see me a week ago. Said his girl friend had been kidnapped by the Russians."

Andrews' face was noncommittal but interested.

"It doesn't hang together and I thought your people might care to have a look around." Clayton pushed his armchair nearer to Andrews' chair and took a swig of whisky before leaning back. "Facts first. The girl has an Irish name. Clodagh Kevan. She's a member of the CP. The chap's a medium-grade clerk in the M of D. His section deals with NATO weapon-design liaison."

Andrews laughed. "Poor sod. Go on, Clayton."

"He is also a member of the CP. About seven months or so. The girl is a real stunner, he left us a photograph. He saw her leaving the flat they use in Kensington. The place over Safeways. She was with an unidentified man. They drove to Heathrow. The car was Soviet Embassy transport and they both boarded the Ilyushin night flight to Moscow."

Andrews put down his glass and gestured for a refill. "Sounds more like a job for your people to me."

"I'm not so sure, sir. There are some odd facts about this. He said they were engaged to be married. That he saw her at about two-weekly intervals and on those occasions they had sex which went on all through the night. And he didn't know whether she was on the Pill or not."

Andrews pursed his lips. "Making up for lost time, no doubt. Those buggers in Defence sit on their arses all day. Don't get enough exercise, if you ask me."

"*Could* be making up for lost time, but why the lost time? They live within walking distance of one another, they're engaged. They could be having it off every night. But they don't even meet all that often."

Andrews looked up at the younger man. "You got a theory?"

"Yes, sir. I think he's been getting the sex as a reward. For services rendered, maybe."

Andrews put down his glass, stretched his arms, and looked up at Clayton. "I can't remember, laddie. Are you married?"

"No, sir."

"By Christ, your wife's going to have a hell of a time when you are. You've got a nasty mind, Clayton. But I think you're probably right. Anything else?"

"We checked with British Airports Authority, but Aeroflot still doesn't give them a proper manifest. Just numbers, that's all."

"Have you tried our photographic unit?"

"Yes."

"Any luck?"

"They've got photographs of all the passengers. The girl was certainly one of them, and she was with a man. They were together at check-in, in the VIP lounge, and they walked out together. Nobody's seen him before. He's definitely not an embassy man."

Andrews stood up. "Talk to Mac about it. It's worth pursuing. How you getting on over there now?"

"Not too bad, sir. I think."

Andrews smiled. "Take care. Keep at it." And he walked briskly to the door and down the stairs. They shared a taxi to Shepherd Market.

chapter
6

By the end of the first month Operation 471 had ground its gears into a smooth-working machine. But Slanski was aware of a problem. And so was Levin. The two problems were quite different.

Levin had gradually become aware of his own feelings of resentment toward Panov. Panov represented the military view. The Pentagon view. And he did it well. But he did it with a dogmatic aggression that sometimes left Levin seething with ill-concealed fury. Panov dealt mainly with facts and figures—the placement of troops and weapons by the Allies, and the Warsaw Pact forces in the satellite countries. When Levin queried the wisdom of some disposition of units Panov would listen, but it seemed that he could not be bothered to argue. He behaved as if his part was inviolate. If Levin wanted to put his oar in, OK, but it would make no difference. Levin began to form the suspicion that Panov's views were not his own. They came from Moscow. And Levin was not a professional soldier; neither were any others on his staff. He was determined to get another military man who could argue the toss with this stocky little major who plagued him so.

Slanski's worry was the girl. It was obvious that she enjoyed her time with Levin. There were glances exchanged between them that indicated a real affection. There was much laughing when they were together, and when they walked in the snow inside the perimeter wall they ignored the guards as if they didn't exist. But Levin's time with the girl was too brief, and Slanski could sense the boredom when she was on her own. It was understandable, but potentially explosive. She was too intelligent, too bright, to stomach this regimen for another five or six months.

He had discussed it with Panov, and had been surprised at his reaction.

"Bring the girl into the operation. She could contribute. I have no doubt about that. He'll feel he's got someone on his side. The poor bastard's already getting paranoid about me."

"Why about you?"

"Because he can't very well argue with my opinion. Well, he can argue, but he can't make it stick. He's got no military training. He couldn't give fire orders to a platoon, let alone thirty divisions. You watch. He'll be pressing for a replacement inside a week. Or an additional military adviser. One who does what Levin tells him." Panov was grinning at Slanski's astonishment.

"This means trouble, Boris. We'd better put it right."

"Nonsense, my boy. It's proof that it's working. You don't imagine that Langham loves the Pentagon, do you? Presidents never do. They give orders, but if the soldiers don't like them they get shuffled on one side. American Presidents are like old ladies who buy themselves a lion for protection but they have to keep it in a cage. OK, they poke it with an umbrella from time to time, to hear it roar, but that's all. Even Roosevelt was never too sure what the military was up to. Kennedy and others didn't know a thing. Levin is feeling frustrated and that means we're all doing our job. It's working, my friend."

"Is the information you give him true?"

"Up to now it is, but it may not be when we start making our moves on the ground."

"So how can he react accurately?"

"He'll have everything that matters."

Slanski looked at Panov. The leathery face, the bulging neck and the barrel chest that strained his uniform jacket.

"You know something I don't know, Boris?"

The piggy eyes looked back at him, alert and guarded.

"Maybe, Ivan, maybe."

They had held a mock press conference, and two men from Novosti who had worked in the United States were the inquisitors.

"Has any decision been made, Mr. President, on next year's contribution by the United States to the United Nations?"

"It's under review at the moment."

"By whom?"

"By a committee under the chairmanship of the Secretary of State."

"Are there any advance indications of their decision?"

"No, sir. And they will be recommending, not deciding."

"Who will decide, Mr. President?"

"I will."

"Will it depend in any way on the contribution made by the Soviet Union?"

"The committee and I will bear in mind all relevant factors when the decision is made."

"Can you give us an idea of what you consider relevant factors, Mr. President?"

Levin shrugged. "The phases of the moon, the Dow-Jones index and the state of the repair work in Red Square."

The meeting dissolved in laughter.

As Levin stood up one of the Novosti men said, "Can you tell us what *you* think the Americans will actually do about their contribution?"

Levin laughed and glanced at Slanski, who shrugged his shoulders. "Yes. Their permanent representative will say nothing until the last possible moment. And then he'll raise hell about unpaid subscriptions and announce that the United States will pay its full quota, but they'll pay it on a month-to-month basis."

There was silence for a moment and then the same questioner said, "And who's going to be the new Secretary of Defense?"

Slanski stood up quickly. "I'm sorry, gentlemen. The Ministry of Culture will have to consult its own crystal ball. That's enough for now."

The visitors had been taken to another part of the building for lunch and Levin had eaten alone with the girl.

As she spooned out the last of her avocado she said, "Do you know something?"

"No. What?"

"You're beginning to sound like Langham. You sound like the President. I can't believe you'll be wrong about the UN thing."

Levin smiled. "I won't be. You see."

He looked at the girl's beautiful face and reached out to touch her hand. "Can I ask you something?"

She smiled and nodded. "Ask me."

"You never really told me how Slanski persuaded you to come back here with him. I think you evaded the question."

His eyes were on her face, intent on her answer. She looked away for a moment and then looked back at him. She smiled.

"You know, Andrei, Slanski is a very shrewd man. He didn't persuade. He talked with me, about my childhood, my background. Why I joined the party and so on. And then he talked about you for a long time. He showed me a photograph too. And then he said you were going to do something special, something important that would cut you off completely from the rest of the world. Particularly girls." She smiled. "He told me about the girl students, and how they didn't last very long. He said you would need somebody physically attractive and intelligent as well. Would I help you? Not help the party, not help the Soviet Union—but you. An individual."

"And why did you agree?"

She looked at him for a long time before she spoke. "When Slanski was telling me about you it was as if he were describing someone I knew. It was a long time before I realized who it was. It was me. The same contradictions. The same flaws. And—I hoped—the same virtues."

Levin smiled. "When I first saw you, all I could think was that you were so beautiful. And then you gave me the box

67

with the roses. I knew that must be you. Slanski or Panov would never have thought of that. And it was as if I had known you all my life, and there was no need to pretend, or establish that I was the professor."

She smiled up at him. "I hope you gave the girls good marks in their exams, Andrei."

He stood up, faintly embarrassed, and loosened his tie. As he sat down again he said, "They were very wise, Slanski or somebody. I would have gone mad in this place without you."

She leaned forward and took one of his cigarettes and his lighter. When she had inhaled she leaned back and said, "Do you miss your wife, Andrei?"

It was a long time before he answered.

"It is a terrible thing to say, but no. It's part of my life that's like a dream. Not a bad dream, just a dream. I think, as always, I was 'in love.' I didn't love. I cared about her, but after she died it seemed—I don't like to say this Clodagh, it might turn you against me—it seemed like the shedding of a burden, a responsibility. I was sad for her, but not for me."

There was silence as he looked at her, and he flinched when she spoke, although it was almost a whisper.

"And your daughter. How did you feel about her?"

Levin shook his head slowly and his voice was low. "Nothing, Clodagh, nothing at all. I made the arrangements for her to be accepted at the orphanage and I closed my mind to it all and went back to my work. I was no husband, no father."

"You know, for a psychologist you're very insecure."

His head jerked up. "In what way?"

"Since Galina died have you ever slept with a girl who was not a student?"

He frowned, his hand slowly rubbing the side of his face as he thought.

"No. I don't think so."

The green eyes looked up at his face, and he noticed how her full soft lips never quite met. Even at this serious moment he imagined his tongue in her mouth.

"You married Galina, but although she was beautiful her mind couldn't compete with yours. And she became a burden on your life. You had enough self-assurance to get by yourself, but she was an extra burden. You had to carry her insecurity as well as your own. And when the burden went you hurried back to the shelter of your work. You sleep with girl students because the relationship is already established. You up here, and them down there. But you don't escape *quite* so easily, Andrei Levin, because you're a psychologist. *You* know what you are up to all right, so when you've had enough there's still some guilt and you make a mess of the ending. And for that you can thank our old friend Josif Vissarionovich Dzhugashvili."

"Stalin. What's he got to do with it?"

"He fixed things so that you went into an orphanage, and orphanage kids are lucky if they end up with enough confidence for themselves. They have none to give away."

Levin looked at the calm beautiful face and then shrugged. "It sounds possible, but maybe too easy. It would be worth a study paper after all this."

She reached forward to touch his hand, smiling up at him as she spoke. "Don't dwell on it, Andrei, I won't be a burden."

He turned his head quickly to look at her. "I never saw you as a burden. It was like another me. Just as you said. I think maybe I am beginning to be a burden on *you*. I feel that although I know more about the science of people's minds than you do, you have something that I *haven't* got. And that's wisdom, or maybe realism."

He looked around the room, and despite the dry warmth he shivered. "I wish that we could just walk together somewhere. Anywhere. A busy street, a quiet wood—it wouldn't matter. Or that we could say, 'Let's go to the Bolshoi tonight, or the circus, or a restaurant.' "

She smiled. "Let me take you for a walk. Sit down and hold my hand."

He sat down, smiling. "Where are we going, Clodagh? Tell me."

"Have you heard of Killarney?"

"No."

"Shame on you. That's where we're going. Now close your eyes. That's right. And listen carefully, because it's very very quiet. It's very green everywhere and it's very springy under-foot. There's a mist along the edge of the lake, but it's early yet. It'll be gone by midmorning. I can hear a skylark. She's coming down lower and lower and fluttering across to lead us away from her nest on the ground. The seagulls are still here, so it must be windy in the bay. Take a deep breath, Andrei, smell the wet grass and you'll just get a breath of the peat smell from alongside the small stream over there. Tomorrow we'll bring a lunch basket and our rods. We could hire a boat today and come here at first light in the morning when the fish are feeding. And by noon it will be too hot on the lake and we'll walk up the scree to the first trees and have our picnic, and then you'll love me and we'll go to sleep until the light starts to go."

She stopped and watched his face. His eyes were still closed and there was a smile on his lips. Without opening his eyes he said, "How do you say 'I love you' in Irish, Clodagh?"

She laughed. "I've no idea, my love."

"I say it in English, then. Dear, beautiful Clodagh, I love you."

"I'm afraid I love you too, Andrei. Now you tell me a story about wolves and witches and dark snow forests."

He laughed. "No. I want to stay in Killarney."

Slanski and Panov had asked for a special meeting the next day. The girl had been asked along, too. They had assem-bled, the four of them, in the conference room. And Slanski opened the meeting.

"I took the liberty, Andrei, of speaking to Moscow about our press conference yesterday. I mentioned your forecast about the American attitude at the UN because I felt they might be interested. They *were* interested. So much so that they discussed your opinion with Kolchov at the UN. He doesn't agree with you, neither does the Presidium. But the Novosti people thought you'd be proved right. We'll know in a few weeks' time. However, they raised two points. They request no more forecasts on any subject in front of out-siders. And having said that, they ask for your opinion on the appointment of the Secretary of Defense."

Levin half smiled. "They want to test me out, is that it?"

"I gather not. A month is too early to do that. No, I think they genuinely want your views."

"You want them now?"

"If it's possible. Take your time if you wish."

Levin shrugged. "There's no point. Not unless something extraordinary happens before he makes the appointment."

"So."

"So he'll appoint Larsen."

"Tell us how you decided that."

Levin leaned back, his hands in his pockets, his legs stretched out. He didn't look at any of them as he collected his thoughts. His eyes were on the Washington clock.

"Let us look at the two candidates. Larsen is one, and Warrender is the other. The newspapers in the United States have all gone for Warrender. He's an old friend of the President. He's young, about fifty-one or fifty-two. He's not an old party hand getting his turn at the controls. He's from California, so he's got a strong base. He'll bring fresh ideas and attitudes. He's tough enough to ride the Pentagon. He is well off but not wealthy, so he's reasonably independent. And he's not in anybody's pocket politically. He got where he is more or less on his talent. He served in Korea, so he knows what it's all about." Levin sat up in his chair, smiling, as he looked around the table. "An excellent candidate. So why not Warrender?"

He went on. "The President knows that his military problems are going to be in Europe. NATO, the Mediterranean and the Middle East—Africa maybe. Warrender has barely been outside the United States. Larsen has been around Europe since Marshall Plan days. He's trusted and admired. Langham always plays the balance. He leaves the party professionals with their clothes on even when they are wrong. He lets them share the kudos when he is right. They won't like Warrender, they'll see him as a whizz-kid upstart. And at the Pentagon end Langham's going to need a man who grinds away diplomatically. Not a rough-rider. The Pentagon has finished that type every time they've been landed with one. Larsen has helped those military guys a hundred ways, on committees and in NATO meetings. They won't trust him, but they'll listen, and that's the most Langham can hope for. And Larsen *is* a politician, he knows how to drag Congress along with the President. Warrender would be like Jack Kennedy, a great guy but never getting his legislation through Congress. And finally—I just *know* Langham will choose Larsen."

He smiled faintly as he looked around the faces. Nobody spoke, because nobody knew what to say. He had argued the case for Warrender and then pulled his own reasoning to bits. They had no feel for whether he was right or wrong. He was on his own, a long way away.

Levin and the girl were sitting on the bergère couch, their feet up on a long low stool as they watched the TV. They were both wearing only light dressing gowns and they were eating thick T-bone steaks after the clear chicken soup.

The color from the late news presentation dissolved to the station-identification logo and then dissolved again as the credits came up in black and white for the late-night film.

The girl said, "You'll like this film, Andrei. I do."

"What's it about, *Casablanca*—a war film?"

"I suppose it *is* a war film." She looked at her watch and looked back at the screen. "In forty-one minutes from now she's going to say, 'Play it again, Sam,' and the pianist's going to play 'As Time Goes By.'" And she looked at him smiling as she hummed the tune.

"How do you know all this?"

"Because I've seen it ninety-nine times or thereabouts. That bit's famous. It's a classic."

But the film didn't hold him, the flickering image bored him like those other classics, the Russian ones like *The Battleship Potemkin* where everyone waited awestruck as the baby carriage jolted its way down the steps.

He looked at her lovely face, the curve of her cheek and the small neat nose, and his eyes went down to her stomach where the silk dressing gown had slid away. The light from the screen touched the bush of black hair that emphasized the mound between her legs. When he looked back again at her face she was looking at him and smiling that amused smile.

"You're not watching the film, Andrei."

"I'd rather watch you."

"Still?"

"Still."

She stood up, the dressing gown sliding from her shoulders as she moved across and stood in front of him, her legs apart. There was no coyness and no embarrassment. She had stood like this for other men, and she had learned that this man was a looker, a toucher, a fondler, and she was happy to please him. When his hand went up between her legs she stood there patiently for a few moments as it moved on her. When it grew more avid she gently held his wrist as she turned away.

"Let's lie on the bed, honey, it's easier."

It seemed a long time later when, with him still lying on her, kissing her mouth gently, she whispered, "Listen, they're playing the tune. Look, that's Ingrid Bergman, and the man's Humphrey Bogart."

When it was over he turned back to her. " 'And when two lovers woo, they still say I love you.' What does 'woo' mean?"

She looked up at his face. "What we're doing now."

"So I say, 'I love you'?"

The green eyes sparkled wet and the soft upper lip quivered. "You don't have to say that, Andrei."

"I know. But I say it all the same."

chapter

7

At the end of January, Langham had announced the appointment of Erik Larsen as Secretary of Defense, and the congressional committee had endorsed his selection in the record time of two weeks.

But it was the end of March before the American representative at the UN had stood up to say his piece about the United States's contribution to United Nations funds. Even some of America's oldest allies had been shaken by his excoriating commentary on those who used the UN for their own ends and then welched on their contributions. And against expectation he had named names—or one name: the Soviet Union, whose representative had walked out of the General Assembly followed by the more alert representatives of the Warsaw Pact and the members of the Organization of African Unity. The United States would once again meet its obligations in full, he said, but, in future, payments would be made quarterly and, like the Soviet Union's, in arrears.

Levin's forecasting had had several effects on the Kiev operation. The staff of specialists had been strengthened on orders from Moscow. Panov was recalled to Moscow for two weeks' special briefing, and the conference room had been converted into an operations room with computer links to Red Army headquarters in Moscow and a tactical headquarters on the outskirts of Warsaw. A high-grade cipher and radio unit took over from the old signals unit, and the new facilities included a high-grade link to the Soviet embassies in Washington and London.

The other effect was on Levin. He longed for the sight of houses, cars, and people going about their normal business. The hangar had become a prison and he recognized the neuroses. Just one day outside the perimeter, maybe just one hour, and he knew the tension would go. But Moscow was adamant. Levin would stay where he was and no outside contact. The messages he gave to Slanski for passing to Moscow would have got any other man a lifetime in Siberia, and even Slanski's diplomatic translations brought terse replies.

The operation itself was growing more intense and the flood of paper across his desk kept Levin occupied night after night. At the beginning of April Levin had sensed a tension in the unit. Both Slanski and Panov seemed cautious in their replies, not willing, as they normally were, to discuss things to conclusions. A few days later Slanski had asked for a special meeting.

They sat in the operations room at the far end of the long table. Just Levin, Slanski and Panov. It was Panov who leaned forward to speak.

"Andrei. We have reached a new phase in the operation now. We have received new orders from Moscow. Sometime in the next three months the Red Army will take Berlin, and we shall be part of that operation."

Panov's cold eyes watched Levin's face and waited for him to speak.

"What does it mean, Boris, 'take' Berlin?"

Panov shrugged his broad shoulders. "We shall know in due course. Meanwhile you should check on the American situation in Berlin. I've told them to put up a large-scale map in your operations room and to flag the present dispositions. The time may be shorter than we expect. There will be queries from Moscow in the next forty-eight hours."

Levin lit a cigarette and watched the flame of the lighter before he snapped it off. "I assume that 'take' includes military action, Boris."

Panov nodded. "It includes everything, Andrei." And he

got to his feet clumsily and walked to the corridor door. Then he turned, digging in his jacket pocket, and he walked back to the table.

"Moscow sent you that, Mr. President. Langham has just had one."

It was a small quartz-crystal watch, and as Levin pressed the button the red diodes lit up, the seconds flicking quickly. There was an inscription engraved on its face, and he held it slanted to the light so that he could read it. In a delicate script it said: "'God helps them that help themselves.'— Benjamin Franklin, June, 1736." As Levin looked up, smiling, Panov nodded and walked into the corridor.

The girl had sensed Levin's tensions and had planned an hour each evening when they listened to music, talked about books and read poetry. It was on one of these occasions that she had first realized the magnitude of the pressures on Levin and their effect on his mind. It was the first time that she had completely recognized that this was not some elaborate and eccentric game, not even a military exercise. From what he had hinted it was the buildup to what could be a war. It was as real as the news they read every day, and it was only a small part of what was going on elsewhere. In the closed-in atmosphere in which they operated, Levin's work seemed vastly important, but she guessed that in fact Levin would be used effectively only when the first aggressive moves were made. Meanwhile he was their modern soothsayer. An expensive piece of pink litmus paper.

She had read him one of John Clare's poems and was telling him about Clare's life when he turned to her, his face drawn. He was looking at her, but she knew he didn't see her, and she heard him say softly, "We're all going mad."

She put down the book of poems and looked at his face. He was extraordinarily handsome, and part of his attraction was his apparent unawareness of his looks. But the real attraction for her was his vulnerability. From the first day she had been aware of the cutting edge of his mind. It was the first time in her life that she had recognized a mind that had greater clarity than her own. A clarity that came, unlike her own, not from analysis but by instinct, as if his mind were already programmed with solutions. His awareness of people and their motivations was amazing. But it had one flaw. The perception was like some lens with a long focal length, unable to bring into focus the immediate foreground. He seemed unaware of the abuse of his mind by Slanski and Panov and their masters in Moscow. He saw himself as a leader of a team, when it was all too clear to her that he was their captive. He hadn't even noticed the subtle changes that had left Slanski still as head of Operation 471 but with Panov in direct and separate contact with the authorities in Moscow. Panov still played his role of Pentagon "hawk" in their meetings, but somehow he was not part of the charade. He was watching the performance from the wings.

And she was aware of Slanski's and Panov's subtle pressures for her to stay aligned with them, to leave Levin with his delusions. But for the first time in her life she cared more for somebody else than she did for herself. She was attracted by him physically and she admired his brain, but it was much more than that that moved her heart. She was his only protection, and she knew that whatever the implications she was totally committed to him, far behind this complex operation.

Michael Andrews walked from Petty Prance up to Buckingham Palace, then across Green Park and through the side streets to the back entrance of the Hilton.

The meeting was in one of the penthouse suites, and he hesitated as he stepped out of the lift. A young man in a checked sports coat, crew-cut and with an ominous bulge where his shoulder holster had been pulled forward, came toward him.

"Can I help you, sir?"

"I'm sure you can." Andrews opened a small red leather folder that displayed his photograph and an identity card.

The young man turned and knocked, and then held the door open as Andrews passed through.

A man in slacks and a sports shirt got up from the armchair where he was sitting. His hand was outstretched. "Mike, how ya' doin'?"

"Fine, Harry. How about you?"

"Not bad. Come and sit down. Have a drink."

"A malt, please, Harry. Neat."

The man suddenly stopped pouring and straightened up. "My God, Mike, I nearly forgot. Congratulations on the knighthood. There was much rejoicing in Langley and Washington when we heard about it."

"Not too much, I hope, or they'll take the bloody thing back." Andrews arranged his broad back in the chair and held up his glass. "Cheers, matey. What's the trouble?"

"Who says there's trouble?"

"Batman outside. Your telephone call. This place instead of the embassy. And what the little dicky-birds are saying."

"What are they saying, Mike?"

"Aw, c'mon. Let's have it."

"Do you remember the six months before Cuba? You were in Washington then. Every goddam Soviet intelligence outfit was checking out to see if the U.S. was mobilizing. We were not, and we couldn't understand why the hell they thought we might be."

"I remember, Harry."

"Well, as we all found out, they were checking that we were not mobilizing because we had found out that they were setting up the missile circus in Cuba. Well, it's happening all over again."

"Which bit is happening again?"

"For six months all the reports we've been getting show that the Soviets have been putting their main intelligence effort into checking us out all over the globe. We've pulled in three of their people in the last two months. Important people. And every darn one of them was working on orders of battle, training, recruitment—that sort of stuff. They've all been KGB, and the GRU usually covers that kind of stuff. And one last thing. They were all legals, all based at the Washington embassy. No illegals, no foreign nationals. We don't like it, Mike. How about we compare notes?"

Andrews leaned over and put down his glass and then leaned back in his chair. "What do the Samos pictures show?"

"Nothing special, just the usual average movement of units. Nothing out of the ordinary."

"Where d'you think they've got their eye on this time?"

"Our evaluation says Turkey, Korea, the Balkans or Berlin."

"Any preferences?"

"Yep—Berlin."

"Absolutely certain. Out of those four, anyway. If it was Turkey or Korea they wouldn't need to worry about your readiness. They're both on the Soviet doorstep. They could be in and have it all over in forty-eight hours and you couldn't do a thing. No, it'll be Berlin—if anything."

"You got any doubts about it?"

Andrews turned his big head to look at his American opposite number. "Afraid not, Harry. Those buggers have never forgotten that bloody nose they got over the Cuban missiles, and Berlin is worth fifty Cubas."

"Have your people picked up anything?"

Andrews took a deep breath and pursed his lips, and looked at his companion speculatively. "Nothing specific, but the signs are there, and they're increasing. Something's up, and it looks like Berlin to me. But you never can tell with those bastards—it could be a feint. I'd be prepared to set up a liaison team with Langley if that would suit your masters. I would suggest you include NSA as well."

"Let's do that, Michael. Let's get it going in the next few days before I go back." Harry tapped out his pipe in the ashtray. "Was there any particular reason why you wanted the National Security Agency included?"

"Yes. There's some very fancy radio traffic coming in and out of their embassy here. High-speed Morse with some sort of signal bias wound in, and a code that we haven't come across before. We haven't cracked it, but we've only had two weeks of it. NSA could do a better job. Our people in Berlin have reported similar stuff coming out of Warsaw."

"Any source identification?"

"Very general. The opinion at the moment is that it's coming out of Lvov. Somewhere round about there, from the signal strength. My chaps can give yours anything we've got, and maybe between the two outfits we can build up a picture."

"Fine. What do you think your government's attitude would be to a move by the Soviets against Berlin?"

Andrews stood up, smiling. "They'd be very strong for you guys doing something about it." He shrugged. "For Christ's sake, Harry, what could we do, apart from making a noise? Everything's run down in the past five years. The whole of NATO wouldn't stop 'em for more than a few days, unless somebody pressed a nuclear button."

He bent down to put his glass back on the small table. "Be seeing you."

Murphy and Peters had found the atmosphere at the New Scotland Yard office restrictive and they had suggested diplomatically to Clayton that the flat at Sloane Square would be more conducive to inspiration. Clayton took the hint, and the three of them had settled down with note pads and a tape recorder.

Duplicate tapes of the radio traffic to the Soviet Embassy had already been sent to CIA headquarters at Langley, and the NSA had reported back through the CIA to London that they had equivalent traffic into the Soviet Embassy in Washington and that the code had not been broken. They also confirmed that the code was not in use on any Red Army, political, or KGB network. The CIA had been requested to carry out an on-the-ground identification of the signal source.

The three of them dredged up all those loose ends that had lain around unexplained in both organizations for the last year or so, and one of these was an identity check by both sides on unidentified Soviet officials. Out of this session came recognition of the Russian who had accompanied Clodagh Kevan to Heathrow and onward.

It was Murphy who had recognized the face. "Yeah. That's one of ours. I can't remember his name, but he was at their embassy in Washington. We had him placed as positive KGB. Rank, captain or above."

Murphy turned to Peters. "Remember that fellow we gave the shove to after that incident at the diner? What the hell was his name?"

"Ustachi—something like that."

"Ustenko, that's him. Well, he took over from this guy in the photograph. Central records will have him on file."

80

Murphy looked at Clayton. "Can we use your security signals facility or do we have to go to Grosvenor Square?"

"All facilities, Sir Michael said. Help yourselves. There's a scrambler on the red phone."

A messenger brought the reply two hours later, and Murphy slit open the double envelope. There were two pages of computer printout, and a photograph.

Murphy read the first page and then looked up. "Slanski his name is, Ivan Slanski. Was promoted to major after his recall to Moscow—KGB, First Directorate. After Washington he went to Directorate S. That's about it. The picture is him, I'd guess. There'll be plenty of others on file."

He read the second page quickly and then shoved it aside. "Just general crap about the function of Directorate S."

He whistled softly and inaccurately the opening theme of the *Pathétique* and looked thoughtfully at Clayton. "I reckon we'd better have a closer look at your files about the girl. Do you agree?"

"The man concerned—Jephcott. He's available, too, if we need him."

Murphy turned to Peters. "You go to the embassy, Pete. Get the CIA to run a check on this dame and check if Slanski has any current record in London. Check with SIS records as well on both of them."

Slanski and the girl were watching the first cutting of the grass in the compound. Boxes of plants had been brought from the Crimea and they were being planted out in the border alongside the hangar. For security reasons there were no trees in the compound, and Levin and the girl, who were not allowed out, had never been able to look to a horizon. Two hundred yards in any direction was the maximum range. But now there were leaves on the trees outside, and despite the coming and going of army vehicles they could hear the calling of wood pigeons and, in the early morning, the drumming of woodpeckers.

"How do you think he is, Clodagh?"

"Tense, very tense."

"And you?"

She looked at him and laughed. "You must know already, Ivan. This life is a kind of madness. But I shall put up with it for Andrei's sake."

"Is there anything we can do to make it easier for him or you?"

She looked up quickly. "Too damn true there is. Let us out of this dump for a couple of hours."

"Moscow says no."

"Why?"

"For security reasons."

"So what about you and Panov? You both get out."

"Not very often, I'm afraid. And we're not so classified as Andrei."

"But you can go out when you want."

Slanski snorted. "I've been out three times and Panov maybe four times. Each time you'd have thought we were defecting. Two guards went with me every time."

"And with Panov?"

"The same. Why should he be different?"

The girl looked at him without turning her head. "He seems to have a special position, independent of you or Andrei."

Slanski stopped walking and turned to look at her. "What makes you say that?"

She shrugged. "At meetings he ignores anything you or Andrei say about military things. He just sits there, silent."

"I guess he recognizes that neither of us knows enough to make sensible comment."

"It's more than that. He despises you. Both of you."

"Did Andrei say this?"

"No. I say it."

"On what grounds?"

"The way he looks, the way he talks, or doesn't talk. I've seen Andrei playing you off against Panov. *You* always respond. One way or another. You justify a view or an attitude. Panov just sits there like a Buddha. Watching. Observing. Secure. Not involved."

Slanski sighed and turned away without answering, and she followed him. He spoke without looking at her.

"Do you regret the choice you made?"

She turned on him quickly. "Never, never, never. I came out of interest, out of curiosity, but that finished a long time ago. Make no mistake, Ivan. I stay only for Andrei's sake."

"There's something I always wanted to ask you."

She frowned. "So. Ask me."

"Do you remember the day I met you and first talked with you?"

"Not the date, but I remember the occasion."

"Do you remember what you did the day before? The evening before?"

She stopped walking, her hand over her eyes as she bent her head. Then her head came up.

"Yes. I went to a concert at the Albert Hall."

"They played some music. The words were about 'mother of the free,' and so on. Do you remember?"

She nodded. "Yes, they do it every year. Elgar's 'Pomp and Circumstance.'" She looked at him with curiosity.

"There were tears on your face. Why was that?"

The green eyes looked at him sharply. "How do *you* know?"

"I was there. I watched you through glasses from a box. And you didn't sing with the others."

She arranged her cardigan carefully on each shoulder in turn. Not because she was cold, but to give herself time to think. "I was moved by the music. I hate the words, they're so typically English. Nevertheless the music is magnificent, and the words are, too, if they weren't about England. The crowd singing made me feel terribly alone and I thought about when I was a small girl." She laughed sharply. "It was self-pity, Ivan. Disgusting."

And he changed the subject to food and the fresh fruit that had come up from the Crimea with the flowers.

On the slope of the hill there were women stringing up the hop poles. Wire, top and bottom, and creosoted string in the strands between.

A man with a donkey stood watching them and waved back as one of them waved to him. His belongings were in the two hampers slung over the donkey's back. The hampers were of soft plaited straw, each one fastened with a long wooden skewer. Zhitomir produced some of the Soviet Union's best hops and flax, but the standard of husbandry was low. There were groundsel and the first threads of convolvulus trailing along the side of the field, and in the ditch itself were thick banks of dock leaves among the stocky thistles. Their seeds would have germinated in the hop fields long before the hops were harvested.

He squinted toward the sun where it was sinking behind the low hills and then looked toward the east. He walked on with the donkey another mile, then stopped. He eased out one of the long skewers and, spreading a red handkerchief on the donkey's back, took out a knife to slice a piece of cheese. After one bite he pulled the hamper further open. There were a kettle, boots, underwear. A block of tea and a loaf. One hand held the loaf, the other lifted the crust just far enough for him to see the two dials for a moment, and then the crust was laid back carefully in place.

The reading was nineteen degrees magnetic, and the radiated strength was fifty kilowatts. It must be just north of Kiev, and about seventy-five kilometers due east. It would be the skip distance that carried it to Washington, or a relay from London.

He put up his bivouac tent for the night, and he signaled his position to the British Embassy in Bucharest as the village of Gubochitsa on the Kiev road. He was asleep about eight o'clock local time.

Levin was standing half in the bathroom, half in the bedroom, wearing a toweling bathrobe and rope sandals. The girl was sitting in the armchair and they were both looking at the CBC news program.

The first item showed the crashed plane, and sweating helmeted men struggling with sheeted stretchers. The plane had crashed on takeoff out of Las Vegas, and the latest count was thirty-four dead, with more expected.

But it was the second item that had been in the headlines that they were waiting for. The film ended and the camera was on the newscaster; behind him was a picture of Checkpoint Charlie taken from Friedrichstrasse. The newscaster was reading from his notes.

"In East Berlin today the authorities announced the arrest of an alleged group of spies. A spokesman for the East German government said that over thirty people were taken into custody, including an American citizen. No names or further details have been given as yet, but unofficial sources suggest that the Soviet Union will be raising the question of American espionage networks based in West Berlin at the forthcoming session of the General Assembly of the United Nations." The newsman looked up to the camera and added, "There have been no comments so far from official sources in Washington. . . . In Johannesburg fierce fighting was . . ."

The girl leaned forward and turned down the sound. She turned to look over her shoulder at Levin.

"Is that the start, Andrei?"

"I guess so."

chapter
8

The evergreen forests of the Harz Mountains drew visitors in search of both relaxation and health, and the small town of Bad Harzburg was both a winter ski resort and a health center with its famous chloride and ferrous waters.

It had escaped the ravages of war, and its special camp where young SS men were officially encouraged to copulate with selected Rhine maidens became a rest camp for Allied troops whose intentions, although not officially encouraged, were to carry on this worthy tradition.

When present-day visitors pull on their walking boots or heavy shoes, they are warned that the frontier with East Germany is just a few kilometers to the east of the resort. Not that all that much warning is needed, because the green-flashed *Grenzpolizei* of both sides are separated by taut barbed-wire fencing, a fifty-five-yard depth of mine field, and, it is rumored, a whole selection of electronic devices that can detect the difference in weight between a field mouse and a stoat. And the watchtowers house their complement of military with machine guns on fixed traverses that cover 180 degrees.

In the early days sheep and cattle had grazed right up to the barbed wire, but before long the Russians had stopped this on their side of the border. A sheep or a cow could give cover to a human being.

Most of the visitors to Bad Harzburg were middle-class, looking for a quiet time, and even in winter the après-ski had a very low profile. But there was a disco just off Braunlagestrasse, and its owner and operator, Otto Faller, was a popular man with both locals and visitors. From a whole raft of virtues, they valued most his broad-mindedness and his discretion. His broad-mindedness was evidenced by the plethora of small rooms on the first floor, and his discretion was a byword. He knew which of the pretty girls did what, and for how much, and, of course, he knew where they could do it. On the first floor. Afternoons he was officially closed, and that ensured that visiting fathers were not engaged with visiting daughters. The local lovelies were there in strength and variety. Otto Faller was a popular man, respected by all, summer and winter alike.

Otto Faller had spent fifteen years in the Gehlen organization, and when that august body was broken up in the interests of détente it meant that anti-Russian intelligence out of West Germany came to a grinding halt. The Gehlen people were professionals and the CIA had provided most of their funds. They were the favorite sons of Allen Dulles, and the only organization in the West which had penetrated Soviet life at most levels from the bureaucrats to the KGB, and the general machinery of Soviet government.

A handful of enthusiasts still worked on, in great danger from their Soviet target and from their fellow countrymen in the rear. The East German spy Guillaume had sat in Willy Brandt's office while détente was being negotiated, but that was another story. The enthusiasts were well paid. About the same as the combined salaries of Helmut Schmidt and the President of the United States.

Otto Faller was one of the enthusiasts. The checkpoints in Berlin and at Helmstedt were all right for run-of-the-mill agents, but for the ex-Gehlen boys they were far too dangerous. Human nature, that standby of all intelligence operations, was at its most primitive level along the frontier at the Harz Mountains, and the nubile girls were paid well to hoist their skirts for the guardians of the frontiers of democracy. And if, on odd occasions, two men went back through the electronics and the mines, where only one had journeyed over, well, who was to know, or care, when those long legs were ready to open on demand?

The man who sat with Otto Faller in his private suite at the top of the disco was not a customer for the girls, although he contributed most of their earnings. He brought the money from his masters and he passed on specific instructions. His base was in the sleepy university town of Göttingen, and he knew more about what was going on in the Soviet Union than half the members of the Presidium knew. And despite his comparative youth, at thirty-seven he was a full colonel in the CIA. And he was, of course, a lecturer in American history at the University of Göttingen.

Otto Faller was a businesslike man, he never played games with the CIA, and as they settled around the oak table he got down to business. They had asked him to check on Slanski.

"Slanski has disappeared. Nobody knows where he is. He's not in Dzerdzhinski Square and he's not at the new place on the ring road."

"When was he last seen?"

"Just before last Christmas."

"Any indication that he's fallen out of favor?"

"No. Just the opposite. He was promoted to full colonel about August last year."

"What was he working on then?"

"He was officially with Directorate S and he had been running the United States desk."

"Has he left the Soviet Union, do you think?"

"Not under his own name, anyway. I've had that checked."

"Any ideas?"

Faller leaned back, turning the stem of his pipe in the bowl so that it squeaked as he lined it up. He sighed. "There's talk of some special unit."

"Where?"

"Somewhere in the Ukraine. No more than that."

"And what's the unit's function?"

"Nobody knows. They've got the Tokama nuclear-fusion unit down there, of course. That's in Kiev. Fantastic security there."

"But they would have known if Slanski was there, surely."

"I'd have guessed so. And it's not his sort of operation at all. He's a specialist on organizing networks in the States."

"Anything on the girl?"

"No. Nobody's heard of her. We're trying to check the passenger list for that flight, but it's difficult. They'll keep trying."

"Anything else?"

"Yes. They picked up Simmonds in the roundup in East Berlin. They took him straight to Moscow. He's in the interrogation unit down the road at Podolsk."

"Is he talking?"

"Yep."

Georgi Velichko was one of the two secretaries to the Presidium. A survivor from Khrushchev's days, a ruthless, untiring organizer. A ready tool for the variety of despots who had been his bosses. A peasant whose vulgarity and excesses had made him enemies, but whose power and usefulness to the powerful had kept him immune from attack. Derided as a messenger boy of his masters, he had nevertheless carried bad tidings without fear, and had always stayed on to clean up the blood and press the message home. In America he would have been designated a troubleshooter. But in the Soviet Union the shooting was for real, and as a young man he had achieved a reputation during the collectivization when he was dispatched to accelerate the liquidation of the kulaks in the Ukraine. He had fulfilled the same bloodthirsty role when Stalin had liquidated the trade-union leaders.

He sat now, with Slanski, in the communications room office, his piggy eyes missing nothing as he watched the operators through the open door.

"Is he behaving, Slanski? Doing what you want?"

"He is proving very successful, Comrade Secretary."

"So I've heard. So I've heard. You keep the bastard up to the mark. This operation is costing us a lot of money. There are those who wonder if it's worth it."

Slanski had opted out of reacting to this sort of goading

years ago. He knew how to deal with it. "They may be right, of course, comrade."

Velichko hawked loudly and spat on the floor, grinding the residue with his boot. The small, faded eyes watched for a reaction on Slanski's face. They found none, and he belched and went on.

"I'll have a go at that girl before I go back. These foreign women make a change. I'd say she was a real *baralka*. She's got the tits for it, anyway."

"I'd better explain something, comrade. The girl is for Levin, and there is a genuine affection between them. It would be unwise to disturb that. Extremely unwise."

The bloated face was red with anger. "Don't give me that, Slanski, the bitch is here to get screwed. That's what she's paid for, she can find out what it's like to get it from a real Russian, not a damned schoolteacher. You fix for her to come to my room after we've eaten and if the damned President wants to put it in her he can damn well wait."

Slanski looked at the turkey-cock face, the jowls quivering with rage, and he said quietly, "She's not paid for anything, Comrade Secretary. And I'll make any arrangements you want when Moscow orders me to." He stood up. "And not before, comrade. I'd watch my step if I were you."

And without waiting for an answer he walked out.

Velichko's tour of inspection had concluded and Slanski had taken the precaution of phoning direct to the head of the First Directorate. A message came at midday from Moscow. "Eyes only" for Velichko, it ordered him to return to Moscow immediately.

The shrewd, angry eyes looked at Slanski after reading it, but Slanski stayed silent. Velichko decided that the military plane could take him back to Moscow after dinner, and he ate with Levin and Slanski in the operations room.

Levin was amused at the strutting cockerel of a man, noticing his constant, agitated shifting of the beefy shoulders as he wielded his knife and fork, as if his jacket were too tight. Levin recognized those overt signs of frustration and tension, and kept the conversation moving. The subject, the early days of Velichko's career. The meal was almost over when Velichko first mentioned the operation in Berlin.

"They're not going to need you, you know, Professor. Our people know how to deal with the Americans."

"Let us hope I'm not needed, comrade, but anything that helps us solve the Berlin problem satisfactorily is useful."

Food sprayed from Velichko's mouth as he threw down his knife in quick anger. "To hell with Berlin, mister, we'll really bury those bastards this time—just as Khrushchev said. It won't be just Berlin."

Slanski saw Levin's head come up, his mouth open to speak, the quick glance in his direction and the hesitation before he carried on eating. Levin barely spoke during the rest of the meal.

The commercials had come on after *Kojak*, and Levin had watched them all, his legs crossed and his feet up on the small table.

The girl laughed and said, "They would be so flattered, Andrei, if they could see your face."

He turned to look at her. "I don't understand."

"You study the commercials as if they were feature films or documentaries."

Levin wagged his finger. "Clodagh Kevan, I regret having to say this, but you're a snob. I like the commercials, and clever people have spent much thought working them out. And as a psychologist I learn a lot from them about Americans and the West."

"Tell me, Andrei, reveal all."

He laughed. "I'm serious, Clodagh. After this is all over I shall do a paper on this. Just take that last commercial. The photography was better than in many shows we see. Why? Because they recognize that the pictures are more important than the words—fantasies are pictures, not words. It's just a furniture polish, but they make a small symphony in three movements—you, your home, your man. And they choose a daisy—that's so clever. No woman would buy herself roses. Daisies, yes, but not a rose, the man buys those. The daisy is cleanliness, freshness and modesty. A model flower. The

91

problem: dust and dirt. The solution: the product. The reward: the man and the roses."

The girl looked at him gently and with affection. "Dear Andrei, the last of the romantics. Honey, all they want is your dollar."

He shrugged. "I know, I know, I accept that, my love. But I don't mind. I would rather be . . . what was the word in the song in the film?"

"What film?"

"*Casablanca.*"

"Ah, yes—woo."

"That's it—woo. I would rather be wooed than ordered."

"You know what it was all about really?"

"No. What?"

"Symbols. Sexual symbols."

"For God's sake, do you make that out?"

"The tube of product is a phallic symbol, the girl's hand in closeup presses the button and out comes the product. The daisy is purity despite all. And the man coming in the door—well, it's obvious."

"But Freud is so old-hat, Clodagh. Unproved statistically, even today. Psychoanalysis itself is unproved. Nobody knows if it works. Most things in the world are upright or holes. It's too easy to make them all symbols of sex."

She smiled indulgently as mothers do at bright children. "I love you, Professor."

In the last week of May Moscow gave Slanski the narrative of a military exercise which included the closing for twenty-four hours of all the crossing points into East Germany from the West. They asked for Levin's assessment of American reactions. He was given four hours in which to consider the issues.

When Slanski saw Levin with the document, Levin walked over to the window behind his desk and stood there silent and preoccupied for five or six minutes. Then he turned and, leaning against the wall, looked across to where Slanski was sitting on the other side of the shiny desk.

"There would be an official protest. The ambassador would be called in, probably by the Secretary of State himself. The words would be sharp, but it would be implied that the State Department took it for granted that it was a one-time event. I'm assuming, in saying this, that the military exercise would have been publicized in advance. They'll be angry, but they won't take any action except diplomatic protest."

Slanski nodded. "And the President's view?"

"He'll welcome the little bit of tension. It will be his first brush with the Soviets since he came to office. There is tremendous anti-détente pressure on him now, and his instinct will be to meet Soviet pressure with counterpressure. This incident would give him a chance of showing the American public that he isn't going to rush into anything. So when the next pressure comes he can react toughly and nobody's going to say that he's just temperamentally quick on the draw. Mind you, our people are wasting a wonderful cover story for the real thing."

"What do you mean?"

"They're going to need to move troops and supplies around immediately before the Berlin operation. If the summer exercises were held over they would provide a cast-iron cover story."

"But you see no tough action from Washington?"

"None at all."

Slanski discussed Levin's view about the exercise with Panov, who reacted positively, and Slanski's report to Moscow covered this point.

They had walked around the inside of the perimeter wall three times, and according to Levin's calculations their afternoon walks were the equivalent of forty kilometers in the last month. Allowing for holidays, it would take them another three years to get halfway to Moscow.

They sat on the grassy mound that covered access covers to the drains, and Levin was aware of the girl's inertia. She seemed tired now, every day. And she seemed to have to make a big effort to talk at all. Her long slim fingers were plucking blades of grass, and her hand rested on her drawn-up knees, her eyes focused in the distance, despite the big wooden wall.

His hand took hers and she turned her head sideways to

look at him, her other hand pulling aside the curtain of long black hair. He saw the faint blue smudges under the big green eyes. Even her eyes seemed to have lost their sparkle. They looked, but he was not sure that they saw. He had seen too many patients like this not to know the signs. He opened his mouth to speak, but she spoke first.

"Have you noticed the birds, Andrei, on the wall?" And she pointed toward the perimeter wall. There were pigeons, thrushes, a blackbird or two and dozens of smaller birds, fieldfares and buntings.

He looked back at her face. "They're probably looking for food."

She shook her head. "I brought crumbs out this morning when you were working. I threw them down, but the birds stayed on the wall. I've watched them for weeks. They never come inside the perimeter. They just sit there watching. They don't sing, they don't move. It's as if they knew."

"Knew what?"

"About this place. That it's a prison, a sick place."

"Would you like me to see if I can get leave for you to have a break outside?"

She shook her head slowly. "Forget it, Andrei. The answer will be no. I asked them to give you a break. Just a day, I said. An hour even. A walk in the woods. The answer was no."

"But it may be different so far as you are concerned."

"If it were I wouldn't go."

Levin realized that he would hate it if the girl were away for a day, an hour even. He spent far too little time with her, but while he worked he knew she was there. She would never be farther away than two hundred feet.

The girl shivered. "They don't care about us, Andrei, neither of us. We might just as well be prisoners. I think that's what's wrong with this country. The people in power care about the Soviet Union, but they don't care about individual people. They would think me crazy. They give the orders, and the citizens get on with the job. We've got a roof over our heads, food, TV, and all that jazz, so they would say what the hell am I complaining about? Is that really what our lives are meant to be?"

"Disillusion of the convert?"

"No. Just a realization that this isn't a Communist country. It's just Bolshevik. A change of tsars."

"I wouldn't say that to Slanski or Panov."

"I shan't, Andrei. Panov is just a crafty soldier and Slanski's a faintly civilized KGB man. They haven't got enough imagination to be Communists." She looked up at him, her face serious. "I won't let you down, Andrei."

He looked at her and she saw tears at the edge of his eyes. He spoke very quietly. "You're all I've got, my love."

Levin stood up and reached down to help the girl up, and they walked slowly back to the building. Somehow the tension had been relieved, and somehow they were closer together.

The girl left him to take a bath, and Levin had half an hour before he need go back to the operations room.

He stood aimlessly and preoccupied in front of the bookshelves. He had read the two John O'Haras. That was America as Pravda said it was, but the Louis Auchincloss was more like Chekhov. Those old families and their money, their dynasties and their feuds. He reached for the Walt Whitman paperback. Now there was a Russian, a fundmentalist who could tell a tree from a forest. He looked back to the shelves and pulled down one of the big illustrated books. Clodagh had called them coffee-table books.

The book fell open at a panorama of New York Harbor, and on the next page was a photograph of the Statue of Liberty. There was a table of its dimensions, and pictures of the details, the torch, the head, the base. There were words chiseled into the base and he read them slowly and carefully.

He walked over to the bathroom and knocked. The girl shouted to him to come in, and he waved his hand at the steam and sat comfortably on the toilet.

"Something to read you."

He looked at her for a moment, aware of her wet body and the lather that touched her breasts and stomach, and the long legs pushed up beside the taps. She held a wet sponge against her neck as she waited for him to speak. His eyes went back to the book as he read slowly and clearly.

"Give me your tired, your poor,
Your huddled masses yearning to breathe free,
The wretched refuse of your teeming shore,
Send them, the homeless, tempest-tossed to me."

He looked over to her. "There is great kindness there, a big heart, generosity and love."

She smiled. "I told you, Andrei, you're the last of the great romantics."

He looked disappointed. "Doesn't it move you, Clodagh, doesn't it make you like Americans?"

She shrugged. "I bet they wish now that they could send them back. All those bloody Irish, and the Poles, and the Puerto Ricans."

"But that isn't what matters—well, it isn't *all* that matters. What matters is that a group of men felt that way. Cared enough to have it carved in stone. I like it."

Clodagh Kevan looked at his earnest face. Defiant, like a small boy's.

"That's good enough for me, Professor. From now on that shall be our personal national anthem."

He laughed and his eyes were on her body and when they went back to her face she was smiling and the green eyes actually sparkled again. He reached out and his spread fingers closed over a wet, smooth breast and she watched his face as his fingers kneaded the firm resilient flesh.

In the first week in June trucks and private cars formed long lines at the crossing points into East Germany. East German troops were manning the posts, and tanks and armored vehicles lined the roads on the other side as silent crowds watched over the barriers. At Helmstedt a jeep had edged its way along the line of parked vehicles, and at the barrier the crowd had parted as its radiator touched the gate. An American major with infantry insignia, a British major of the Royal Engineers and a major of the Chasseurs Alpins sat in the jeep blowing long blasts on the horn. On the other side nobody moved.

All over the world editors briefed journalists and photographers as they waited for airline tickets and cash. There was much to-ing and fro-ing in London, Bonn and Washington. The more efficient editors who had got their staffs away in the first couple of hours found themselves going through the same operation later in the morning. By midday the media had discovered that the real story was in West Berlin.

There had been phone calls from a spokesman of the East German government to the world's press in West Berlin. There would be a press conference at noon precisely, at the TV tower. An important announcement would be made.

The press veterans of the Cold War wondered if their day had come again, and there were demands for photographers, and hurried conversations with home offices in the world's capitals. It looked as if somebody was going to fire the starter's gun.

The guards at Checkpoint Charlie had never been more gracious, familiar faces were let through on the nod, and documents were barely scanned before the cars and passengers were waved through.

The conference hall at the TV tower was packed, and experts on military tactics, the Berlin airlift and the Americans were much in demand. A mass of TV cameras, microphones and lights were already in place and there was a hush as a group of men came onto the stage. There was a swell of conversation when the crowd identified the Russian commandant of East Berlin in civilian clothes. Then silence as a last lone figure walked from the wings to stand in the spotlights in front of the triple bank of microphones. It was the Deputy Prime Minister of the German Democratic Republic. He looked up into the glare of the lights as the cameras zoomed in for a closeup, and then he looked down at the paper in his hand. He read carefully and slowly.

"The Government of the German Democratic Republic announces that the protective wall which was erected in 1961 in the city of Berlin is to be demolished. It is felt that with the spirit of détente beginning to show positive results, this protection against revanchist elements is no longer necessary. It is hoped by our government that this positive and significant step will be reflected in the attitude of the warmongers in the West. Once again the members of the Warsaw Pact countries have demonstrated their total commitment to peaceful coexistence. Volunteers will commence the demolition of the wall tomorrow morning, and there will be no restrictions on movement in Berlin and the German Democratic Republic."

The Deputy Prime Minister nodded toward his silent audience, and then, as the shouted questions came, the group on the stage filed off, and a man from the East German Press Service spoke into the microphone.

"There will be no questions, gentlemen."

The TV lights dimmed and the crowds of journalists headed for the exits and telephones.

For the first time during the second phase of Operation 471 Levin was told of an outside event as it happened. It was clear that the symbolic closing of the crossing points would go virtually unchallenged.

The report from CIA Langley on the location of the high-speed radio traffic had not helped the joint intelligence team in London, but a separate CIA report the following day had concentrated their efforts regarding the girl. A special and highly reliable source had provided the information that the Ilyushin flight to Moscow had had only two women on board. One of them was a ballerina from the Kirov Ballet who had been taken ill in New York and had returned to Moscow via London. She had been met at Moscow Airport by two representatives of Stateconcert, the Soviet artistic booking agency, and there was no possible question of mistaken identity.

The second woman passenger had come in on a passport under the name of Nadia Galinova Myaznikov. Madame Myaznikov was the wife of a press officer at the Soviet Embassy in London. However, a discreet check with her family had indicated that neither she nor her husband had been seen in Moscow for a year. All of which seemed to explain how Clodagh Maria Kevan had gone through the passport control at Heathrow without problems.

The National Security Agency reported nil progress on breaking the high-speed code.

World press reactions to the announced demolition of the Berlin Wall had been friendly but cautious in the first few hours, but when, early the following morning, the demolition started with massive teams of workers, backed up by equipment and strings of vehicles to remove the debris, the headline writers had a field day.

By the following day the editorial writers had their turn, and the demolition of the wall was hailed as a turning point in East-West relations. The dawn of a new era.

The event was received with much less rapture in the White House, and the officer commanding U.S. troops in Berlin was surreptitiously recalled for discussions in Washington. The British ambassador in Washington had been called to the talks and the full implications of what had happened became clear.

The Soviet Union and its East German satellite had borne the opprobrium of the Berlin Wall for years. But the Allied commanders had probably benefited more than anyone else. The wall had been a symbol, a rallying point for the West, and Kennedy's *"Ich bin ein Berliner"* had put the Good Housekeeping Seal of Approval on who were the good boys. But now, suddenly, the city was open. The carefully orchestrated protocols of the past decade had disappeared overnight.

Anyone could go anywhere. It was far too late to go back to the old demarcations of Russian, American, British and French sectors. Those had died the death years ago when the wall went up.

Now East Berliners were swarming over West Berlin like American tourists. The shopkeepers were praying that it wouldn't be stopped, and there were even West Berliners wandering into East Berlin without permits, checkpoints or any other hindrance. And the significant fact was that they were not just wandering into East Berlin. East Berlin was an integral part of East Germany. West Berlin was an integral part of nowhere. Just a small island that had suddenly been washed over by the sea. West Berlin was no longer really an island; you couldn't, except with lines on maps, say where it began and ended.

As far as the world was concerned the Russians had done what the Western Powers had been demanding for years. Like it or not, there was nothing the West could do now but grin and bear it.

Allied troops were "unofficially" ordered not to enter the "old" East Berlin, and even when they did they were brought back courteously by the East German police. They had committed no offense in walking over an imaginary line on the Unter den Linden.

Russian troops were wearing their best uniforms and were hardly to be seen in the city center.

A week later there were paragraphs in the more serious Western papers noting that the Soviet summer maneuvers would be held this year in the second week in July. New bridge-building equipment and rocket transporters would be tested under field conditions, and several Warsaw Pact allies would be cooperating to test top-secret communications equipment.

chapter
9

Faller had insisted that they should not talk inside, and they had walked out of the town and up toward the woods. The heat of the sun was still lifting a mist from the side of the hill and where they sat there was still a dampness from the night dew.

The American lit a cigarette and slid the lighter back into his shirt pocket. He was blond and fresh-faced and looked more like a German than Faller himself. He looked at Faller's tanned face and waited for him to speak.

"We've traced Slanski, and the girl."

"Tell me."

"You ever heard of Velichko—Georgi Velichko?"

"No. But he's probably on file."

"He was one of the two secretaries to the Presidium. A real bastard. One of the old faithfuls from Stalin's days. He was chopped a month ago. Designated an 'enemy of the state,' and he's in the Lubyanka now. When he was a hatchet man he was responsible for wiping out thousands of Ukrainians. They've never forgotten him. They've been waiting for years to get him. He had been to Kiev for two days and got called back. We don't know what happened then, but we do know he went out and got pissed. He was caught screwing one of the girls who hang around the railway station. They were doing it in a taxi. The police picked them both up and took him to the police post by the Manege Metro station. They didn't know who he was, but he kept shouting about the President of the United States screwing some chick in a secret place in Kiev. The cops laughed at him and he went berserk. Said he was secretary to the Presidium, and at that point they contacted Dzerdzhinski Square. While the KGB were on the way he was raving about a guy named Slanski and what he was going to do to him.

"One of the cops was originally from Kiev and last week he was on leave there. Half the damned town knows the story now. There are Velichko jokes now."

"What do you make of it, Otto?"

"Slanski is somewhere in Kiev. At some top-secret installation, and the girl is with him, I'd say. That's where we've got to look now."

"And all that stuff about the President?"

Faller shrugged. "There have been those books about the chicks that Kennedy was screwing, maybe it was that."

"I don't see the connection."

"Neither do I, but who looks for sense when a drunk's shouting the odds?"

The American was silent as he looked over toward the town, and then he turned to the German and looked at him before he spoke.

"Your network's pretty good, Otto. Can they find out any more about the installation where Slanski is supposed to be?"

"Maybe. I've already given them my instructions."

The National Security Agency reported to the liaison team in London that the Russian code had still not been broken. But the CIA was now able to give them the map reference of the source of the radio traffic. It was just north of the city of Kiev and unapproachable nearer than five miles.

Two days later they received a Samos-satellite photograph of the site, and a brief report.

SAMOS III NUMBER 801149/USSR/GRID 12
STRUCTURE 240 FEET BY 170 FEET. MATERIAL OF STRUC-
TURE FERROUS (POSSIBLY CORRUGATED STEEL SHEET). UN-
USUAL FEATURES—NO WINDOWS. LATTICE AERIAL ESTI-

MATED 27 FEET HIGH WITH DISH RADIATION, LOCATED AT SOUTHEAST CORNER OF BUILDING. RADIATION BEARINGS— SEE SEPARATE REPORT NSA 12/147/4951/TKU.

VEHICLES IDENTIFIED. 3 CIVILIAN CARS. 9 MILITARY TRUCKS (LIGHTWEIGHT), 3 MILITARY ARTICULATED (TEN TONS). 3 TROOP CARRIERS (ONE-TRACKED/ONE-WHEELED).

PEOPLE IDENTIFIED. 24 UNIFORMED MEN (UNIFORMS UN-IDENTIFIED) 1 WOMAN (CIVILIAN CLOTHES).

IDENTIFIED WEAPONS. 8 HEAVY MACHINE GUNS (SEE GRATICULES 7, 13, 19 AND 27). 15 MEDIUM MACHINE GUNS. 3 LIGHT MACHINE GUNS (ONE MOUNTED ON TRACKED TROOP CARRIER).

SITE. CLEARING IN PUSHCHA-VODITSA FOREST. PERIMETER WALL (WOODEN) APPROX. 10 FEET HIGH. SITE SHOWS VE-HICLE TRACKS IN DIRECTION OF CITY OF KIEV AND IMME-DIATE SURROUNDINGS. TRACKS NOT OLDER THAN SEVEN MONTHS. NO APPARENT ANTIAIRCRAFT DEFENSES IN VI-CINITY. AREA BETWEEN STRUCTURE AND PERIMETER UNDER GRASS.

SPECIAL NOTE. HEAT PHOTOGRAPHY SHOWS NO CAMOU-FLAGED AREA INSIDE PERIMETER.

A few days later the NSA informed London that the build-ing in the Samos photograph had been identified as a studio for documentaries previously allocated to SovFilm but not used as a studio since 1975.

The girl could tell that it was going to be one of those nights when she had to stay behind. He had come back to the shop in midafternoon and his face had had that tight look, and his eyes were on her breasts as he stood watching her serve the last customer. She slid in the four batteries and eased the radio back into its carton. She gave the customer two dollars change, and the old man went over to the door, locked it, set the security alarm, and lowered the lights in the showroom.

She had been working for him for two years and from the start there had been these sessions in his office after hours. She didn't mind because he paid her a good basic wage and a good commission on sales. There were no other places where she could make ten thousand dollars a year. He was easygoing and frequently left her in charge, and the sessions were only about once a month. If you're young and pretty you get used to men making passes, and she reckoned that from time to time it paid to go along with it. He had asked her to marry him several times, but she had kept him happy with the sex instead.

She had the wad of receipts in one hand, and the checks, credit slips and cash in the other, and when he had closed the showroom door she stood waiting. He turned and looked at her and she smiled at him.

"It's been a good day, Sam."

But for once he wasn't interested and she stood patiently as his hands closed over her breasts. After a few minutes she said, "You want me to stay for a bit, Sam?"

He nodded.

"Let's go in your office, then."

She put the money and the receipts on his desk and he stood watching as she slid off her sweater. He never got undressed himself, it was part of the routine that she unzipped him, but that was all. She unbuttoned her skirt and tossed it onto his desk.

He was sitting on the couch waiting for her as she slid out of her pants, and she walked over to him slowly so that he could get a good look, and she saw him staring. All men stared when they saw her naked, but this was a different sort of stare. And then he spoke, his voice slurred with anger. He pointed at her.

"What the hell's been goin' on, Julie?"

She stood still in front of him, frowning.

"What d'ya mean, Sam? What is it?" Her eyes followed the pointing finger, and then she saw them. The red marks on her breasts and on her arms and legs. She'd forgotten about the fellow. She hadn't realized that he had held her that tightly.

"It's OK, Sam. It's nothing, forget it."

"They're fresh, you little bitch. Who was it?"

"Calm down, Sam. It's nothing. I told you."

He stood up, his face suffused with anger. "Who was it, you bitch? Tell me."

"It was a customer, Sam. If you want to know. He's been propositioning me for months. That's all."

His hand grabbed her arm and pulled her roughly to him. His voice shook with rage and she realized that he was actually jealous. "Who was it, you little tramp?" And she screamed as he twisted her arm up her back.

"For Christ's sake, let go, you're hurting. It was that fellow Mason. He spends three thousand bucks with us every month, for God's sake."

He loosed her arm violently and she swung around to face him. He was panting.

"What did he do, Julie? What did he do?"

She shrugged. "He made love to me, that's all."

"How many times you do this?"

"Two or three times. We wouldn't have gone on getting his business if I hadn't."

"You could have told him to go to hell."

"He's spent fifty thousand dollars with us since last New Year. I had to."

He stood looking at her and then he said, "Right. Get dressed. We'll settle that bastard."

And he reached for the phone and asked for the police precinct on Second Avenue. When they came on the line he told them he wanted to report a rape, and after a short conversation he hung up.

The girl dressed in silence, and the old man was silent, too, as he paced back and forth across the room to ease his tension.

The police arrived in five minutes. A lieutenant in plainclothes and a sergeant. The lieutenant showed his card.

"Rafferty, Mr. Siwicki. What's been the trouble?"

"One of the customers forced my assistant to have sex with him."

The lieutenant looked at the girl. "D'you know the man's name, miss?"

The girl sighed and looked away. "Mason, Rodney Mason."

"What happened?"

The old man chipped in. "He spends a lot with us and he said if she didn't do it we'd lose his custom."

"What's your name, miss?"

"Julie Seymour."

"Where did this take place?"

"At Mason's place."

"Where's that?"

"A few blocks up at Twenty-third."

Lieutenant Rafferty had doubts by now, but he decided to go on a little longer. He turned to the sergeant. "Take Mr. Siwicki into the showroom, Sergeant. Take a statement from him."

The old man looked at the lieutenant desperately. "The young lady's very upset, Lieutenant. I think it'd be better if I stayed."

Rafferty nodded slowly as if he were agreeing. "That'll be OK, Mr. Siwicki. You just go on with the sergeant. It'll be all right."

He stood watching as the old man left, and stared at the door after they had gone. Then he turned to the girl and sat down.

"This guy Mason. Is he your boy friend?"

"No. He's a customer."

"Mr. Siwicki said he was a good customer. How good?"

"One of the best we've got."

"What'd he do—proposition you?"

"Kind of."

"What kind of? He threatened you?"

"Not physically. Just said he was a good customer."

"When was this? What time?"

"Just on lunchtime."

"He spend any money?"

"Yes."

"How much?"

"Nine hundred dollars."

"You got the copy of the receipt?"

"Yes." She made to get up.

"No. Leave it for now." He looked at her for a few moments.

"Did you have sex with Mason?"

"Yes."

"Willingly?"

106

"More or less."

"You get commission from the old boy?"

"Yes."

"How much on nine hundred dollars?"

"Ninety dollars."

"You done this before with Mason?"

"This was the third time."

"Is that every time he comes here?"

"No, he'd been here lots of times before he spoke to me."

"How much has he spent altogether?"

"About fifty grand."

"Rafferty looked sharply at the girl. "What does he do?"

"I don't know."

"Is the old man jealous?"

She nodded.

Rafferty stood up. "Where's the receipt?"

The girl went to the desk and sorted through the papers and handed one to him. He read it slowly and carefully and then looked at her.

"I'll take this." He pursed his lips. "You realize you could get the old man into trouble?"

"I didn't want him to call the police. He insisted."

"Not that, honey. You get a commission on sales. You agree to sex with customers. That makes the old man a pimp and you a prostitute."

He walked to the door, and as he opened it he turned back to look at her. "I would stick to the old boy, sweetheart."

Outside he called to the sergeant, "That's OK now, Sergeant. We'll get back to the station house."

When they were outside he handed the sergeant the invoice. "Drive me to that address. We'll have a word with Mr. Romeo Mason."

The sergeant checked the address and handed back the invoice. When they were in the car he said, "You know, the old boy's screwing her, Lieutenant. Seems like this guy Mason's just one of the circle."

The lieutenant leaned back. "Sure he is. I just wanna have a look at a guy who spends fifty grand in six months on hi-fi stuff, screws shop assistants and lives in this part of town.

The car pulled up and they looked at the building. It was one of those narrow-gutted houses that still survive as if they were physically trapped between the big blocks.

The name card showed that Mason was Apartment 17 on the third floor. They went up through the smell of boiled cabbage and knocked on the door.

A young Negro about twenty-five years old came to the door. He wore faded blue jeans and was naked from the waist up, except for a towel slung around his neck.

"Lieutenant Rafferty, NYPD. Are you Rodney Mason?"

"Yeah." The brown eyes looked them both over; he didn't open the door any wider.

"Can we come in, Mr. Mason? We want to ask you some questions."

"What about?"

"You prefer to come down the station house?"

Mason opened the door and they went in. It was a clean, well-furnished apartment, and a pretty black girl was watching the TV. She turned around.

"What is it, honey?"

"The fuzz."

She turned to look at Rafferty and the sergeant. Then she looked at Mason, but she didn't speak.

Mason stood, hands on hips. He was a good-looking young man.

"Well, Lieutenant. What's the trouble?"

"Who's the lady, Mr. Mason?"

The big eyes flashed with anger, and Rafferty saw the sleek biceps tense.

"That's my wife, Lieutenant."

And Rafferty half smiled because he knew then that there'd be no trouble.

"Maybe we could talk in another room, Mr. Mason?"

"We can talk right here, man."

"OK. Did you purchase equipment from Solita Electrics on Second Avenue today?"

"Yeah."

"About one o'clock?"

"Near enough."

"Where did you go from there, Mr. Mason? What did you do for the next hour?"

"I came back here to the apartment."

"Any witnesses? Was your wife here?"

"No. She was at work."

"Anybody else with you?"

"No." The hesitation was barely perceptible.

"How much did you spend?"

Mason hesitated. " 'Bout nine hundred bucks."

The girl's head came around with surprise.

"What d'you do for a living, Mr. Mason?"

"I'll come down the station house with you, mister."

"Let me explain your rights, Mr. Mason. You are—"

The young man's teeth were clenched. "Don't give me that Miranda crap, I know my rights."

At the station house they had read Rodney Mason the words from the Miranda-Escobedo card and had put him in the interrogation room at the end of the corridor.

Rafferty brought in two cups of coffee and shoved one across to Mason and sat down facing him. He pushed his fingers through his thick black curly hair.

"You got a choice, you know, Mason."

"You tell me."

"Either your wife finds out you screwed the young chick from the radio shop or you talk."

"Talk about what?"

"Where you got fifty grand from to spend at the shop in the last six months."

"Seven months."

"OK. Seven months."

"I won it at the tracks."

Rafferty sighed and reached for a pad and a pencil. "Now we got to go through all the jazz of dates, and races, and horses' names, and how much. Is that what you really want?"

Mason's eyes looked toward the window and the bars, and Rafferty waited. Mason turned to face him.

"You know this money was a hundred percent legit. I swear it."

"No need to, Mason. Just tell me."

"A guy gives me the money to buy this stuff twice a month."

"What stuff?"

"The videotape. Ampex standard."

"Why so much? And why doesn't he buy it himself?"

Mason shrugged and held out his hands.

"How should I know? They pay me each time a hundred and fifty bucks. That's it."

"Who's the guy?"

"I dunno."

"Aw, come on, Mason."

"Why should I care who he is?"

"Where did you meet him to hand the stuff over?"

"At the Wollman Memorial in Central Park."

"And you never tried to find out who he was?"

Mason looked at Rafferty, and he decided against the lie. "OK. I followed him."

"So who is he?"

"He's one of the Russians at the UN."

"You willing to identify him?"

"And no charges, and no blabber to the wife?"

"No charge, no nothing."

Mason had identified the man. He was KGB. Yuri Butenko. The CIA put a six-man team on him that night. They watched him load the tape cartons and an overnight bag into the Volkswagen, and then they followed him to the Washington embassy.

There was a clerk in the cipher section of the Soviet Embassy in Washington who had been playing footsy with the CIA for almost a year. He had offered a cipher deal for citizenship and a regular income, but they had kept him on ice. The details of the new deal were worked out with Joe Shapiro at Langley. He was handling the case.

Four days later Shapiro had the information they wanted and the man was flown out to Pasadena that day. It seemed that the videotapes recorded every day's programs from WRC-TV in Washington. They were then sent in a special top-priority diplomatic bag to Moscow. Butenko bought the tapes in New York, and they were taken by car to the embassy in Washington. They were for a high-priority high-security operation in the Soviet Union. The recordings had been dispatched every day for seven months. The priority was so high that the reels were not even rewound before dispatch. That was all he could find out.

Apart from the routine report up the line, Shapiro sent a copy to Murphy in London, and a copy of the old file on the radio tapes from the diner. He had sent out his secretary for a packet of forget-me-not seeds, and he included them in the stiff envelope.

The late-afternoon sunshine whitened the superstructure of a police boat and a couple of pleasure cruisers as they idled past Sycamore Island, and George C. Patton (no relation) turned the Mustang off the George Washington Memorial Parkway and kept his left hand down until the big sweeping curve brought him to the CIA's main parking lot.

As he stood beside the car he looked toward the sun and hoped that the fine weather would hold until the next evening, when he would be meeting the girl's father for the first time as a prospective son-in-law. They had chosen the neutral ground of the golf club for the skirmish. Golf clubhouses in the wet can lead to talking for the sake of talking, and George C. Patton wasn't a talker. Which, in a middle-level operator for the CIA, was a distinct advantage, but in mortal combat with a professor of English Lit could be a distinct drawback.

The young man wound his way through the routine security to the satellite interpretation unit where he worked, and took over from his counterpart on shift two. His predecessor's notes were pinned to the board and he checked the last grid number read before he switched on the lights. Now that the photographs were on resin-coated paper there were no problems of dampness and long drying times, and frequently the team was checking photographs that had been taken over the Soviet Union or Poland or North Korea only thirty minutes earlier.

He entered the grid codings and references on the report sheet and then pushed it aside as he bent over the board. He

111

was putting the third photograph of the Berlin series into the "collect" tray when something caught his eye, and he lifted the photograph back onto the board and swung over the magnifier until it covered the edge of the woods where they came down almost to the side of Ruppiner Chausee, about 550 feet before the railway bridge. The six guns were there with their camouflage nets just as they had been for the last six months. He opened the file cover and checked the last six reports. The guns were logged as M-30 howitzers, and he adjusted the magnifier and the lights. And then he saw the muzzle brake, and the big recoil system above the barrel. The final check was the small shield, and as he registered it he picked up the phone. The old-fashioned M-30s had become D-30s during the night, and D-30s were current equipment for line units. And three grids back at the edge of Hermsdorf village the battery of twin ZPU-2s had clearly got their ammunition boxes in place. He could actually see the sun-spray design on the strengthening swages on the sloping covers.

The two reserve teams were brought back on duty, and they worked solidly for the next ten hours. It was the first Monday in July.

chapter
10

Levin sat opposite the girl, the chessboard between them. Her hand hovered over a white pawn. As her hand went toward the ivory head he spoke.

"Don't do that, Clodagh. It loses you your advantage."

She looked up, smiling. "How can it, Andrei? I haven't got any advantage. Neither of us has lost anything."

"Not so, my love. You are white. You had first move and that gives you control and *tolchok*—what's that in English?"

He stood up and walked over to the bookshelves. His hand reached for a book and he turned the pages slowly. Then he turned to her, his head bowed as he read and spoke.

"Ah, yes. Thrust—it gives you thrust." He closed the book with one hand and walked back to the small table and sat down. "And if you take my pawn like that you have doubled up your pawns. The rear pawn will be disadvantaged."

She was smiling at him, gently, and with affection.

He sighed. "Why do I talk of this? It is all a waste of our time. I feel that in my bones."

"Are you afraid, Andrei?"

He looked up quickly. "Why do you say that?"

She shrugged. "I can feel it in the air. I am afraid. Maybe you too."

"Afraid of what?"

"Afraid of everything. The world outside. Your people.

113

The big machine that seems to be grinding us to pieces. I feel so cut off that I don't really believe the world still goes on outside."

"We shall feel normal again once this is over." And he waved one hand slowly, as if to encompass the whole building.

"And when it is all over, Andrei? Then what?"

He shrugged. "Back to Leningrad. The university."

"And I?"

He looked startled. "But . . . won't you come with me?"

She smiled. "Maybe they won't allow me to."

"Of course they will. That will be no problem." He stood up, his knee catching the chessboard, and as he bent to adjust the pieces he looked at her face. "Please say you'll stay with me, Clodagh."

She reached forward and her hand covered his. She said softly, "I'll stay with you, my dear. Don't worry about it."

Suddenly he was cheerful again, energetic and alert. He walked over to the hi-fi shelf and took out a cassette.

"I forgot all about this. I got them to do it and somehow it slipped my mind."

And as he pressed the key down the slow piano chords came through, and the sandy voice: ". . . on that you can rely. The world was only made for lovers, as time goes by. . . ." And when it was finished he said, "It seems a long time ago when I first heard that. Nearly six months." He turned to face her, his face serious.

"Would you marry me, Clodagh?"

She looked up at his face and saw the tension as he waited for her answer.

"Of course, Andrei, but I would be an embarrassment to you."

"How ridiculous. How an embarrassment?"

"I'm not Russian. I don't speak Russian. And I'm too independent."

"But you're here. You are part of all this. You have a sharp mind. You would be a tremendous asset."

She laughed and shook her head. "They wouldn't like the sharp mind. Outside this setup I should cause trouble. They wouldn't want the sharp mind then."

"I think you're mistaken, Clodagh." He hesitated. "I've got a meeting in the operations room. What are you going to do?"

"Escape." She laughed as she saw the horror on his face. "To a bath and Rachmaninov."

He smiled and sighed heavily as he retied the belt on his dressing gown. As he went through to the conference room he looked back at her and was pleased that she too had turned to watch him.

The girl stood in the silence of the room after Levin had gone, looking at the books on the shelves and the neat rows of cassettes alongside the hi-fi. She slid a cassette from its plastic container and loaded it into the deck. She stood with her eyes closed as she listened to the first few bars. It was Rostropovitch playing Tchaikowsky's "Variations on a Rococo Theme," and the languid cello melody matched her mood. Just this side of sadness, a touch Irish, an elegy for dripping leaves in a wood.

She walked to the bathroom and slowly closed the door. She didn't want to hear any more, but she couldn't bear to switch it off. It would be a sign, a confirmation of her mood.

She lay in the water until it was cold, beset by inertia, her mind reluctant to face the facts her logic paraded. Slanski was a shrewd man, and he was educated enough to recognize that Levin's mind was something special. But basically, she felt, he was weak. A clever implementer, but more used to analysis and assessment than action. Panov was the man of action. Those shrewd peasant eyes looked at them all, Levin, Slanski and her, from behind a screen. A screen of control, of immunity, that they didn't share, not even recognizing that it existed. Slanski cooperated with Levin naturally and easily, but Panov seemed to stand outside the situation. Cooperating superficially, but mentally aloof. She hooked out the bath plug with her toes, and, as if her fears would flow away with the water, she lay there until the bath was almost empty.

Back in the bedroom, she sat wrapped in the big towels and phoned for hot chocolate from the kitchens.

In the conference room Panov was standing in front of the fast printer as it clacked and hesitated, trembling for the next set of characters. The paper was feeding into the big plastic bin, and Panov was looking through some of the residue. He turned, nodded as he saw Levin, and then carried on reading the printout. Levin noticed that Panov was wearing his uniform again, and so was Slanski when he came in from the corridor.

Levin sat down at the long table and shifted a space among the files and papers for his cigarettes and an ashtray. "I gather that you have some news from Moscow, Ivan?"

Slanski nodded and looked across at Panov. "You go ahead, Boris, explain about the new operational headquarters."

Levin realized that the two of them had already discussed whatever it was between them. He watched Panov's face as he looked at his note pad. When he looked up Panov spoke slowly and quietly, not in his usual brusque phrases.

"We're going to move this operation, Andrei. There are two reasons for this. The more important one is that if we move we can decrease the time lag on the TV and radio programs. We hope to cut the delay to one day from the present two. The second reason is security. We have been here over seven months now and there are indications that our security has been degraded. Everything will go on as usual, and the facilities will be improved, if anything."

"Where are we moving to, Boris, and when?"

It was Slanski who answered. "We shall be moving tonight, Andrei."

"And where to?"

"We want to keep it on a need-to-know basis, and you don't need to know."

"Need or no need, I am entitled to know. What the hell is all this?"

Panov leaned back, looking at Levin through half-closed eyes. "Don't make us any more problems than we've got, Andrei. It has all gone well so far. The operation in Berlin starts in a matter of days. We need all the help you can give us."

"Have you told the girl?"

Panov shook his head slowly. "There's no need for her to come, Andrei. It should be over in a week or ten days. She can go back to Moscow. We'll fix her an apartment until you get back."

Levin lit a cigarette and inhaled slowly as he looked at the other two. His voice was harsh with tiredness and tension when he spoke. "I want her to come with me."

Slanski leaned forward. "It's going to complicate things so, Andrei. In a few days' time we shall be operating in reality. There won't be time for anything but work."

"Nevertheless the girl will come with me. Let that be understood."

Slanski started to speak, but Panov put up his hand to silence him.

"If that is what you want, Andrei, then that is what we shall do. Forget it." Panov leaned back, relaxed and unconcerned, to ease the tension. "Have you seen the Berlin situation report tonight?"

"No."

"The Americans have asked for an urgent meeting."

"In Berlin?"

"No. In Moscow. They're scared."

It was too late to eat a big meal, and Levin and the girl were watching the late news on TV as they ate strawberries and cream.

The Secretary of State's request for an urgent meeting to consider "current problems" between the two countries was being discussed, and the views of various experts were given without comment. There were shots of a huge fire in a furniture warehouse on the outskirts of Tulsa. And a clip showing a map with the fault line superimposed of the latest forecast for earth tremors in California. It was in the middle of a zoom shot on the representatives of OPEC entering the UN Building that Levin felt the sensation. He leaned forward slowly, reaching out to put the fruit dish on the small table. He couldn't make it, and he saw the dish fall in slow motion, the cream and the fruit slowly pouring splash by splash on the green carpet. He tried to turn to look at the girl, but his head wouldn't move. His eyes were out of focus and the lids slowly closed. He could hear noises, but they seemed far away.

He was vaguely aware of lying on a bed and the noise of a car door closing. He seemed to be only just unconscious, and from time to time he could see some fleeting snatch of vision. The stars in the sky as he seemed to be lifted, the face of a woman in a nurse's uniform, the portholes of an aircraft, and then the even roar of well-tuned jets. A flash of daylight, and then darkness again. Another car door slammed and then the whiteness that got whiter and whiter until it became a ceiling and a sensation of falling that made him jerk out his arms into the softness of a bed. Then like a half-submerged log he sank back into a hazy limbo of nothingness.

James Watson was twenty-six, and as he lay on his belly in the windowed blister on the lower fuselage of the KC-135 he quietly cursed the commander in chief of Strategic Air Command, the President of the United States, the CO of the 384th Air Refueling Wing, and the radio operator who had tracked him down to the beach hut.

Way down below, the first plane was responding to the tanker pilot's instructions. In the next two minutes the SR-71A had eased its way up to the slot. Sergeant Watson moved the control stick, and the boom came up slightly and he held it there for the Lockheed to get the boom into the receiving mechanism. After it made contact he watched the fuel gauges as the JP-7 gushed from the tanker. The operation from now on was automatic, and a few minutes later he felt the slight surge as the SR-71A unlocked and fell away, banking in a shallow dive as the next aircraft came up. There were five planes to fill up from the thirty-thousand-gallon capacity, and it went in at a thousand gallons a minute. They'd be back at McConnell in an hour. He wondered what the fandango was all about. It had a funny smell about it. Like when he had originally joined SAC and the first operational missions had flown out from Okinawa to Hanoi.

Levin had struggled back to consciousness, and as he sat on the edge of the bed he felt no ill effects from the

118

drugs. His head felt clear and his mind was alert, as if he had awakened from a long and restful sleep.

He looked around the room. It was smaller than the bedroom at Kiev. White walls, no windows, and modern furniture. All the personal things were there, the hi-fi and the cassettes, the TV and the radio, and his bathrobe lay across the foot of the bed.

It had been a long plane journey and a short car ride. Levin reckoned that they must be right down near the Chinese frontier. It could be Irkutsk, near Lake Baikal, or perhaps even farther east—maybe Khabarovsk, which was right on the border.

And then he noticed the bed. It was a big double bed and where he sat on the edge it sagged with his weight. On the pillow he could see the impression from his head. But on the other side of the bed it was empty. Not even matching pillows. The girl had not slept in the bed.

He stood up and walked to the corridor door, but it was locked. The door in the side wall opened easily and he was in the operations room. There were three young men in civilian clothes, sports jackets and jeans, and they were busy at the maps and the printer. He walked on through to the oval office, but it was no longer a replica of the President's office. This time there were no windows, just white walls and ceiling. A big desk but no Stars and Stripes; a framed photograph of Langham was hung on one wall, and an aerial photograph of the White House and the grounds leaned against the far wall, waiting to be hung.

He lifted one of the phones on the desk and asked for Slanski to come in.

He was sitting there, at his desk, clad only in his crumpled pajamas, when Slanski came in from the corridor.

"How do you feel, Andrei?"

"Was it really necessary? The drug?"

"Part of the security system, that's all."

"Why me, not you?"

Slanski sat down in the chair alongside the desk. "We want you to be away from any Russian influence. In Kiev you were cooped up, but you knew where you were. Here you're in the

White House. Anyway, if all goes well we shall all be back in Moscow in a week or ten days."

"And where's the girl?"

Slanski's brown eyes looked at him carefully. "They wouldn't let us bring her, Andrei. I tried very hard, but they were adamant. I spoke to the Director personally. He was sympathetic, but he stuck to the point that it was only a matter of days before it was all over."

Levin reached for another cigarette, and without a glance at Slanski he said, "You tell them that I want her here immediately, otherwise I go back to the university at once."

Slanski watched Levin as he lit his cigarette, and when he spoke his voice was soft. "Andrei, listen to me. You are suggesting that we threaten the Presidium, blackmail them. About a personal relationship. In a time of stress and tension. You can't be serious. You would be saying that because you cannot wait for a week to see a girl, you will disturb, even jeopardize, a military operation." He stared at Levin, his eyes hard. "You are still a citizen, remember, you must not forget that all of us—you, I, Panov—do this because we were ordered to do it."

Levin looked back at him, conscious of his own unshaven face, his uncombed hair, his crumpled pajamas. Slanski watched him light yet another cigarette. Levin leaned forward, his arms on the table, his shoulders hunched.

"Maybe you chose the wrong man, Ivan. Or maybe I'm too right. Perhaps I think differently after playing this game for so long." He smiled across the desk. "Maybe I've become too American, no longer a good citizen."

"For Christ's sake, don't talk such stupidities, Andrei." Slanski stood up jerkily, his fingers fiddling with papers on the desk, patting them together. "Just be sensible, be patient. It's days we're talking about, not a lifetime."

When Slanski had gone Levin stayed sitting at the desk and smoking. He felt anger, fear and shame. Anger that he was treated like a pawn, that his wishes were ignored, fear as to what could happen to the girl and shame that at this moment his body and mind should lust for the girl, with visions of soft lips and faint blue veins on outthrust breasts. And slowly his head came down as the drug took over again, and he slept at the desk with his head resting on one bent arm.

Faller had insisted that they meet somewhere outside Bad Harzburg, and the rendezvous had been fixed at the Guldener Krone in Breitestrasse in Göttingen. The bells of the market church were ringing the hour as the American pulled out a chair and sat down to face the German.

"I can't stay long, Otto. What is it?"

"I've just had one of my people cross over. Do you remember my telling you about a guy named Velichko? Got pissed and was picked up screwing a girl in a taxi?"

"I remember. Said he was going to screw the President's wife or something."

"That's the boy. The girl with him in the taxi was only sixteen. You heard of Kilometer 101?"

"No."

"It's a prison. A camp for corrective training for under-age girls in moral danger. If they're not pretty enough to interest the KGB they get shipped down there. I got one of my people to make contact with the girl from the taxi. It seems Velichko talked to her too. She didn't understand what he was talking about, and she could see he was blind drunk. He told her he was one of the Presidium secretaries and she thought he was trying to pull rank for a free screw. But he said he'd just come back from Kiev and he was raving about a man named Slanski who had done him dirt. There had been a quarrel about a girl, and this guy Slanski had put the burn on him in Moscow. The girl was a foreigner and very pretty. The only other thing was this raving about the President of the United States and a room with the American flag in it. That's it. But you know where Slanski is now, and I guess you know where the girl is."

"Is this the same place your man figured the radio stuff was coming from?"

"I'd guess so."

"Can you get him to check?"

"No way."

"Why not?"

"They picked him up on his way back to Warsaw."

"And?"

"And nothing. They found his DF equipment and after they'd interrogated him they shot him."

"Christ."

Faller wondered sometimes if the CIA really knew what it was all about. But he said nothing.

"Any chance of getting this girl out so that we could interrogate her thoroughly?"

"We could, but it's not worth the risk. Our man knows what he's doing. If there had been any more he would have got it."

The NSA circulated all concerned that the special code had still not been broken and that all radio traffic from the Kiev location had ceased forty-eight hours previously. Traffic in the special code had increased between Moscow and Washington and had ceased between Kiev and Warsaw. There was still traffic between Warsaw and East Berlin but much reduced in volume.

chapter

11

All the crossing points into East Germany had been closed.
Not only the four from West Germany but also the Warne-
munde ferry from Denmark and the Sassnitz ferry from
Sweden. Behind the white-barred gates and the guardhouses
Red Army engineers and equipment had sliced great can-
yons across the roads. Eighty feet wide, and twenty-five feet
deep. The rock and spoil had been spread on nearby fields,
and electricians and engineers were repairing cracked pipes
and sliced cables.

By sunrise the area looked like the aftermath of a tank
battle, and no observer could doubt that the obstructions
were meant to last.

All along the frontier, from Lübeck to Hof, the frontier
guards had been replaced by units of the People's Army, and
in the Baltic the patrol boats of the Transport Police had
given way to armed cutters capable of thirty knots. On
the Elbe the East German patrol boats were on red alert.
The West German customs on the Elbe, at their headquarters at Hitzacker, reported cannon and machine-gun fire
as the East German patrol boats tested and cleared their
weapons.

The Field Security Unit at Helmstedt had radioed the frontier closure to the commander of British troops in Berlin. The

123

U.S. Fourteenth Armored Cavalry at Fulda had similarly informed the American commander in Berlin.

In Berlin all East German border guards, customs posts and police were withdrawn from the perimeter that marked off West Berlin from the East German hinterland.

In Washington it was barely midnight on July 14, and the President was told of the developments while he was still celebrating with the French at their embassy.

In Moscow it was already 7 A.M. on the fifteenth, and Pravda carried news of détente with Peking and predictions of a record wheat harvest.

BERLIN, 10 A.M., JULY 15

On the Berlin underground on Routes 6 and 8 the trains stopped at the Stadtmitte station and Heinrich-Heine-Strasse, and the blue-uniformed guards emptied the cars. Nobody was particularly alarmed; the East Germans played their little games from time to time and the Berliners ignored them.

Aboveground the S-Bahn trains all stopped at the Steglitz station and the passengers were advised to walk. The East Germans controlled all S-Bahn traffic in both West Berlin and East Berlin, and everywhere the trains were stopping at the old zone borders.

Herr Anton Lemke was one of the West Berlin undertakers. One of the more macabre results of the Berlin Wall had been the problem of West Berlin corpses whose relations wanted them to be buried in family graves in East Berlin. The procedure was simple. Herr Lemke would send a telegram to the state undertaker in East Berlin, and the two hearses would meet at one of the checkpoints to transfer the coffin. Not even for those last rites could the relatives pass into East Berlin. Herr Lemke now had his first coffin transfer since the wall had come down. He had sent the standard telegram and now he was at Checkpoint Charlie. Except that Checkpoint Charlie wasn't there anymore. You could see where the wall had been, but that was all. A Vopo sergeant walked over to him, and Herr Lemke explained that he was waiting for his opposite number from the other side.

When he was told that there was no longer anything to stop his hearse from going to the cemetery at Pankow he found it almost unbelievable, and when he was told that his clients could have gone over for the burial he sent one of his men to the telephone to give the good news.

TV and film crews were dispatched to the border crossing points, and cameras were shoved up on hired cranes to film the yawning chasms in the roads, but there was nothing else to film apart from the crowds who had come to watch the action.

All over the world radio and TV programs were interrupted with news flashes. But except for the closure of the crossings there was no news.

Moscow, 4 p.m., July 15

The American and British ambassadors had requested interviews with the Soviet Foreign Minister, which had been granted for 4 p.m. The media had not informed the Russian public of the events in Germany, but the state trial in Moscow had been announced of seven residents of West Berlin and an American citizen named Simmonds, who were accused of being spies for the CIA. Three of them, including the American, had already confessed to the charges, it was announced.

The Soviet Minister of Foreign Affairs received the ambassadors of the United States and the United Kingdom together. When they came into the big paneled office he waved them to two chairs alongside his desk. They both chose to stand, and the Russian remained standing, too, as they placed their documented protests on his desk. He made no move to examine the papers. When it was over he stood silently for a few moments. Then he spoke, quietly and clearly, and he watched their faces as he signaled to his interpreter to speak.

"The Minister informs you that your documents are not acceptable to the Soviet government. The matter of the crossing points is entirely for the German Democratic Republic to control. Your governments must address themselves to those quarters. As for your complaints about the situation in Berlin, that too you must refer to the government of the GDR. But the Minister wishes to make clear to Your Excellencies that the countries of the Warsaw Pact will no longer tolerate a part of the city of Berlin's being used as a base for espionage by the Western Powers."

The Russian Minister, who spoke excellent English himself, spoke again in Russian. A few moments later the young interpreter licked his lips and translated. "The Minister has to inform you that there will be no aggressive moves by the Warsaw Pact countries, but the Soviet government demands that all foreign troops shall be withdrawn from Berlin immediately."

The two ambassadors made reference to the Potsdam Agreement, reiterated their countries' right to garrisons in West Berlin, bowed and left.

WASHINGTON, MIDDAY, JULY 15

The President had left the French Embassy just before 1 A.M. and, back at the White House, had given instructions for Ex-Comm II to be set up, with its first meeting at mid-morning. It had then been postponed until noon so that the Defense Secretary could fly back from Omaha; and meanwhile the President had seen the Director of Central Intelligence and the Secretary of State. He had seen them separately, but they were of the same opinion. The Russians meant business.

The Soviet ambassador had been called to the White House by the Secretary of State. The interview had not been unfriendly and the ambassador had realized early that the meeting was a fishing expedition to find out his government's intentions. He had to inform the Secretary of State that he had received no instructions.

Back at the Soviet Embassy the switchboard had been jammed by calls from the media. All pleas for interviews, statements and information had been fended off brusquely and with open contempt. All except one: that of a free-lance White House correspondent whose column was syndicated in the United States and Europe, an old China hand who had had to move to London to earn a living when the McCarthy era was in full flower.

The ambassador was a comparative new boy to Washington, but he spoke excellent English and had been an Olympic gold medalist when he was a young man. He was cautiously liked by the press for his calculated indiscretions—not a feature of Soviet diplomats in the West and all the more news value for that reason. (It had started when he first landed at Dulles and purloined the story of the Soviet diplomat who had been warned against the Washington press corps and, briefed to plead ignorance on all subjects, had been asked by a reporter if he intended visiting any nightclubs in Washington. The diplomat had said, "Are there any nightclubs in Washington?" Next day the major newspapers all carried the same headline—"Soviet Diplomat Asks If There Are Any Nightclubs in Washington.") And there were lady journalists who thought they detected a faint resemblance between Ambassador Saratov and Cary Grant.

Yuri Saratov had poured out the whiskies slowly and carefully, and now, as he pushed the tumbler across the desk to the journalist, he said, "What did you want to see me about?"

He leaned back, smiling broadly at the journalist's raised eyebrows, and Fowler noted the confidence behind the charm.

"What's happening in Berlin, Mr. Ambassador?"

Saratov shrugged. "You tell me, Bob. By the way, is this on the record or off the record?"

"Whichever way you say."

"Let's make it off the record, shall we?"

"OK."

Saratov moved his shoulders around in the chair, making himself comfortable. "The East Germans are tired of the CIA circus in Berlin. Otherwise there's nothing happening so far as I know."

"What about the closed crossing points?"

"That's probably temporary."

Fowler put down his glass and leaned forward. He spoke very quietly as he watched Saratov's face. "All personnel of SAC and the North American Air Defense Command are on standby, Ambassador. They don't do that just because you're digging up the autobahns."

"So?"

"So what's going on?"

Saratov tapped on his desk with a sword-shaped letter-opener, and it was several seconds before he spoke. "We've warned your people for years, Bob. You know it. It's on the record. Khrushchev told Kennedy when they met in Vienna. We've told you time and again since then. Berlin is part of the GDR. West Berlin is a trouble spot for us. Your people abuse it. The British abuse it. The French abuse it. We've had enough, we're going to stop all that."

"They'll never let you get away with it."

Saratov's nostrils flared with anger as he leaned forward across the desk. "They won't stop us this time, Bob. There are over two hundred known CIA operators in West Berlin, not counting the military-intelligence people. I'll give you a list of their names if you don't already know them."

"Makes no odds, Saratov. Maybe you can pressure them into lifting out the CIA bodies, but they won't give up Berlin."

The ambassador leaned back angrily, and his fist was clenched as he bounced it up and down on his desk.

"They gave up Saigon, they gave up Angola, they'll give up Berlin, or the responsibility will be theirs."

"Responsibility for what?"

Saratov stood up, his face turned toward the window. Then he turned to look at Fowler. "Responsibility for all that will happen."

There was a few moments' silence before Fowler spoke. He too had stood up. "I understand that there are two Soviet planes scheduled for Dulles this evening. The grapevine says they're for evacuating families."

Saratov's hand smoothed his jaw as he looked at his wrist-watch. "Call me tomorrow, Bob, if you want to talk. Call me any time. I've warned the switchboard. They'll know where to get me if I'm not here."

As Fowler stood in the sunshine waiting for a taxi, he realized that he was going to be used. Used as a catalyst, an unofficial channel where information and reactions could be fed in and digested. Certainly by the Russians, and probably by the White House. Back at his apartment, he telephoned the White House press secretary.

Since the wall had come down Berliners had gradually got used to the fact that they could now travel freely over the city, and it was in the suburbs that the panic had started. Not only had the wall that sliced across the center of the city come down; so had all the defenses that marked off the perimeter of West Berlin from the rest of East Germany. What had seemed like the bars of a cage had gone, and people were not sure now where the lions were. Maybe the bars had previously provided a security that had now disappeared. But East German police and officials kept well away from the old borderlines.

It was the TV news and the radio that pressed the panic buttons. There is something particularly disturbing about international concern for the safety of the place you happen to live in, and when, on the ground, there appears to be no problem it is easy to get the impression that it's only you who can't see what's wrong. Memories of the Russians in 1945 had been suppressed into the subconscious, but the commentators created a feeling of crisis, and suddenly the wall coming down was a threat, not a victory.

The signs of panic were not obvious, and they ranged from merely burning one's copy of *The Gulag Archipelago* or Yevtushenko's poems, and one's CDU membership card, to the overbooking of flights to Bonn and Hanover.

By midevening there was a tension throughout the city. Cinemas and theaters were empty, but cafés and restaurants were packed. Those who remembered the last days of the war recognized the unspoken need to be outdoors, to congregate with others.

Despite the concentration of interest on Berlin, the media had played it cool. It was the radio news bulletin of the East German radio station Stimme der DDR at 7 P.M. that really started the rot. The bulletin had ranged over the world news, briefly touched on the "new wave of optimism in Berlin," and then given its usual list of share movements on the Federal German and West Berlin exchanges. The share values of any company based or dependent on West Berlin had fallen by fifty percent in the course of the afternoon. All other German shares had taken ten percent drops. It was only two o'clock in New York, but there had already been massive selling, with two hours of trading still to go. For those who tuned immediately to the Voice of America there was the news that the President of the United States had sent a letter to the Soviet Prime Minister. Contents and subject undisclosed.

chapter

12

There was computer printout in piles along the table, and
on the visual display unit new text flashed up every few
minutes. Slanski and Panov sat opposite Levin at the long
table in the operations room and Levin was smoking a new
cigarette, with half of the old one still burning slowly in
the ashtray.

Slanski was now fulfilling his role as dove adviser and
Panov the role of hawk. Both were taking an entirely United
States stance, and, indeed, most of what had happened that
day had been unexpected. Moscow no longer kept them informed of its moves. They received printout of all communications between the two governments, they had access to the
current U.S. radio, TV and newspapers and a selection of
intelligence material that the KGB evaluated as being available to the White House. All day long Moscow had asked
for Presidential reactions to moves already made. Sometimes
it gave an hour for the response, sometimes the response was
required without any time for reflection or discussion. Levin
was responding now solely by reflex and instinct.

Slanski stood up to take off his sports jacket as he
spoke.

"They're asking what instructions will have been given
to the U.S. Berlin commander. The situation report says that

radio traffic has been almost one-way nearly all day. From Berlin to Washington. They've given them a duplicate link to Cheyenne Mountain, Colorado."

Levin looked across at Panov, who sat hands in pockets as he put in his comment.

"Cheyenne Mountain is North American Air Defense Command. They give the orders to Strategic Air Command. There was a report about noon today that SAC had put up a second Boeing EC-135C."

"What the hell is that, Boris?"

"EC-135Cs are permanent alternative airborne battle staff aircraft. If SAC on the ground gets wiped out, then the EC-135C staff takes over. There's one of those permanently in the air, twenty-four hours a day, with a general in command on all flights. There's an overlap of ten minutes as aircraft are relieved, but the second one has been up there for six hours now. We can take it as permanent."

"Have they ever done this before?"

"No. Not all the time of Vietnam. Not even in exercises."

"What does it mean, then?"

"It's defensive. Precautionary. They're taking the possibility of nuclear attack very seriously."

"All because we've taken down the wall and closed the crossing points. Isn't it overreaction?"

Panov smiled coldly. "Maybe it's a guilty conscience."

"I don't understand."

"Maybe the Americans have had plans to move against us, and the scenario started with something mild like what we've been doing in Berlin. And now they can't make their minds up whether we're doing the same or it's just what we say it is—a gesture of peaceful intention."

"And their troops in Berlin?"

Panov sighed. "There's nothing they can do. The American, British and French sectors in Berlin don't exist anymore. They're just part of one city now. They have no function now. They're guarding an empty stable."

Levin nodded and turned to Slanski. "The President's orders will be to keep a low profile, minimum troops on the streets, and send back troops from Berlin who are on leave, to see if the East Germans or the Russians try any hold-up tactics."

While Slanski was phoning the communications room Levin looked at the next query on the pile. "They want us to answer a cable from the West Berlin Oberbürgermeister on how to react to the current situation."

Panov grinned. "That bastard must be really sweating."

Levin turned in his seat and waved to Slanski. "Ivan, Message 9401. Tell them the reply is a message of encouragement to the Oberbürgermeister and the city council. They have our full support and we are instructing our military commander and our consul to keep them fully informed."

It was almost midnight Washington time, 5 a.m. the next day in Berlin, when the long printout was put in front of Levin. He read it in silence and then looked up at the other two.

"The President of the GDR has invited the West Berlin Oberbürgermeister and the whole city council to continue functioning for the next six months to avoid unnecessary obstruction of the life of the city. Their salaries will be increased to the level of the East Berlin authorities and their pension rights guaranteed. A friendly but cautious reply was received and a full council meeting will be held in a few hours. Ten o'clock tomorrow Berlin time, four o'clock in the morning our time."

Panov laughed and stood up, stretching his arms. Oddly, he look genuinely American in his denim trousers and hunting jacket. "They're really squeezing the lemon now."

Levin leaned back, tilting his chair. "But the Americans and the British will be isolated, humiliated. They'll be a laughingstock and they'll react. Overreact probably."

"Let 'em."

"But we've as good as got Berlin, and we haven't done a thing. Nothing aggressive, we'll have world opinion on our side. But this way the Americans will pick up a challenge we haven't even made."

Panov swung around to look at Levin, and the little eyes were amused. "Who says we haven't?"

Levin looked at him in silence, and the stocky major returned his stare unblinking.

They had worked for another two hours answering queries, giving reactions, and then Levin had gone to his bedroom.

He sat on the edge of the bed as he unbuttoned his shirt. Then, holding his trousers up with one hand, he walked over to the shelf and slid the cassette into the deck. He stood there as the film sound track slowly wound through and played the song she liked— ". . . It's still the same old story, a song of love and glory, on that you can rely. The world was only made for lovers, as time goes by." The books were on the upper shelf, level with his face, and he saw the blue-covered book with the gold lettering. She had read him poems from that book and he reached for it. It was Palgrave's *Golden Treasury*, and he opened it where the blue ribbon marked a page. It was one of the poems she had read to him. A piece of Shakespeare: "Love is not love which alters when it alteration finds, and bends with the remover to remove . . ."

And he watched as a piece of paper fluttered to the carpet. Bending, he picked it up. It was the lines that he had read to her. The lines from the base of the Statue of Liberty. She had written something in the margin—"Remember these lines and remember me. I love you. Clodagh"—and the date. The date was the day they had drugged him. She must have written it after he was unconscious. He read the lines again:

> *Give me your tired, your poor,*
> *Your huddled masses yearning to breathe free,*
> *The wretched refuse of your teeming shore . . .*

He had never felt so lonely, so lost, in all his life, and he walked blindly to the bed. As he lay on his back the lights seemed dim and the fat hot tears leaked from the corners of his eyes. He thought he could hear them as they hit the pillow. He was back in the orphanage again as his eyes closed in sleep.

In Washington, Ex-Comm II was in session. Langham was in shirtsleeves listening to the report of the Secretary of De-

134

fense on the day's happenings in Berlin, his arms on the table, his head shoved forward as if to listen more closely to the words. When Larsen had finished Langham looked around the table, but nobody spoke. He leaned back slowly, collecting his thoughts before he spoke.

"Well, gentlemen. You've heard the situation. What do we do?" The President looked at the Chairman of the Joint Chiefs of Staff.

"We see the situation like this, Mr. President. The Soviets have removed the wall in Berlin, and the city's perimeter has been opened so that we now have a completely open city. Anybody can go anywhere unhindered. There are no longer any restrictions imposed by the Soviets or the West Germans. Our own military has been instructed to maintain a low profile and that means that we no longer control those areas which were previously the American, British and French sectors. Berlin, both West and East, is now just part of East Germany. If we attempted to assume any stance of control of movement we would be in the invidious position of seeming to rebuff an attempt by the Russians to do what we've been demanding that they do for the last ten years or more. There has to be a political decision now before we can make any move."

"What is morale like with our people there?"

"They're confused, but no more. They await their orders from Washington."

The President nodded at Erik Larsen, Secretary of Defense, who looked around the table slowly before he spoke. "Mr. President, of all the situations for which we have contingency plans, this is not one. Maybe we should have, but that's water under the bridge. Superficially the Soviets have made no aggressive move. On the contrary, they have made a magnificent gesture. That's how the man in the street will see it. I have not long ago been speaking to our ambassador in Moscow, and he reports nothing but smiling faces there. But we have all seen the CIA and NSA current reports. There are massive troop concentrations all around Berlin. The signals are quite clear: they're going to take Berlin. They've played their cards well. To the rest of the world they look like the good guys. But all over Europe governments are

135

waiting. Waiting to see who's bluffing who. It's our turn to call, and the position is clear. We either throw in our cards or pay to see their hole card."

Larsen leaned back, glancing at his watch, and somehow the gesture emphasized the enormity of the decisions they must make. They were dealing in hours now, not days.

The President pointed a finger at the Deputy Director of the United States Information Agency. "How *are* the people at home taking it, Lloyd?"

"I'd say they are confused, Mr. President. The media have played it very low-key. Not at the request of the White House. They just have. I think they sense that this is no time for rocking the boat. I'd take that as a bad sign, not a good one. They're well-informed, they know the game. I think they're holding their breath. There's been no unusual load on the telephones, not here nor with Congress. The media are on continuously, but they're polite, and that's bad, too. Sort of not kicking their man when he's down."

The President looked at a paper handed to him by a Marine and pushed it to one side. "Any other comments, gentlemen?"

There were none.

"My letter to the Soviet Premier has been acknowledged, but so far I have received no answer. My feeling is that we have no real choice here. As Erik Larsen said, we've got to pay to see their hole card. If we don't, then we lose Berlin, we lose credibility and we'll be on our own. We *could* forget NATO and every other security pact on the books. We could just grit our teeth and accept that. But then we could count the months before they were in Venezuela or Colombia. With missiles and troops. The only choice we have right now is how much we pay to see that hole card, and I'd like your comments on that. You first, General."

The Chairman of the Joint Chiefs reached for his briefcase and took out a file. He lifted out a single sheet of paper and looked at the President. "Sir, we have enough troops in West Germany to cross the border with East Germany in three places. The Red Army reserves from the recent exercises are fifty miles back from the border. We could be well up the autobahns before we made contact. We estimate that

136

with neither side going beyond tactical nuclear weapons we could hold those positions for seven to eight hours. Strategic reserves could be available by air drop in five to six hours. From then on in—"

It was Larsen who interrupted. "Mr. President, with due respect, there is no point in considering such measures. To the rest of the world it would be outrageous. May I make a suggestion?"

Langham nodded, and Larsen looked across at the general. "How many troops have we on leave from Berlin at this moment?"

"Five hundred, maybe six."

"OK. Recall them from leave and send them back by air. No civilian aircraft, just military. Notify the Soviets that we have an air corridor exercise and give the transports fighter escort. Thirty minutes' notice as prescribed in the agreement. Not a second more, not a second less. That way we lift the ante, but we still are doing nothing that we aren't entitled to do. Anybody who knows what's going on behind the scenes will see that we're still in the ball game. Not punching, just counterpunching. Meantime we see what we can do on the diplomatic front. Even if our troops in Berlin are exposed and isolated I want the Soviets to make the first aggressive move. It's their timing. They're in the hurry, not us. Let's get all the time we can."

And that was how it was left for the next four hours, at the end of which they were to meet again.

Half the units of Strategic Air Command were ordered to civilian airfields around the country to lessen their vulnerability, and the B-52A's and FB-111A's were ordered into the air fully loaded with atomic weapons. As one came down to land, another immediately took its place in the air.

Five infantry divisions were put on standby in Europe, all of them outside West Germany, and the Polaris submarines put to sea with sealed orders from Holy Loch in Scotland and the Spanish base at Rota.

chapter
13

Levin had been shaken awake by Slanski after only a few hours' sleep, and he had taken a bath to rouse himself while Slanski sat on the toilet reading a long situation report from Moscow. Levin lay still in the bath as Slanski started to read the letter from the Soviets to the American President.

"DEAR MR. PRESIDENT:

"I have received your message of the 15th July indicating your concern regarding the city of Berlin. You will know that a week ago the defensive structure which the Soviet government was forced to erect in August 1961 in the city of Berlin was demolished. This gesture by the German Democratic Republic was fully supported by my government. I am sure you will agree with me that there could have been no more obvious indication of our will to consolidate the policy of détente. My government and the government of the German Democratic Republic have removed all restrictions on movement within the city of Berlin.

"For a decade the United States government has used the western sector of Berlin as a base for provocations against the Soviet Union and the Warsaw Pact countries by the CIA and other revanchist cliques under United States protection. I can provide you with extensive documentation of this claim if you yourself are not aware of the situation. May I refer you to your own newspaper reports of Congressional committee investigations into the well-known illegal activities of the CIA.

"To avoid the continuous provocation in the heart of the independent German Democratic Republic and to avoid the possibility of such provocations proving intolerable, the Soviet government demands that all foreign troops should be withdrawn from Berlin immediately.

"The world has seen the gesture made by the Soviet government to ease tensions in Berlin, and my government and I, Mr. President, join the waiting world in eager expectation of a reciprocal gesture from your government and the peace-loving American people."

Slanski looked up from the paper and raised his eyebrows in query. "They want your reaction, Andrei. One hour." He looked at his watch. "Forty minutes left now."

Levin slowly soaped his chest and arms and reached forward to turn on the hot tap. After a few moments he turned off the tap and lay back in the bath, his wet hands covering his face. Suddenly the months of being cooped up seemed to concentrate in his mind and he felt an almost overwhelming urge to stand up and smash things. To enjoy the pleasure of breaking tiles and glass, to hear wood splintering and cloth tearing. To see a crack, a hole in a wall, letting in light and air. There was a layer of pumping pain just under his scalp, between the bone and the soft mass of his brain. Violence would cure it, and for a microsecond the anger almost focused to that fatal center of destruction as when a boy focuses a magnifying glass on dry wood in the sun. His hands moved to the sides of the bath and the terrible strength helped him upright and the orgasm of rage flowed like the water from his body.

He walked into the bedroom, a towel around his shoulders, another around his waist, wet footprints on the carpet. Slanski pulled up one of the armchairs and sat facing him as he toweled himself dry.

"What do you think, Andrei?"

Levin laughed brusquely. "I think that we are hoping for a negative reply."

"Why?"

"Just one word—'demand.' They won't swallow that."

"What will their reply be?"

"They'll go straight to the United Nations and ask for an immediate session of the Security Council."

"That won't get them anywhere."

"Oh, but it will. Not in practical terms maybe, but they will take the shine off our framework of goodwill. Even their allies and friends will have a sympathetic appreciation of our present attitude, but when it goes to the UN the interest will divide on the usual lines. That letter was a mistake."

Slanski put Levin's views on the high-speed coded tapes, and they were transmitted to Moscow.

An hour later Bob Fowler reached blindly for the telephone as it rang beside his bed. He listened almost without comment for ten minutes and when he finally hung up he looked at his watch and reached again for the telephone. He crooked the receiver against his collarbone as he reached for his lighter and a cigarette. He had lit his cigarette and inhaled before there was an answer at the other end.

"White House press secretary."

"That you, Walt?"

"Yes. Who's there?"

"Bob. I've just been contacted, Walt."

"Don't go on, Bob. Can you come around?"

"OK. Ten minutes. Where?"

"Stay put. I'll come to you."

Fowler smiled as he hung up. It seemed a long way from the days of McCarthy.

Walter H. Harcourt II looked and dressed like a J. Walter Thompson vice-president, which is not surprising, because two years earlier that's what he had been. He tried not to take in the untidy room or the photograph of Castro on the far wall.

Fowler stood leaning against the bedroom door, a glass of milk in his hand. "The message is: If the President goes to

140

the United Nations they'll physically occupy West Berlin within the hour."

"Who said we were going to the UN?"

"Nobody. They just said *if* we do, then that's what'll happen."

"What are these bastards after, Bob?"

"Berlin."

Harcourt shook his head. "No way, Bob. If that was what they wanted this isn't how they'd go about it."

Fowler put the empty glass on top of the radio and, wiping his mouth with the back of his hand, said, "What do you think they want?"

Harcourt's eyes watched Fowler's face as he replied. "I think they want a fight. They want World War Three."

The two men looked at each other in the dim light of the room, each searching the other's face for clues as to what he was thinking. When Fowler made no reply after a long silence, Harcourt knew that they shared the same views. When he stood up Fowler didn't move from the doorway.

"Is there anything you want me to tell them?"

Harcourt shrugged. "That's for the President to say, Bob. Like you, I'm just a messenger boy. Where are you going to be in the next hour or two?"

"Right here."

"I take it this is all off the record?"

"I've got a living to earn, Walt, but I won't use it at this stage."

When Levin had gone to bed exhausted, Slanski and Panov had sat together drinking black coffee in the operations room.

"He's been right time and time again, Boris. They must be pleased in Moscow."

Panov, in his bright-red lumberjack's shirt, looked more American than some Americans, but he remained stubbornly and aggressively Russian. Despite Slanski's seniority, Panov was beginning to have the air of a man who knew he had power that he hadn't yet exercised. And it was Panov now who was liaising direct with Moscow. There had been no discussion, no new instructions, it had just seemed to happen.

"In three days' time we'll know. That will decide success or not."

"What's going to happen in three days, then, Boris?"

Panov shoved his coffee cup away with the back of his big hand. He smiled for a moment and then his face was turned toward Slanski. "What do you think will happen in three days, comrade?"

And Slanski noticed the "comrade," which nobody had used for over seven months.

"We take Berlin?"

"It's much more than that, Ivan. We want the world to see the Americans back down. To learn that when it comes to the final threat the Americans will defend nobody but themselves. The rest of Europe will know that from then onward they will do as we wish."

"And if they don't back down?"

"Then, my friend, we shall wipe them out."

"Have you discussed this with Levin?"

"Of course not. It is not for him to know."

"What do they plan for him when this is over?"

Panov shrugged. "Whatever he wants. He's not important when this is over. He'll be rewarded."

"And the girl?"

"What about the girl?"

"He wants to marry her."

"He must be crazy."

"Why? He loves her and she loves him."

Panov folded his arms. "She's a foreigner. Forget it."

"But that need make no difference. She has helped us, Boris."

"I said forget it."

Slanski looked at Panov's bulldog face. "Tell me, Boris."

"I understand that she's dead, Ivan. She was a security risk. A complication."

"God Almighty, Levin will go beserk."

"Let him. He doesn't matter in a day or two, either." As he saw the shock on Slanski's face Panov leaned forward. "We're talking about the final reckoning, Ivan. One way or another Europe will be ours three days from now. By occupation or by the American surrender. That is all that matters. This is

142

what we have been planning. This is what the sacrifices have been for. For the first time ever we are stronger than the Americans. And they know it."

Levin had noticed a change in Slanski, but he had put it down to the pressures of the operation and the demands of Moscow which kept them all continuously occupied for hours on end.

It was noon Moscow time when the President's reply came through to them. They had not been asked to comment.

> DEAR MR. CHAIRMAN:
> No situation since World War II has brought our two countries to a position of such tension as we have today. Your letter of the 16th July is couched in words that we have to interpret as completely contrary to the dé-tente agreement that our predecessors signed in Helsinki in 1975. And your demands that Allied troops should evacuate Berlin are in direct contradiction of the Potsdam Agreement.
>
> It is my belief that any problem there may be in Berlin would best be solved by negotiation rather than unilateral declarations. To this end, Mr. Chairman, I suggest after due preparation we should meet, with our advisers, to discuss those problems which both the Soviet Union and the United States consider to endanger their good relations.
>
> T. LANGHAM

When Levin had finished reading the reply he looked up from his desk at Slanski. "About what you could expect, reasonable and ignoring the demands."

Slanski did not reply, and Levin found this disturbing.

"Don't you agree, Ivan?"

Slanski stood up and walked silently from the room, and Levin half rose to follow him and then sat back in his chair.

He walked through to his bedroom for another pack of cigarettes. He switched on the TV and it was the main evening news. The President's reply was being read out, and in the background was a map of Germany showing the crossing

143

points and colored arrows showing the air corridor. There were interviews with shoppers in Berlin complaining about hoarding of food and rising prices, and with Americans on Pennsylvania Avenue, looking at the White House, who thought it was time the President told the Russians that Berlin wasn't Vietnam or Angola. This time the Reds had gone too far. They wished the President's reply had not been so "soft."

The picture cut to a stadium in Los Angeles where an American was breaking the current world record for the 100 meters. It reminded Levin of sitting one summer with a girl at the Leningrad Stadium. He could remember that she was very pretty and very loving, but he couldn't remember her name. They had stayed that weekend at a friend's dacha, and he remembered driving her for miles on the road alongside Lake Laduga, almost up to the Finnish border. She had had a straw hat with flowers on it, and she had left him sleeping the next morning and was sitting on the side of the bed when he awoke. She had pushed forward a big old-fashioned rose from the garden for him to smell. It wasn't just a lifetime ago, it was a world away from his present nightmare of print-out and documents. He tried desperately hard not to think of Clodagh Kevan. It could only be days now before he saw her again.

It was well past midnight when the second letter from the Soviets came through. It was very short.

> DEAR MR. PRESIDENT:
>
> I have received your letter suggesting a meeting to discuss current problems, particularly Berlin. We should welcome such a conference immediately after the withdrawal of all foreign troops from Berlin.
>
> Respectfully yours,
> L. GRECHKOV

Levin telephoned for Slanski. When Slanski came, Levin couldn't ignore the pale, drawn face and the brown patches under his eyes.

"Are you well, Ivan?"

Then Levin noticed that there were tears on the rims of Slanski's brown eyes and that his upper lip trembled. Levin stood up slowly and walked around the desk. With one hand gently resting on Slanski's shoulder he leaned forward to look at the sad face. "What is it, Ivan? Tell me. Have you had bad news?"

Slanski looked up at him slowly and his voice was thick when he spoke. "It's not what I planned, Andrei. It's not what I thought."

"What isn't?"

Slanski looked at the half-open door, and Levin walked over and closed it. He walked back and sat on the edge of the desk facing Slanski. "Now tell me, Ivan."

"It's not just a question of Berlin, Andrei. It seems it never was. They want a war, a world war, now or next year."

Levin was silent, waiting for Slanski to say more. The man was trembling with all the symptoms of an ague. His fingers were interlaced as he tried in vain to steady his clenched hands on his knees.

"Take deep, deep breaths, Ivan. Very slowly, very slowly. That's right. Deep breaths."

Slowly Slanski recovered his composure. "Panov is in charge of the operation now. The orders have just come through from Moscow. I think he was in charge all the while without my knowing. They want the Americans to back down so that all the world can see them do it. We are stronger now than they are. In everything, arms, men, tanks, planes, ships—everything. And they know it, the Americans know it. When the Americans back down over Berlin, then Europe will be a continent of satellites to Moscow."

"And if they don't back down?"

"They will threaten nuclear war. Drive the Americans to desperation, taunt them openly. The Americans will do anything to avoid a war now. They are one, maybe two years behind us. Berlin is just a tethered goat. An excuse."

"Why are you telling me, Ivan?"

"There is nobody else I can tell. The other people in Moscow who thought this was just about Berlin have been pushed aside. The Red Army is riding the politicians now. There are many in jail."

Levin swung his leg slowly to flatten his own tension as he tried not ask the question. But it was impossible. "Where is the girl, Slanski?" And there was an unusual rasp of determination and command in his voice.

Slanski sighed deeply. "She's dead, Andrei. They had her killed."

Levin's eyes half closed as if he had been hit, and the blood drained from his face. His knuckles were dead white where his hands gripped the edge of the desk. His voice was a harsh whisper. "How do you know?" He stood up, his face distorted as his hands gripped the lapels of Slanski's jacket. "Tell me—how do you know?" And he shook Slanski as if he were a bundle of rags.

Slanski put up his hand to hold Levin's wrist and it dropped back limply beside him. He gasped for air. "They'll hear you, for God's sake."

"How do you know?" Levin's voice was strident and harsh.

"Panov told me, Andrei. I don't know how he knows. Don't tell him I told you, or he'll kill us too."

"But why, Slanski, why in God's name should they kill her? She helped them. She was part of the operation."

"Her part was over, Andrei." Slanski tried to stand, but he sank back into the chair, and as he spoke he was gasping for breath. "In two days' time they're going to make the American and British troops in Berlin prisoners. And that will be the beginning of the end."

"But the Americans will retaliate."

"That's what they want, Andrei." And as he finished speaking Slanski's face drained of blood, and he fell forward from the chair to lie prone along the front of the desk.

Levin reached over and picked up the phone and asked for Panov.

Panov looked harassed but alert, but he didn't notice Slanski until Levin had pointed to him. He hurried over and turned Slanski's face to the light. His hand went inside Slanski's jacket and he looked up at Levin. "Phone for the doctor quickly, Andrei."

Slanski was put on a stretcher and taken down the corridor, but Panov stayed behind.

"What happened, Andrei?"

146

"We were talking and he collapsed."

"Talking about what?"

"The Party Chairman's second letter to the President."

Panov nodded and turned to go. At the door he stopped. "You'll be able to relax in a couple of days or so. You better get some sleep."

Levin went back to his bedroom. There was a meal laid out on the small table, but he sat in the chair alongside, without eating. His body felt unbelievably heavy. There was no response in his legs and arms, and he could feel ice-cold sweat running from his forehead down his face, the taste of salt on his lips.

How did you kill a beautiful girl in cold blood? With what weapon? In what place? A crazed film cut and dissolved in his overloaded mind. Her green eyes out of focus near his face. The uneasy birds sitting unmoving on the perimeter fence. Her long legs pink in the soft light from the lamp as she sat naked in the armchair, her head to one side as she listened to the Dvorak. He shuddered and reached in slow motion for the brandy and a glass. The glass clashed against his teeth as he drank, and the fiery liquid seemed to trace his veins and arteries, working its magic slowly and purposefully. He could hear the dull roar of aircraft high above the building. They sounded like bombers, that sullen relentless thunder of heavy aircraft on course to some distant target. All over the world men and aircraft would be carrying out their orders, and at missile bases the covers would be rolled back, with the white plumes rising like steam as they were fueled. His body was cold and his mind dull with a kaleidoscope of random thoughts. Whenever a rational pattern emerged for a few moments the pieces fell apart to make way for some new unhappiness. The clues had been there all the time, the things Velichko had said, the things Panov had said, and Slanski's strange behavior over the last few days. Even the girl's death seemed inevitable with hindsight. He groaned as he remembered that he had once imagined her receiving an Order of Lenin, or at least a Red Star. Without realizing it he was standing, and his knuckles beat against his lips till the blood ran salty in his mouth. The clinical symptoms of trauma went through his mind, his brain reaching for the

147

brief descriptions, but they dissolved and faded. And all the time he knew what he was going to do. His mind had not dwelt on it for a moment, but it had threaded through all his thoughts like some haunting contrapuntal theme.

He found it almost unbelievable that his own people, who had fought against imperialism all over the world, would actively pursue a policy that they hoped would lead to war or to the abject surrender of Europe by the United States. With so much to achieve at home. What would be the gain? It was conquest, nothing more. And if there were a war, then there would be millions dead before the issue was decided. One false move by the Americans and the buttons would be pressed. And the Americans were misconstruing the Soviet moves all along the line. They were seeking reason without knowing that reason wasn't available to them. They would mobilize too late because they saw Berlin as the problem. The killing of the girl was a small-scale model of Moscow's ruthlessness, and his own fate would be equally unimportant. Two minutes' consideration about whether he would be better dead or promoted to head of faculty at Moscow. He had little doubt as to what the decision would be. There could be a million Americans and Russians going about their daily tasks at this moment who had no idea that in three days' time they could be dead in the smoking ruins of their cities.

He was already at least twenty-four hours behind the real events, maybe more, and the thundering aircraft were indications that the tensions must be high. They were probably patrolling the Chinese border to keep the Chinese out of the struggle. At most he was no farther than thirty miles from the frontier, and for the Peking government he would be a welcome defector. They would help him contact the Americans if it meant defeating the Russians. In his mind he realized that he was talking as if he himself were not a Russian, too.

He had no weapons, no identity documents, and no money. It was almost impossible, but he had no real choice. The sooner he went, the better.

chapter
14

The Samos-satellite photographs had shown batteries of D-30 howitzers clustered in farm buildings about half a mile back from the crossing points. The central jacks were down, the wheels off the ground and the outer trails spread out at 120 degrees. They were ready for firing, their muzzles were uncovered and their seven-man crews were sprawled under the trees and along the hedges. Their insignia were unidentifiable, but on the side of one of the towing vehicles was the Soviet armored troops' sign, stenciled on the door panel.

The Joint Chiefs of Staff situation report indicated ninety-seven Soviet and Warsaw Pact divisions assembled in East Germany and Poland. The forty armored divisions were in attack positions facing Hamburg, Hanover, Brunswick, and Göttingen. Forty-five miles deeper into East Germany they had identified seven hundred SCUD A's and SCUD B's already mounted and elevated on JS-111 transporters. This was four times the number that had previously been assessed as the total available to the whole of the Warsaw Pact forces. They had ranges up to 170 miles and they could all accommodate optional nuclear warheads.

The Red Army troops deployed from the Soviet Union for the summer military exercises had not returned to their many bases in the Soviet Union but were strung out along the border with Poland and East Germany. It was 6 A.M. Washington time on the seventeenth of July. In Moscow it was three in the afternoon.

The first news of the situation in the West was given to the Russian people on Moscow's four-o'clock news bulletin. It was the third news item:

"In an official note to the President of the United States the Soviet Prime Minister warned of the serious consequences of the continued use of the so-called area of West Berlin as a base for their spies and saboteurs against the peaceful members of the Warsaw Pact. The hysterical outbursts by warmongers in the United States against the Soviet Union's attempts at détente are no longer tolerable. The peace-loving American people have already exposed, through their own Congressional investigation committees, that the Central Intelligence Agency spends hundreds of millions of dollars a year to assassinate national leaders, to bring down governments and to sabotage the structure of those countries which they decide are hostile. The Prime Minister reminded the United States President of the words of one of his predecessors, 'There is no burden we will not bear, no price we will not pay, to preserve our freedom.'"

At the same time, the statement was being broadcast on thirty Communist short-wave transmitters in a hundred languages and dialects. The announcement was followed by extensive quotations from American newspaper reports of congressional committees investigating the CIA.

The U.S. President had a 6-A.M. start with a working breakfast with the Chairman of the Joint Chiefs of Staff and the Secretary of State.

The Berlin troops returning from leave had not been harassed in any way by the Russians, but there were divergent views as to the significance of this. The State Department saw the move as showing flexibility on the Russians' part; the Pentagon and the Defense Secretary saw it as a sign of the Soviets' indifference to pinpricks and of their complete self-confidence.

In Moscow it was already one o'clock in the afternoon, and the Presidium had been given a presentation by a Red Army staff team on the likely first-strike damage and casualties if the Americans chose to press the button first.

From 11 A.M. the same team had given its evaluation of the effect of a United States counterstrike if the Soviets committed their forces first in an aggressive situation that the Americans could consider as a declaration of war. The deaths were estimated to be in the region of 3.9 million, the target areas being Moscow, Leningrad, Sverdlovsk, Kiev and roughly a hundred missile installations beyond the Urals. Compared with the estimated American deaths of 21 million in the first forty hours there was no doubt about ultimate Soviet victory, but day two could begin to raise problems. The problems had been those outlined in a report of highest security from the KGB. Public morale in the USSR would become a major problem if the United States did not capitulate between the sixteenth and twenty-fifth hours after the first strikes.

There had been argument for a Soviet first strike, but a majority, without the necessity of the Chairman's vote, had opted for nuclear missiles to be used only tactically in Europe and for the ICBMs to be used only if the United States appeared to be ready to use nuclear weapons to resist Soviet pressures.

The test point for next Presidium consideration would be the roundup of United States and Allied troops in Berlin. This would take place in two days' time. If the Americans made no aggressive move to free their troops, the Americans would be finished so far as Europe was concerned. If they took action, the Presidium would consider opening general hostilities against the United States itself. At that point there would be more information available. All Soviet diplomats abroad were instructed to concentrate on putting the Soviet case as nonaggressors and to emphasize the Americans' own revelations concerning the CIA.

Four members of the Presidium met later that afternoon at an apartment just off Sudovaya Ulitsa. They later contacted a marshal of the Red Army and a general in the Red Army's Missile Command. One of them sat next to a Chinese student at that evening's performance of *The Flames of Paris* at the Bolshoi.

At noon exactly Panov had brought in a sheet off one of the radio message pads and handed it to Levin. It was written in pencil because it was too urgent to type.

> *471/97048/17. What reaction to closure Berlin air corridor and takeover Tempelhof. Stop. Immediate. Stop. Ends.*

chapter
15

Levin had put aside bread from his breakfast tray and wrapped it in a newspaper between shirts in the chest of drawers, and a pack of cigarettes was left unopened on his bedside table. He realized that he had no idea what he should try to take with him or what clothes he should wear. And he had no idea of how he could escape from the operational complex.

The morning had been occupied continually with giving his opinion on Presidential reactions to a dozen situations, and he had lunched with Panov in the operations room.

Late in the afternoon he had been asked for his reaction to the various American military and administrative buildings in Berlin being put under guard by Soviet and East German troops, with all Allied troops being confined to their quarters. Panov sat opposite him, one arm on the desk top, his raw face smooth and his small blue eyes as alert as an eagle's.

"Will there be a big show of force, Boris, tanks and the like?"

Panov grinned. "Let's say there'll be enough troops and hardware to make it impossible for them to break out. At least, if they do there'll be none left to tell the tale."

"And when would this be?"

"The day after tomorrow. About ten in the evening Berlin time."

"What about troops outside the buildings? At cinemas, with their girl friends, or whatever?"

"We'll let them in if they come back, and we'll issue radio orders for all troops to report back immediately to their units."

"Any warning to Washington or their commands in Berlin?"

Panov shook his head, half smiling at the naïveté. "No. No warning."

Levin leaned awkwardly in his chair, his fingers squeezing a small eraser on his desk. His eyes were on the digital clock on the wall. The red diodes had been extended to six digits and the sixth digit constantly flickered as it registered hundredths of a second. As he looked it showed "WASHINGTON 15.30.14—July 17." His eyes moved away to the chandelier and his ears again picked up the heavy drone of aircraft throbbing their way in the distance. It was the first prediction he had had to make when he was certain that the American President would make the fatally wrong choice. The Americans were relying on changing world opinion, diplomacy with the Soviets and time to cool the pressures so that some compromise could be negotiated. The Americans would have already recognized that there was an even greater threat behind the threat to Berlin, but it would be a major decision to react to the present pressures as if they were the prelude to real hostilities. Each side was intent on making the other commit the first openly aggressive act, and the Soviets were applying pressure after pressure on the Americans to that end. There was no country in the world that was unaware of the activities of the CIA in Berlin and the rest of the world. The American Congress and the American news media had done the KGB's job all through the middle seventies. The use of West Berlin as an espionage base was obvious enough and the Soviet case was overwhelmingly and sympathetically accepted by enemies and even friends of the United States. A physical reaction, a military response, to the Soviet pressures would leave the United States isolated completely. Levin was sure that the President would take no aggressive stance, but he knew that only a sharp

154

military reaction could halt the holocaust. He toyed for a moment with the thought of predicting the aggressive reaction, but he realized that it would be pointless. He wasn't used as an oracle, merely as an early warning system.

He looked back at Panov. "They will call for a meeting of the Security Council and they'll raise some hell in the General Assembly. They'll be mounting all the diplomatic and financial pressures they can muster."

"No military action at all?"

"No. None."

Otto Faller sat smoking in the Volkswagen. It was parked near the crossroads on the Northeim side of the road to Göttingen. The American was late, but Faller guessed that the CIA must be hard pressed in these last few days.

The Merc had pulled up facing him, and the American walked down the road and climbed in alongside him.

"I can only stop for minutes, Otto. Is it important?"

"That's for you to decide, my friend. You remember the inquiries I made for you about the KGB man named Slanski and an Irish girl called Kevan?"

"Yeah."

"Do you remember my reporting about a guy named Velichko who had been down to an installation just outside Kiev?"

"The guy who got drunk and went into the Lubyanka?"

"That's him. He's in a labor camp now, outside Leningrad. My people have a contact there. Velichko will talk in return for our getting him out."

"What'll he talk about?"

"The installation at Kiev and anything else he knows."

"Is he trying a con?"

Faller grinned. "If he doesn't talk or if it doesn't add up we can easily put him back in the Soviet Union. He knows that as well as I do. He'll talk."

"How much will it cost?"

"Fifty thousand dollars, and you take him over for the rest of his life."

"Jesus. Is it worth it?"

"Maybe. Maybe not. It's up to you to decide."

"How long have I got to refer back in?"

Faller shrugged "As long as you like. He's gonna be there a long, long time."

The American phoned two hours later. He ordered Faller to make the deal to get Velichko out of the camp and the country. Half the money had already been deposited in a Bahamian bank account.

Levin had worked solidly until nine in the evening and he had eaten a full meal and kept aside an apple and a pear. He had drawn a rough map of the Chinese-Soviet border near Irkutsk and Khabarovsk from the wall map in the operations room. The sketch map, and the printout asking for his view on the operation against American troops in Berlin, he folded carefully and put into his shoes. He had read somewhere that that was where espionage agents put their secrets. It seemed faintly ridiculous and overdramatic.

He went back to his office to check the digital clock. It read "WASHINGTON 20.17.34—July 17." That meant that the real time outside was three o'clock in the morning Moscow time. It would give him another three or four hours of darkness to get clear of the installation.

At 20:27 Washington time he took a deep breath and reached up to remove the electric-light bulb over the bed. He pushed the bone-handled knife into the bayonet fitting, and the blue flash was instantaneous. The explosion took the knife out of his hand as the lights went out. He pushed the bulb back in and shone his flashlight onto the bed. He found the burned knife, slid it into his pocket, and made for the corridor door. He bumped into a shadowy figure and there was the rattle of a rifle sling on a gun barrel. The figure cursed in Russian and moved on. There was light from a flashlight at the far end of the passage, and Levin moved to his right. He passed another man, and then the lights came on.

He was by a door with a big handle. The handle turned and he could have opened the door, but he left it closed. Hurrying back down the corridor, he walked past the operations room door and his bedroom door. He could see Panov at the far end of the corridor. He hurried down toward him.

"It's OK, Andrei. The circuit is fused, we've put the emergency installation on until we can correct the fault."

"How long will it take, Boris?"

"There's no hurry, Andrei. Get your sleep, we'll check the generator tonight and the circuit tomorrow."

"What about communications with Moscow?"

"Leave it to me, comrade. We can use the emergency twelve-volt for the radios. Just get some sleep."

He watched the midevening news on TV, and the first fifteen minutes showed the Berlin troops returning from leave and filing out of the transports at Tempelhof airfield. It cut to the President with a putter on the lawn at the White House, smiling cheerfully at the camera crew as he bent to lift the ball from the cup. The Vice-President was shown boarding a U.S. Army plane at Dulles, his destination London. The network defense specialist was interviewed about a report in the *New York Times* that Soviet troops were massing in East Germany. His answers were defensive and cautious. After the second commercial break there was an interview with the British ambassador to Washington, who appeared to be as unwilling as everyone else to be caught with the hot potato of being the first to let unspoken fears become discussable facts. The rest of the news was sports and an interview with an environmentalist protesting against pollution by automobiles and its effect on the weather. As Levin switched it off he wondered what the weather would be like in a week's time after the missiles had exploded. Maybe all the old *babchas* were right and nuclear explosions *would* affect the weather.

He had suppressed all thoughts about what he was attempting to do. The food, the cigarettes and the documents were his only precautions. He didn't even know his way around the building, let alone the terrain outside. All he knew was that it was early morning and somewhere near the Chinese border. His eyes would quickly get used to the darkness, and what happened outside the building would be his fate, whether it was escape or a pounding hail of bullets. There was no point in thinking about it. He wasn't a man of action, he would move on by instinct. Inside the building it was the seventeenth of July, outside it would be the eighteenth or even the nineteenth.

He took the knife out of his pocket again. The short circuit had taken a jagged piece of metal from its tip, and around the edges it was blue from the burning. It was an hour since the electricity had been restored. There would be no need to put the bulb back this time, every second would count; all their attention would be concentrated on restoring the circuit, and this time it would take longer, there was no secondary circuit to bring in. For a moment he hesitated, and then, shielding his eyes, he thrust the knife up to touch both contacts. The current flashed and turned the knife in his hand, there was a smell of ozone and he turned and made for the corridor door.

There were voices and shouts at the far end again, and two men pushed past him in the darkness. His hand held out before him, he made his way to the near end of the long corridor. His fingers moved around on the cold steel door to find the handle. He pressed it down slowly and opened the door gently. He closed it quietly behind him. There was a faint light coming from another door ahead, and he went forward. The second door opened and a searchlight blazed in his face. He threw his hand up instinctively to shade his eyes and he caught a glimpse of a yard and metal silos. It wasn't night, it was daylight on a bright sunny day. Something was terribly wrong.

As his eyes focused he saw a big house, painted white, with a wooden fence marking off a small garden. Alongside the two massive silos was a long barn, and two men were leaning against a low gate. They were too far away for him to see their faces, but as he looked at them one of them waved to him. Hesitantly he waved back. Across to his left was a long brick building and a tubular metal gate that led onto a paved path that sloped down and curved to a wood of conifers and beeches.

Red dust came up as he walked to the gate, and it groaned on its metal hinges as he swung it open just enough to ease through. On the paved road he started to run. He could be at the border in an hour. He tried to remember the greeting he had learned in Chinese, but it had been too long ago. Beyond the wood the ground sloped upward steeply, and instinct made him leave the road. He crossed the ditch and shoved backward through a thorn hedge and headed for the hill. The grass was rough and coarse, and as he ran the thick tussocks squelched with underlying water. Another hundred yards and he was at the bank of a river.

The banks were steep and the red sand ran down to stone and gravel. The river must be big in the winter, for the bed was almost forty feet across. But now there was a three- or four-foot-wide stream, not more than a foot or two deep. He could see nothing on either bank now, and there was no sound except the stream on the stones and the noise of his own footsteps as he ran along the shingle. At the first bend in the river he stopped, breathless and sweating from his efforts. He sat down against the foot of the sandbank, his head back to take in air.

As he sat there his senses slowly returned; he could hear a skylark and as he lifted his head he could see the small bird rising and falling as if it were on a jet of water. He shaded his eyes and looked for the sun. It was high in the sky, and that meant that the time as well as the date inside the installation had been deliberately put out of phase. Wherever he was it must be just after midday. The border would be south-southwest and he was already heading in the right direction. He loosened the laces in his shoes and as he stood up he heard shouts in the distance. Carried on the summer wind they sounded like children's voices or women's voices, but they were too far away to the south to be pursuers.

There was a wide bend in the stream that curved across the front of the hill, and Levin followed the bed of the small river until it formed two branches around an outcrop of rock. There was a small pool, and the slow current barely moved the surface of the water. Levin took off his shoes and socks and sat with his feet in the cool water. There were clumps of blue water-speedwell and forget-me-nots and a bulbous yellow flower that he had never seen before. As he sat quietly a water vole plopped down from the sandy bank and swam across to disappear in a cluster of lily pads.

Levin wondered what Panov and the others would do when they discovered that he was missing. In the confusion it would probably be some time before they even noticed, and when they did, Moscow would be preoccupied with the greater realities of Berlin. They would cover the border, but for hundreds of miles it was scarcely defined. The gorges and the riverbeds sliced up the terrain in a network of watery hazards that made troop movements by both sides extremely difficult. There were hundreds of minor border infringements every day, and both the Russians and the Chinese accepted them as accidental. When they appeared to be deliberate both sides reacted aggressively. A few tribesmen a month defected along the lonely border, and Moscow put on a show of force from time to time. On the Chinese side the patrols were for observation rather than control. Perhaps he could find a local smuggler to take him across, with the promise of reward when he was on the other side. After that, everything would depend on persuading the Chinese to let him contact the Americans.

He dried his feet in the sun and checked the time. It was about four o'clock, maybe a little later. He would be able to move more easily when it was dark. It took an hour to skirt the base of the hill and to struggle up the lower slopes to the clumps of trees. Ten minutes later he stumbled across a gravel path, and he followed alongside it through the thickly wooded area that stretched up to the summit. Right at the top was a clearing. He stood looking back to where he had come from. On the distant horizon he could see the sparkle of water. A large lake to the west. Too big to be anything but one of the lakes that dotted the border area. He must be right on the Sinkiang frontier. To the north and east were tree-covered hills and deep gorges.

He had to walk across the clearing to look to the south because of the trees, and there the gravel clearing gave way to a path and another clearing large enough to take turning vehicles. A ray of sunshine slanted through the tall trees, illuminating a white-painted post. The pointing signs said "CAYUGA COUNTY. Lake Ridge 4m. S. Lansing 10 m. ITHACA 20m."

chapter
16

Levin closed his eyes and in the silence wood pigeons called from the treetops and in the distance he could hear the heavy drone of aircraft again. His heart was thudding, up near his throat, and his breathing was shallow. As he stretched out a hand to the trunk of a big pine tree he felt the first spirals of vertigo and he shivered with cold in the summer sunshine.

So often he had lectured on the tunnel vision that constricted the imagination to the narrow sector of the expected and familiar in the sciences, the creative arts and human relationships. Yet his own mind had been incapable of imagining a plane journey outside the Soviet Union. And now it seemed so obvious. The two-day time lag for TV, radio and the newspapers had been intolerable once the operation against Berlin had started. Everything he had been getting since the move from Kiev must have been instantaneous. And that explained the sunshine too. It was so obvious, so incredibly obvious, but he hadn't seen it. The Soviet citizens' indoctrination worked well, even on psychologists. Pavlov's bell still worked.

He looked back at the signpost. He had never heard of Cayuga County, but somewhere or other he had heard of Ithaca.

Panov and the others would be in difficulty coming after him now, they wouldn't have any real resources, and they needed to keep a very low profile. So far as he remembered, Soviet citizens were limited to a small circle around Washington, like the foreigners in Moscow. Maybe Ithaca was near to Washington. Wherever it was he would be able to phone Washington and warn the President.

Levin stood up and brushed down his jacket. He must make for a road. It was not illegal here to give a ride to a stranger.

It took an hour's walking down one of the gravel roads before he approached the highway, and he had to check with the sun again to find which direction would take him to Ithaca.

The first car he waved to didn't stop. It was a boy and a blonde in a Mustang. The next car was a big white station wagon and it pulled over and rolled to a stop a few yards past him. The driver was a stocky man in a woolen plaid shirt who looked remarkably like Panov. The driver leaned across and opened the nearside door as Levin approached.

"You in trouble, Mac?" he said, squinting upward to look at Levin.

Levin bent down to the window and spoke carefully as if the man might not understand what he was saying. "Are you driving to Ithaca, sir?"

"I'm going just south of Lansing on State Thirty-four. You can get a lift there at the filling station."

"Thank you, that would be excellent."

For a moment the pale-blue eyes screwed up as they looked at Levin's face. "OK, then. The door's open."

Levin slid in beside the driver. He had white silky hair and a deeply tanned face and arms. His sleeves were rolled up and his left arm rested on the door where the window was rolled down.

As they swung out onto the highway the driver said, "You on holiday in these parts?"

"Er . . . yes. Well, perhaps more business than holiday."

The driver half turned to look at him. "Say. Are you a Polak or somethin'?"

"What's a Polak?"

The driver laughed. "A Pole. You speak sort of funny. Kinda like a foreigner. An Englishman, maybe."

162

"Am I difficult to understand?"

The man laughed. "No, friend. It's just you talk like a schoolteacher."

The driver was silent for a few minutes as he changed lanes around a string of trucks. Ten minutes later the car pulled in at a big filling station with a restaurant and self-service cafeteria alongside. The driver edged the car along to a vacant pump, and a girl in overalls unscrewed the gasoline cap and thrust in the hose.

"How many, mister?"

"Fill her up. It'll take ten, maybe twelve."

The driver turned to Levin. "You wanna grab a coffee, mister?"

Levin flushed and hesitated. "I came out without my money."

The shrewd blue eyes looked at him. "Are you on the run or somethin'?"

"My car broke down. I just want to get to Ithaca."

"You one of the foreign professors at Cornell?"

And Levin suddenly realized where he had seen the word "Ithaca" before. It was on Professor Railton's invitation to Cornell for the autumn seminar.

"I'm a colleague of Professor Railton."

The driver nodded, his curiosity gone. "Let's go over and get a coffee." He turned to the girl. "I've left the keys in. Shift it when you've finished."

She nodded.

The self-service was busy and it was ten minutes before they'd drunk their coffees. The driver paid the bill and while he was waiting for the change he turned to Levin.

"I'll take you down to Ithaca, you'll get a lift there easy enough and I can get my stuff at the supermarket."

When they were back on the highway the driver leaned forward and switched on the radio. A man was singing a cowboy song and the driver reached forward again. He grunted. "Let's hear what those goddam Reds are doin' now."

The newscaster was speaking so fast that Levin could barely follow what he was saying. ". . . and the President in his speech to union leaders emphasized the need for negotiation rather than aggressive action—not only between labor and management but between world powers. . . . recent note from Soviet Premier . . . a regrettable . . . and now to the Washington mystery. News agency reports state that Soviet diplomats in Washington are concerned about the disappearance of one of their number, Andrei Levin. The Soviet Embassy spokesman hints that the disappearing comrade is the victim of current tensions between the Soviet Union and the United States. It seems that the embassy medical adviser has been treating Levin for the symptoms of a nervous breakdown. . . . in the early hours of today . . . some violent action against the President of the United States. . . . At Albany this afternoon representatives of the—"

And the driver switched off the radio. "Those bastards ought to be packed off back to Moscow along with the goddam United Nations."

"You don't like the Russians?"

"Who the hell does?"

They were approaching Ithaca, the signs said, and Ithaca welcomed careful drivers. In the center of the town the good Samaritan said, "Aw, hell, I've brought you this far, I'll take you up to Cornell. Ain't never been there myself. But it's up State Seventy-nine."

Three miles out of the town they saw the Cornell University sign and the driver pulled over to the side of the road. "Here you are buddy. Back at the seat of learnin'."

Levin reached in to shake the driver's hand. The man looked surprised, but the grip was friendly enough. The driver waved and then looked behind him to check for oncoming vehicles and eased his way back onto the highway.

It was a long walk up to the university buildings and the sun was low now, casting long shadows across the grass and making the white buildings seem ever whiter. He asked a girl the way to the offices and she walked with him to the long white building.

"Are you one of the visiting lecturers?" she asked.

"Not just now," he said. "Maybe in the autumn."

She pointed. "That's the Arts and Science Building—Goldwyn Smith Hall. Right in front as you go in is the secretary's office. It's late, but she's probably still there."

She nodded goodbye and he restrained a bow and returned the smile.

He knocked on the door, but there was no answer, so he opened it slowly. There were a desk, an electric typewriter and banks of filing cabinets. Otherwise the room was empty. The door to an inner room was open, and there was a young woman sitting at a long desk, the telephone cradled on her shoulder. She looked up at him as she was talking and waved him casually to a chair alongside the desk.

". . . I must go, Pat, I've got a visitor, but remember—the grant covers books and fees, nothing more. The kid's got to live *somewhere*. OK. I leave it in your good hands, as they say." She hung up and looked across at Levin. "And, sir, what can I do for you?"

"Could you tell me please where I can find Professor Railton—faculty of psychology?"

She shook her head. "I'm afraid not. It's our vacation and he's not on campus. I could try his home for you."

She reached for the phone, her finger poised to dial as she turned the pages of an internal telephone book. "Here we are. Railton, James Sinclair, Ph.D." And she dialed and waited. After a few minutes she said, "No luck, I'm afraid. How about I put a message on the faculty board for you? Where can he contact you?"

"Does he live near here?"

"Sure. He's up on the Ridge Road."

"Maybe I could check if he's there."

"OK. But I've got a feeling he's in Europe. There was some talk of a trip to London."

"Can you give me his address?"

"Yes. Here we are. Let me write it down for you, thirty-four Ridge Road." She stood up and turned to point through the open window.

"See the long building—that's the Psychology Faculty building. Go right to the end. Then over the bridge to where the road forks. Take the left fork and then turn right. Don't be scared if you meet a few packs of dogs on the campus. They're on our side. They can recognize the smell of an academic a hundred yards away."

He laughed. "That's fine. Thank you."

As he was reaching for the note she said, "You look like you've been in the wars." And when he looked surprised she blushed. "Very rude of me. By the way, what did you say your name was?"

"Langham," he said. "Andrew Langham."

She laughed. "A good name to have around Washington, D.C., these days. See you."

The young woman had been right. It had taken him an hour to get to the Ridge Road and as people passed by he was conscious now of his beard and his disheveled clothes. He must look like a tramp.

There were expensive cars parked in the driveways, but when he got to Number 34 it had that empty look. Not just that the owners were away, but away for a long time. The dying sun was reflected in the white paint, and the lawn had been recently cut. A gardener maybe. There was still the smell of new-mown grass. He walked slowly up the wide drive past the double garage and up three steps to the veranda. There was clematis in bloom that must be as old as the house itself, for it swarmed over the door and across the tops of the windows to trail upward to the first-floor windows. He rang the bell and knocked on the brass knocker and turned to face the road as he waited.

Everywhere was quiet and peaceful. A pair of blackbirds listened for worms on the lawn, their heads to one side, intent and alert. A small rufous bird scuttered in the clematis for insects, and in the distance he could hear a girl laughing. He walked down the steps and strolled around to the back of the house. There was a swing and a children's slide, and a plastic toy lay in the grass at the foot of an old apple tree. There were geraniums in clay pots along the foot of the wall of the house, and a spade leaned against the small porch. His hand tried the doorknob. It was loose on its spindle, but it didn't turn.

The nearest house was two hundred yards away. The light was going now, the sun half hidden behind the trees. He searched the garden for a stone and touched it to the bottom pane of glass in the upper half of the wooden door. It took three blows before the glass broke, and he thrust his hand through to turn the key. But there was no key.

He looked around slowly, and finally saw the spade. He edged it between the door and the frame and pulled slowly on the handle. The wood creaked, then splintered, and suddenly the lock sprang and the door swung open. He closed the door behind him and pushed the spade against it to keep it closed. Even in the dim light he could see the white appliances in the kitchen, and somewhere a time switch clicked and a motor started and stopped. Through a hall was the living room. He closed the heavy curtains on the front windows and the door to the hall, and then switched on the lights.

It was a comfortable room, with solid old-fashioned furniture, a small color TV and a shelf of hi-fi equipment and a radio. There was a doll half hidden under a cushion, and a sewing basket leaking wool and remnants of material. On the wall were photographs. Photographs of children and adults, family groups and Victorian hand-painted portraits. There was a door on the far wall and he walked over. The door wasn't locked and he opened it and switched on the light. It was obviously Railton's study. The walls were covered with framed diplomas and certificates and one wall was lined with textbooks. The desk was modern and it was clear of papers.

He tried the drawers one by one and none of them was locked. As he went through them he placed things on the desk top from time to time. A small cashbox and its key. An out-of-date driver's license and a green passport wallet. Two fifty-dollar bills and a wad of ten-dollar bills in a bank's paper band. All told there were four hundred and eight dollars. He stuffed the currency and the documents into his inside pocket and slowly stood up.

Back in the living room he switched on the radio and turned the dial until he found a news station.

". . . and medical supplies are being rushed to the Turkish capital from neighboring countries. The weather tomorrow will be much the same as today. Light mists at dawn with sunshine all day. Average humidity, but a high pollen count in all areas. Now a roundup of the headlines. Tension is still mounting regarding the Berlin confrontation. The President in a TV address to the nation said, I quote, 'We shall attempt to negotiate with the Soviets so long as negotiation is possible,' unquote. The search is still going on for the missing Soviet diplomat. Fears were expressed by a spokesman for the Soviet Embassy in Washington that the missing diplomat may make an attempt on the President's life. It seems that the White House is not taking special precautions, but the FBI and other government agencies have been alerted. In London the British Prime Minister cast doubts on the ability of NATO's forces to give adequate protection to its member states, and hinted that his government may withdraw its troops from the Berlin trouble spot. The next news is on the half hour, and now our regular feature, 'A Word in Your Ear,' presented by Danny . . ."

Levin switched off the radio and walked over to the light switch. When he had switched out the lights he drew back the curtains. He stood there looking out the windows. He could see the lights of Ithaca reflected on the night clouds and he tried to work out what to do. More than anything he wanted to sleep. He stumbled back through the darkness of the living room to the study. He switched on the light and sat at the desk. He reached for the telephone and pulled it in front of him and then stretched out his hand for the telephone directory and leafed through the instruction pages, reading them quickly as he turned them. He read the last pages carefully and then lifted the receiver. His fingers slowly and carefully depressed the buttons and he heard a thin voice say, "Operator. Can I help you?"

"I want to speak to the President of the United States—" he lifted the instruction page—"person to person."

chapter
17

The White House operator had dealt with the call courteously and smoothly.

"The White House, can I help you?"

"I want to speak please to the President."

"Just a moment."

There was a click and another voice. "White House secretariat. Can I help you?"

"I want to speak to the President himself."

"Well, sir, the President is in conference right now. What was the subject, sir?"

"I want to warn him about Berlin."

At the White House end Charlie Montagu put his hand over the mouthpiece and said to his pretty secretary, "Another nut on Berlin." Taking his hand away, he said, "I'll pass on your warning sir. Thank you."

"I want to speak to one of the President's senior assistants. This is important. It's a security matter."

"I see." There was a pause. "Just a moment."

There was a long silence and then a voice with an Irish accent came on. "Corrigan speaking, White House security detail. I understand you've got some complaint."

"It's not a complaint. I want to speak to the President about the situation in Berlin. It's very urgent."

169

"That sounds like a State Department matter. Have you contacted them?"

"No. How do I do that?"

"They're in the yellow pages, sir."

And the connection was cut off.

Levin reached into the bottom drawer of the desk and took out a small flashlight. Upstairs in the bathroom he washed and shaved by the light of the flashlight. He dried the razor and put it into his pocket. In the main bedroom he set the old-fashioned alarm clock to wake him in three hours. There was a faint smell of lavender in the room, and the pillow was soft to his head. He lay on his side and was asleep almost instantly.

It was five o'clock when the alarm awakened Levin. The short sleep had revived him. He found a jacket and trousers that almost fitted him, and a turtleneck sweater that was comfortably well worn. There was enough light now to move around the house. In the big Westinghouse refrigerator he found cheese and eggs, and he made himself a snack. The radio had that bright and breezy music that is supposed to get people off to work at unearthly hours. He turned the dial to get something quieter, and the sound of his name made him stop.

". . . the wanted man is Andrei Levin, in his early fifties, six foot, weighing about 190 pounds. Since the Soviet ambassador's new revelations that Levin is an armed and unbalanced killer, intent on assassination of the President, the security network around Washington has been tightened. So far the assistance offered by the Soviet Embassy has been declined, but FBI officials have been briefed by Soviet diplomats. State police forces have been given details of the wanted man, and photographs have been supplied to TV stations and the press. Members of the public are warned not to attempt action against the wanted man. They should report their suspicions to the nearest police headquarters. Now to more cheerful news. In San Diego yesterday sixteen-year-old Molly Fane defeated reigning champion . . ."

Levin switched off the radio and sat back at the small table with his coffee. The energy had drained away so

170

quickly, his vague plans so patently naïve. He might have guessed that Moscow would have put out a cover story to discredit him. Even in the buildup to a war there were enough people to see that every crumb was used. In Russia you would never be able to get through to the Kremlin, and if you did get through and mentioned the Prime Minister or security they would be tracing the call in seconds. Here you could phone through to the White House, ask for the President, be politely turned away, and if you talked about security you were bounced from the FBI to Defense. No suspicion, not even in a time of crisis.

Levin turned to the yellow pages, noted a number and dialed.

Mohawk Airlines confirmed that there were seats on its early plane to La Guardia with stopoffs at Binghamton and Scranton. He booked a seat in the name of Railton, and phoned the cab company with the biggest advertisement. While he waited for the taxi he wrote out a note and put it in the center of the desk:

DEAR COLLEAGUE,

I apologize for the damage I have caused. I have stolen the following items:

1. 408 U.S. dollars
2. 1 razor (Wilkinson)
3. Driving License (out of date)
4. Passport holder
5. Some food
6. Clothes

I will repay all the above as soon as possible and give explanation.

With sincerity,
LEVIN (ANDREI)

Levin stood in the living room. The cab company's operator had said the driver would be there in ten minutes. He looked around at the signs of Railton's family. The room had a homely air, an almost deliberate indifference to impressing outsiders. But everywhere there was life. There was music still on the upright piano as if somebody had been playing moments before the family left for the journey. He picked up the music. It was Beethoven's "Für Elise" and the pages were held together with sticky tape. On top of the piano was a sheet of blue note paper with a scribbled list:

Don's red shirt (buttons)
Pop's watch at repair shop
Check fare reductions for Lyn
? Kodak film? OK for England?
Gardener's money (6 weeks)
Sophie new shoes (sandals)
Flight insurance
Plastic bags (dress size)
Soap?

He put the paper back on the piano and tried not to think of the girl. They could have lived like this, secure and calm. And he still found it incredible that ordinary citizens could leave the country just because they wanted to. No permissions, no papers, no hostages to ensure their return. He looked out the window and remembered the taxi.

He stood halfway down the drive. The radio weatherman had been right, there was a heat mist, but it was already lifting. Then the taxi was there, and as he sat back in the seat the nightmare reality of what he was doing made him shiver.

Despite all that he knew, and all that he had read, he still found it inconceivable that he merely paid a girl forty-seven dollars and walked out to the waiting plane. No identity checks, no permits, no questions. The other passengers were mainly men; jackets hung on the hooks by the windows, no ties; laughing as they joked with a big-built man who was reading something from a newspaper. One or two of them glanced in his direction and after a brief inspection gave him a friendly nod.

The curtain of the pilot's cabin was pulled aside and the pilot leaned against the door opening drinking coffee from a plastic cup. Then the warning red lights came up and Levin fastened his seat belt. Another passenger settled in the seat behind him. The plane's door closed and the engines started up. At the far side of the apron a dozen or more small aircraft shone in the morning sun. Stranger he was, in every way, but he was aware of a friendliness and energy that only emphasized the grim, gray purposefulness of Moscow. These people must be aware that they were on the brink of war, but the faces were cheerful and their lives went on normally. Maybe they didn't deserve what they had, but they didn't deserve nuclear destruction either. He was suddenly conscious again of the urgency of his task. Self-preservation had occupied his mind too much. The vague dream of the last two days had crowded out the purpose of his escape.

The hostess had handed him a newspaper, and he put it on the seat beside him. Looking out the plane's window, he saw the fueling pump being hauled away. The plane turned through a 180-degree arc, and Levin could see a handful of people standing watching at the airport building. There was an elderly woman alongside a pretty girl. A woman holding a child in her arms and near her a group of four men. *One of the men was Panov.* He was looking at the plane through a pair of binoculars.

Levin's hand trembled as he picked up the newspaper and unfolded it. It was that day's copy of the *New York Times*. The main story was the situation in Berlin, but alongside the main headlines was a photograph. He remembered when it had been taken—on a trip last summer with his students. His face, squinting into the sun, had a coarse vitality, more like the face of a criminal than a university professor's. It had been blown up from the original photograph and the fringe on the river boat's canvas awning was just visible. Alongside the picture was an interview with Ambassador Saratov, who had never met him, stating that this member of his staff had, unfortunately, a history of mental breakdowns. He had been angered by the American attitude to Berlin and had left his quarters. Several colleagues had overheard him making threats against the President's life. His Excellency understood that his medical advisers had diagnosed Andrei Levin as a psychopathic personality. An FBI spokesman said that with this latest information the Bureau was treating the matter as serious; all possible steps were being taken to apprehend the diplomat. The senior Senator from Texas had commented that the American people had seen enough of political murders in the last decade to last them a lifetime. Every government agency should be brought into action immediately.

There was a brief paragraph on page seven about an unexplained fire on a farm in Cayuga County. The county fire chief said it had all the signs of arson. A large and valuable outbuilding had been gutted. The building had not been insured; it had been rented out and was being used at the time by a French film company.

Levin folded the newspaper to cover his photograph and slid it under his seat.

Panov waited impatiently as the embassy operator connected him with Ambassador Saratov. But the voice that came on was a strange one.

"Where are you calling from?"

"Just put me direct to His Excellency."

"Give me your number. Don't talk."

Panov looked down at the dial and read out the number.

"Wait there." And then there was the dial tone as the phone was cut off. The embassy line must be tapped and they'd go to an outside telephone booth.

He went through the motions of dialing other numbers as he occupied the box. Then five minutes later it rang.

"Panov?" The voice was cold and formal.

"Yes."

"Where are you?"

"At Ithaca, at the airfield."

"Why did you want Saratov?"

"I think I've traced Levin."

"Go on."

"I think he was on a local flight to New York."

"Why do you think that?"

"I'm almost sure I saw him. I checked the passenger list and I think he was traveling under the name Railton. Professor Railton."

"What did you want from Saratov?"

"I want him to notify our people at the UN or the Consulate General so they can pick him up at La Guardia."

"You must be crazy, Panov."

174

"We'll lose him if we don't. Once he's in New York he's gone for good."

"The Feds and the CIA have been marking our people in New York for six weeks. They couldn't move without a tail. Anyway Saratov is taking control of the shambles now."

"Moscow's instructions are—"

"Forget it, Panov. You're under Saratov's orders now. You just get yourself down here to Washington. Phone Saratov when you arrive, but don't come near the embassy."

"What about Slanski?"

"He's been in touch. We sent him to New York yesterday evening. Levin might accept him as friendly if we can make contact."

"Why not—"

"Just carry out your orders, Panov, you're not Moscow's favorite son right now."

Panov replaced the telephone and stood for a moment with his sweating forehead against the cool glass side of the phone booth. Then he turned and pushed his way out and walked across to the ticket counter.

chapter
18

When the red lights went off Levin unfastened his seatbelt. There was nobody sitting in the aisle seat, and he stood up, ducking his head under the shelf and shuffling alongside into the aisle. He stood up and looked quickly along the seats on his side of the plane. He could see the tops of eight heads, six forward of his seat and two to the rear. He walked slowly up toward the flight deck and took a *New Yorker* from the rack of magazines. As he walked back he looked at all the faces. There were in fact eight men and a woman forward of his seat. He stood aside for the hostess and walked back toward the galley and the toilet. Behind his seat there were four men and three women. He had never seen any of them before and none of them had looked at him with particular interest, with the possible exception of two of the women. One, a teenaged girl, had looked at him and openly smiled. The other was a woman of about thirty, sitting at the rear of the plane. Her eyebrows had raised slightly as he looked at her, and there was a faintly amused smile before he looked away. He sat back in the aisle seat of his row.

Levin was hungry again by the time he was walking across the tarmac at La Guardia, and as he followed the rest of the passengers into the terminal he saw the sign pointing to a coffee shop. As he looked around he wondered what Panov and the others would do about him. They wouldn't inform the police, because if he were arrested the police would be certain to interrogate him. Going to the police himself might be the simplest solution, but they would interrogate him for days and if they kept him too long from contacting President Langham the situation in Berlin would have passed the point of no return.

It was just then that he heard the announcement on the loudspeaker system. "Will Professor Railton please go to Mohawk reception immediately. . . . Will Professor Railton please go to Mohawk reception immediately." It could only be Panov. He must have checked the passenger list and given the booking clerk a description. And there would be half a dozen KGB thugs from the UN delegation waiting for him to go to the Mohawk desk.

He hesitated for a moment and then walked over to the line of telephone booths. He checked the Mohawk telephone number at La Guardia and, holding the page open with one hand, slid in the coin and dialed.

They answered immediately. "Mohawk Air Service, can I help you?"

"I should like to speak to your reception desk."

"One moment."

There were the usual clicks and then a man's voice.

"Mohawk reception, can I help you?"

"You announced that I should report to you. My name's Railton, Professor Railton."

"Was it a message or a booking matter?"

"I've no idea."

"Just a moment. I'll check."

A few seconds later the voice was back. "Yes, that's OK, Professor, I've got it. There's a note here been handed in for you."

"Can you read it to me?"

" 'Fraid not. It's in a sealed envelope."

"Will you please open it and read it to me."

"Isn't it possible for you to pick it up?"

"Not for some time and it may be urgent."

"OK. Hang on a moment."

There was the noise of tearing paper and then silence.

When the man spoke again his voice was guarded. "Are you there?"

"Yes."

"I'm afraid I can't read it to you."

"Why not?"

"It's typed, but in a foreign language, it's either Greek or Russian, it's not our alphabet."

"I see. Maybe you can help me. Could one of your staff bring it to me in the coffee shop? I'll look out for them and I'd be glad to pay for the service."

"That's not necessary. I'll send one of the girls over right away."

"Thank you very much."

"You're welcome."

He stopped the girl short of the coffee shop. She was carrying the envelope and politely refused the dollar bill.

He slid the envelope into his jacket pocket and followed the sign to the toilets.

The note was very brief: "OPERATION 471. THE GIRL IS ALIVE. TELEPHONE IN ONE HOUR OR SHE WILL BE SUPERFLUOUS. 687 1301 PANOV."

Levin walked back to the line of booths and entered one that gave him a wide view of the transit area. He lifted the receiver and there was the dial tone. He lay down a small heap of nickels, and, pressing one into the slot, he dialed, and then turned to check if anyone appeared to be watching him.

"Walters Photographic."

"I want to speak to Panov."

"There's nobody with—just a minute."

There was a pause, and a different voice came on the line. "Who is that speaking?"

Levin hesitated and then said in Russian, "Operation 471."

He could hear someone breathing heavily at the other end and then the voice said in Russian, "Where are you?"

"Just let me speak to Panov."

"Panov isn't here."

"I had a message."

"I know, I know."

Levin wondered if they were trying to trace where he was phoning from, but dismissed the thought. They wouldn't have the facilities in a foreign country to do that. Then the voice spoke again.

"You want to cooperate?"

"Maybe. I want to know about the girl."

There were whispering voices at the other end, and then, "Will you speak to Slanski?"

"Yes."

He waited impatiently, still watching the people walking past the telephone booths. A girl looked at him and half-smiled, but she was quickly lost in the crowd. Then he heard Slanski's voice with that unmistakable and irritating Moscow Polytechnic lisp.

"Is that you, Andrei?"

"Yes."

"Well, I must say you've created quite a stir, but I'm sure it can all be smoothed over."

"The girl, Slanski. I'm phoning about the girl."

"It seems she *is* alive. It was decided to hold her until the operation was over."

"Go on."

"They'll trade her, Andrei."

"For what?"

"For you."

"What do they want me to do?"

"You're in New York?"

"Yes."

"Just come to the address I give you and we'll take you back to Moscow and the girl. You would be promoted to head of faculty at Moscow. No recriminations."

"You must think I really am crazy, Slanski."

"Why?"

"They'd have me in the Lubyanka inside an hour and in my grave the next day, after they'd gone over me to find out if you or Panov were involved in my escape."

"I assure you that—"

"How do I know that the girl is alive, comrade?"

"When you come here you could speak to her on the phone."

"Where would she be?"

"Moscow."

"Oh, sure, one of those fancy tapes that the KGB edit together. Forget it."

"How else can we prove to you that she is alive?"

"That's up to you. I'll give you an hour and I'll phone again."

"Andrei, listen, we have—"

He hung up and pushed his way out of the booth and walked to the coffee shop. It was almost empty, and he ordered coffee and a hamburger. As he sat waiting he realized that he wasn't sure what a hamburger was, but he knew it had meat in it. When it came he ate it slowly with the relish of hunger. As he sat there he realized that you could know all about a country's gross domestic product, all the statistics, how it was governed and its history, and you may have heard of hamburgers but you didn't know what they tasted like. As Langham's doppelgänger he knew all about New York that concerned its political significance to the U.S. President, but he knew very little else. Where would he stay? Where could he find a base. He tried to assemble what he knew. There were four boroughs, or was it five. Manhattan, Queens, Bronx, Brooklyn or was it Bowery? He searched his mind and came up with more names, Central Park, Broadway, Times Square, and a street called Mott Street. He had no idea where any of them was, and he had heard of them only from novels or songs. To him, New York was skyscrapers at night, the *Broadway Melody* of 1935, and the brownstones of Louis Auchincloss. There would be Russians at the UN and the trade missions who knew New York better than they knew Moscow. But all he know was a vague collage of novels and music, a few street names and mental pictures of avenues and tall buildings. He had thirty hours, maybe a little less, to contact the White House and convince the President of the real situation. He looked at his watch. There were forty minutes before he would phone Slanski.

He took a cab from the rank and turned to look out the rear window to see if he was being followed. There were three cabs and two cars following, but nobody looked particularly interested. He had told the driver Manhattan; the driver half turned his head.

"Where d'ya want in Manhattan, Mac?"

"What? Oh, anywhere."

"Jesus, it's a big area. Do you want uptown or downtown —maybe Grand Central?"

"Grand Central, then."

He sat back in the seat and looked out the window. It was just as he had imagined. Different from Los Angeles, but just like the photographs he had seen, and the films.

At Grand Central he carefully counted out the exact fare and as he was unused to the principle of tipping he wondered why the driver swore at him so volubly as he turned away.

Levin walked into the station and found the phone booths. He had to wait two or three minutes before one was vacant. He slid in the coin and dialed the number. He glanced at his watch. It was ten minutes over the hour.

"Walters Photographic."

"Slanski?"

"Hang on a moment."

There was a few moments' wait and Levin could hear music in the background, then Slanski's voice.

"Andrei?"

"Yes."

"Andrei, I have a recording for you to hear. We asked the girl to make a recording that you would recognize as coming from her. It's not good, I'm afraid, but we had to record by telephone from Moscow. Shall I play it for you?"

"Yes."

The line suddenly seemed very clear and there was an indefinable noise as when a child puts a seashell to its ear to hear the sea. Then came the girl's voice.

"They asked me to say something, Andrei, that you would recognize as being from me. So I say it to you now.

"Give me your tired, your poor,
Your huddled masses yearning to breathe free,
The wretched refuse of your teeming shore.

181

Send these, the homeless, tempest-tossed to me:
I lift my lamp beside the golden door.

"They say, too, that I should prove that the recording is made today. So I read from yesterday's *New York Times*, page three, column one. 'Scientists at UCLA claim that they have identified a vaccine against gonorrhea and that small quantities have been produced under laboratory conditions.' And the horse that won the first race at Belmont yesterday was Palomino Blonde. I am in good health and I send you my love."

Levin heard the click of the machine being switched off. And then Slanski came on the line.

"Are you satisfied, Andrei?"

"Maybe. What do you want?"

"They want you to go back to Moscow. The girl will be there. We can straighten it all out."

"What if I don't agree?"

There was a long pause and he heard Slanski's deep sigh. "You know that as well as I do, Andrei."

"They'll kill the girl and try to kill me."

There was no answer from Slanski.

"I'll think about it, Slanski."

"They won't give you long, my friend."

"I'll phone you tonight, late, about midnight."

And he hung up the telephone. They wouldn't be ready to make a deal if they didn't want him desperately. He'd have to figure out right away what to do.

He had walked up Park Avenue for several blocks. The marquee of the building ahead said "Waldorf-Astoria." He walked in through the main entrance and up the steps to the lobby. The phones were by the elevators.

He dialed the Washington information operator and got the Soviet Embassy number, and laid out a pile of coins on the shelf. He checked his watch. It was only eleven o'clock. He dialed again for the operator and gave her the embassy number and his name, asking to be connected person to person with Ambassador Saratov. It was almost four minutes before the operator said, "Go ahead, sir, your party's on the line."

He had given his real name and he spoke now in Russian. "His Excellency Saratov."

"Saratov speaking." The voice was tense and cold and he could imagine Saratov at his desk with his KGB people alongside him listening on extensions.

"This is Andrei Levin. I have spoken to Slanski at the New York number 687-1301. I have a message for him."

He waited for a response, but there was none.

"I want you to tell him that if I am not able to speak to the girl on the telephone tonight I shall telephone the newspapers and tell them about Operation 471."

"Where are you, Comrade Professor?"

"In New York."

"Can we help you?"

Levin hung up without replying.

Joe Shapiro was debriefing Murphy when the phone rang. He listened carefully for several minutes, his chair creaking as he leaned back, his eyes focused on the silver-framed photograph on his desk.

"OK. Send it over. No, there's a deck here we can use."

He put the receiver back slowly and carefully and looked across at Murphy. "Go on."

"Faller's people got Velichko out over the Finnish border. They took him to Helsinki and interrogated him there. He's in London now, but we figured I'd better come over with the stuff about Kiev."

Shapiro nodded. "How long will it take?"

"Two minutes, maybe three. Slanski, the KGB man, was in charge of the operation, and the Irish girl Kevan was there too. We had already gotten a fat file on the installation and the people, but we didn't know what they were doing."

Murphy paused for encouragement but got none. Shapiro treated the pause as an attempt to dramatize the story. He sucked his teeth ostentatiously and waited.

"They were running a simulated White House. They'd gotten a guy they had briefed and trained to duplicate Langham. He was supposed to tell them what the President's reactions would be to various situations. We're still getting the details from Velichko, but according to him this guy was always right on target."

"What was Velichko doing down there? We've got him down as one of the rough boys."

"He was joint secretary of the Presidium. They used him as a ferret. He was sent down to Kiev to check that nobody was playing games. Wanted to screw the Irish girl and Slanski put the heat on him in Moscow for rocking the boat."

"Where's Slanski now?"

"Nobody knows. They folded the Kiev operation, but we didn't get that from Velichko. He didn't know that."

"And where's Levin?"

"He was part—. Say, how'd you know about Levin?"

"Where d'you think he is?"

"No information at the moment."

Shapiro's pale-blue eyes looked at Murphy as if he were putting him to some test. "Levin's here in New York. So is Slanski. Levin just phoned their embassy in Washington. Spoke to the ambassador himself. Mentioned Slanski's name."

Murphy looked incredulous, his lighter suspended halfway to his cigarette. "In New York? How the hell did he get over here?"

"Christ knows. It doesn't matter, anyway. What *does* matter is that he's here."

"How was he uncovered?"

"He did a bolt from wherever he was and their embassy put out a statement that he intended to assassinate the President."

"For God's sake, I've read everything we've got on file about him. He's not an action man, he's a professor of psychology. Where is he?"

"We have no idea. He's on the run. The KGB illegals will be after him. So's the FBI, the State Police and every precinct in the city."

"And Slanski?"

"He's in New York, too. We've got a telephone number."

"How was he spotted?"

"He wasn't. We've got a special tap on all the embassy

lines. Levin phoned the ambassador and gave him a message for Slanski at the New York number. Hagger's put a team on the place now. It's a photo studio in the Village."

"Why did the ambassador take the call? He must have known he'd be bugged."

"No choice, I guess. They want him before we get him. They've got to take risks."

There was a knock on the door and a messenger put a receipt pad and a small package on Shapiro's desk. He signed the pad and handed it back before he walked over to a tape desk in the corner of the room. He shook the small spool from the cardboard pack and laced it across the heads and onto the takeup spool. He pressed the button marked "PLAY" and turned up the volume. They stood listening as the tape wound slowly on the machine, and heard Levin's conversation with Ambassador Saratov, followed by an English translation. When it was finished Shapiro pressed the stop button and said, "I want you to find Levin, Murphy. You've got hours, not days. That man could tell us what we want to know."

"We have no idea how he got here, or where he's been?"

"No idea at all. There was no record of Levin, Slanski or Panov entering the United States, and they were not on the declared staff of the Soviet Embassy. They probably came over the Canadian border."

"What help can I have?"

"You name it. You've got it."

"Can I have a plane to New York?"

"There's a McDonnell Voodoo on the field, get over there now. You can land at La Guardia and I'll fix a chopper to take you from there. We'll fix for you to land in Central Park, and a car can take you to the place on Madison Avenue. Use those facilities and let me know what else you want."

Murphy was in the apartment seventy minutes later, and one of Haggar's men gave him a report on the stakeout at the photo studio.

"Who owns the premises?"

The young man consulted his notes. "An outfit called Gramercy Real Estate."

Murphy stood looking out the window, his mind vaguely aware of the shadows between the buildings and the traffic on the avenue. He turned back to the young man. "Anything in our files about 'em?"

"Suspected KGB dead-letter drop. Nothing more."

"Anything from IRS?"

"No. All taxes paid. No charges. No complaints."

"What do they do? What kinda studio?"

"Local stuff. Portraits, weddings, kids—that sort of trade."

"Porn?"

" 'Fraid not. No indications, anyway."

"How many people there?"

"The owner, Franz Dicker, a German from Stettin, naturalized in 1950. A girl who does the darkroom work. Polish and quite a looker, about twenty-five. And we've seen both of them several times in the last hour. But we haven't seen this guy Slanski."

"Have you got pictures of him?"

"Yes."

There was a knock on the door and a big man came in. Early thirties and ugly in an attractive sort of way. A long scar down one cheek, and a folded left ear. He introduced himself. "Haggar. You heard all you want from him?"

Murphy nodded and pointed to the table where a large-scale map of New York was spread out.

"Let's sit down for a few minutes."

When they were settled Murphy looked at them both. "Let's assume that Levin has been holed up at the embassy in Washington. I'm not sure that he was, because the surveillance team covering the embassy swear that they've got everybody accounted for. But for a start we'll try that. Why does he make for New York?"

Haggar leaned forward. "Wants to get away from where the rough boys are. If he stays in Washington they might just get enough guys out on the streets to nail him. Any indication that he knows New York?"

"No. L.A. yes, but positively *not* New York. So how does he come here—bus, train, air or car?"

"Has he got any identity papers?"

"No idea."

The young CIA man said, "I'd say *not* train, because his pals would cover the station automatically. And not car, because he won't be used to driving over here. Bus is possible, but on the slow side. I'd go for plane myself."

Murphy looked at Haggar, who pursed his lips and said, "We can get the Port Authority police checking on internal and external passenger lists. It will take some time, but we've got no other lead."

When Murphy nodded, Haggar told the youngster to get on the phone in the next room. He turned back to look at Murphy. "You want me to go in and lift Slanski?"

"The embassy will have tipped him off by telephone. And they'll have put the usual pressures on to try and stop him from talking."

"So?"

Murphy took a slow, deep breath and then nodded. "Yes. And get a forensic team to go over the whole place. Have you got the back covered?"

"Sure. But there's only one way out. I'll get moving. Where d'you want him?"

"Here."

Saratov had phoned Moscow and they had left him in no doubt about what they wanted. They wanted Levin dead, no efforts would be spared, and diplomatic niceties could be ignored. Anyone and anything could be sacrificed to get Levin before the Americans got to him.

chapter
19

Walter H. Harcourt II had telephoned Fowler, and ten minutes later they had met in a bar on Fifteenth Street. They
had waited for the drinks to be served at their alcove table
before they got down to business. It was Walter H. who
opened play.

"You picked up any scuttlebutt on the diplomat who disappeared?"

Fowler looked over the top of his glass. "You in a hurry,
Harcourt?"

"Yep."

"Ambassador Saratov phoned me just before you did.
Asked the same question."

"What did you tell him?"

"The truth. I ain't heard a damn thing." Fowler slowly
lowered his glass and put it on the table. "What's the panic?"

"What makes you think there is a panic?"

Fowler half smiled. "His Excellency's voice was about an
octave higher than usual and you're shifting about like
you've got hemorrhoids."

"What else did Saratov say?"

Fowler's washed-out blue eyes looked at Harcourt won-
deringly. He finished his drink and pushed the glass to one
side as he leaned forward. "In 1950 that bastard McCarthy
put out the word so that I was fired from the paper, and no

other piece of the media would touch me with a ten-foot pole. A few Good Samaritans let me do pieces under another name, but in the end I had to go to Europe or I'd have starved, Jenny and the girls along with me. Nobody in the White House lifted a finger to help me. Right?"

Harcourt was silent, sitting back against the wall as he looked at Fowler's face.

"Your old man was one of the Good Samaritans, so I owe you something for his sake, but I don't owe the White House a thing. Agreed?"

"Not agreed, Bob, but I understand. But you've had a square deal from Langham."

"I have from Saratov too."

Harcourt looked like a rich man's son. He was. But that hadn't got him his job with Langham. He was a shrewd assessor of situations and people. Right now he sensed that Fowler's resentment was real but fragile. He put both hands on the table as if he were about to leave and, leaning forward, he said. "I shouldn't have asked you for your help, Bob. It was too much to expect." And he nodded across the room to the waiter and made signs that he wanted to pay.

"You didn't ask for my help, you asked for information."

He only half turned toward Fowler. "Would it have made any difference?"

Fowler lit a cigarette and shook out the match, and then looked up at Harcourt. "They're at panic stations. He sounded shit-scared about this Levin guy. They've virtually made an open offer of a hundred grand for his location."

"Who to?"

Fowler gave a short angry laugh. "To one and all. They asked me to put the word around. They'll be doing it, too, of course."

"Have you got any ideas?"

"Yep. You've got a top-security CIA team watching a photo studio in New York. Maybe he's there."

"How did you find *that* out?"

"Saratov told me. That's about all I know."

Harcourt moved the ashtray around on the table top as he thought, and then his head jerked up. "Would you feed stuff back for us?"

189

"And in return you give me good stories I can print?"

"OK."

"What's the feed material?"

"Tell him we're aware of the operation at Kiev."

"What operation is that?"

"I can't tell you yet, but I'll give you a four-hour lead when it breaks."

The single window had a display of portraits in color and black and white, and there was a hand-drawn price list in a picture frame. A card on a string hung inside the glass of the door, and it said "OPEN." But the door was locked. The lock was low down, a few feet from the ground, and Haggar pressed his foot gently against the bottom panel. The door showed a gap at the side where it met the frame, and Haggar pressed harder. For a moment the door held, then the lock sprang and the door shuddered open. There was a door on the left and Haggar tried it with his left hand; his right hand was holding a snubnosed RM109. There was nobody in the room, but it had a door marked "DARKROOM."

There was a red bulb glowing over a sink where a large print was floating in water from a slow-flowing tap. It was of a young couple, the girl gently holding their baby in its white woolly shawl.

Haggar walked back to the short hall and held his gun pointing upward as he slowly mounted the stairs. He could hear music playing as he neared the top, and when one of the treads creaked it was switched off. The door at the head of the stairs opened.

The man was in shirtsleeves and denims, and Haggar sensed that he wasn't surprised at his visitor or the gun. He had a foxy face, long pointed nose and unmoving suspicious eyes. He said nothing as he stood waiting, with his hand still on the doorknob.

As Haggar pushed past him into the room he saw a small suitcase with the lid open. It was packed, ready for departure. He turned back to look at the man.

"Are you Franz Dicker?"

"Yes."

"Where's Slanski?"

"Who's he?"

Haggar looked at him for a moment or two. Then he pressed the microphone button and lifted it from the inside of his jacket. He spoke slowly. "Bring the search team in and bring the car to the front door."

He detailed two men to escort Dicker to the apartment on Madison Avenue and stayed behind to watch the search team start its work.

The eight-man team photographed the rooms and then went through them one by one. There was no trace of Slanski. The girl came back from lunch, and she too was taken back to Murphy. Chalk marks had been scrawled on walls that had given a negative reading to the electronic stethoscope, and the engineer on the team had set up the big industrial drill with its three-foot masonry auger. They had struck oil in the second room, the darkroom. The auger had plunged through up to the chuck, and they stood looking at the wall. The big Besseler enlarger was shoved on one side and the electrical controls were dismantled. They placed the stethoscope and a thermocouple in the center of the area between the wall struts.

The engineer turned to look at Haggar and spoke in a whisper. "He's in there all right. There's a temperature differential over ten degrees."

Haggar shrugged. "OK. Get him out."

When the panel came off Slanski was white with fear as he crouched in the corner of the cupboardlike space.

"Get down, Slanski. That's right. Put your foot there. Right. Now jump."

Slanski staggered clumsily as he jumped the three feet from the enlarging bench to the floor. Haggar caught his arm to save him from falling. They walked slowly down the stairs and out into the summer sunshine. Slanski was trembling as he sat beside Haggar in the back seat of the car and his eyes were closed as his head rested against the window.

The Port Authority police had also made a lucky strike. At the fifth airline there had been nothing on the passenger lists, but they had shown Levin's photograph to all the counter staff. One of the ground-staff girls had recognized him. She told the two policemen about delivering the note and said it had been handed to her by the assistant manager. They had fetched him from the restroom and he had told them about the Russian or Greek typing. They phoned Murphy direct and he told them to cover the taxi drivers and the car-rental firms. He sent two men from the CIA's Long Island office to assist them.

Murphy had got nothing from Dicker or the girl. Dicker was getting a hundred dollars a month as a dead-letter drop. He was usually phoned, before the packet came in, with a code word that was good for only ten days. The current one was "Raindrop," but he was just a stooge. The girl knew nothing of any of this. Her father was a patrolman in one of the downtown precincts.

He could see across the park to the tops of the zoo buildings. The trees were quite still and there was no motor traffic. He realized that it was Saturday. Boys would be hiring boats at the Loeb Boathouse, and girls would be leaning back against the stiff cushions wondering how the day would end. The phone rang and he turned away to walk to the table.

They had traced the cab driver and he had recognized Levin immediately. He had put him down at Grand Central Station, Forty-second Street. The man didn't know his way around New York and he was carrying no luggage. That was all he could tell them.

Then Haggar came in with Slanski. Murphy waved the Russian to a chair.

"What's your name?"

Slanski shrugged and shook his head. Murphy nodded to Haggar, who left the room. Murphy sat down at the table opposite Slanski.

"OK, Slanski, where are your identity documents?"

"At the embassy."

"You know it is illegal to be in New York without identification and a special pass."

"Please speak to the embassy."

Murphy looked grim and reached for the phone. The embassy wouldn't get Slanski off the hook. They'd throw him to the crocodiles. But it would help if Slanski could hear them do it. He dialed three figures and asked the CIA operator to connect him with the Soviet ambassador. He looked at Slanski while he waited. Then Saratov was on the line, his voice constricted and tense.

"Saratov. Who is that?"

"New York Police Department, sir. We have a man under arrest, Ambassador. He claims to be a Soviet diplomat at your embassy. He has no out-of-town permit and no identification. And he was found on suspect premises. He asks that you confirm his status. I've checked with Immigration and he's not on your list."

There was a long silence. Then Saratov said, "What name does he give?"

"Slanski. Ivan Slanski."

Another long pause. "I can't help you, I'm afraid. He is not on my staff."

"Not on your staff?" Murphy looked across at Slanski as he repeated the words.

"Correct."

"Thank you, sir." And Murphy hung up. He leaned back, smiling at Slanski.

"They've thrown you to the wolves, Slanski. You'd better talk."

Slanski's voice quavered as he spoke. "What do you want to talk about?"

"Where's Levin?"

"I don't know. He said he would phone about the girl."

"When is he phoning and where?"

"He just said later, maybe midnight. He was to phone me at the photo shop."

Murphy stood up with the telephone in his hand and told them to bring the car around.

They were back at the empty shop half an hour later. Haggar's men had taken only two calls. Both were from customers wanting to make appointments. Murphy phoned Shapiro, who agreed to provide extra men.

Murphy sat at the battered table with Slanski. "Tell me why Levin is phoning."

"What's going to happen to me?"

"Depends on how you cooperate."

"And if I do cooperate?"

"We won't send you back, Slanski, provided you play ball. Now what about Levin's phone call?"

"It's to make a deal with Moscow about the girl."

"The Kevan girl?"

Slanski looked as if he had received a physical blow. "You know about her?"

"Sure. Velichko told us." Murphy watched Slanski's face as it seemed to fall apart.

"But Velichko is in one of the camps."

"We got him out, Slanski. He's in London right now."

Murphy could see that Slanski was near the end of his tether. He walked through to the head of the stairs and told one of Haggar's men to phone for a CIA-approved doctor. He went back in to Slanski, who was sitting with his head down on his folded arms on the table. Murphy reached over and shook him.

"I'm in a hurry, Slanski. Tell me about the Moscow deal."

Slanski lifted his head, his eyes bloodshot and the pulse at his neck visibly pumping. "Moscow wants Levin, *he* wants to save the girl. They tried to trick him, but he was too smart."

"Why do they want him?"

"They're afraid that he will contact the President."

"Why should he do that?"

"Because of the situation in Berlin. Levin knows too much."

Slanski's eyes closed and Murphy shook him roughly.

"What does he know, Slanski?"

"He knows what Langham will do."

"I guess Langham knows that, too. So why the sweat?"

"He knows that Langham is going to be wrong."

"What way wrong?"

Slanski slowly shook his head. "I don't know. I really don't know. Only Levin knows, and if Langham is wrong it will be a war. All the time . . ." And Slanski voided a pool of yellow frothy bile across the table as he fainted.

Murphy raced for the door and clattered down the stairs. Haggar was coming in from the street.

"Have we got a secure telephone, Haggar?"

"Sure. It's in the front office."

Two minutes later Murphy was talking to Shapiro, outlining his plan. Shapiro had big doubts but would check with the Director, who would probably check with the President personally.

At 3 p.m. Washington time Saratov had received an angry call from Moscow. The American ambassador in Moscow had handed over United States diplomatic routine to the British ambassador and had left only clerks and a platoon of U.S. Marines at the embassy building. The ambassador and all his senior staff and families were boarding two French Concordes at the airport. Surely Saratov must have been warned of this. Gromyko sounded angrier than the situation demanded. There were no diplomatic courtesies.

"We'll find out, Saratov. Call on the Secretary of State. Demand an explanation."

"Immediately, Comrade Minister."

The ambassador was in no great hurry to contact the State Department. He wanted to do a few sums before he decided on his tactics. The Americans' move in Moscow looked as though they were pulling their people out because they were expecting an actual war. Or maybe they were planning a preemptive strike themselves. No wonder Moscow was on the boil. It was the first move the Americans had made that wasn't just reacting to Soviet pressures. He dialed Fowler's number and leaned back waiting, with the receiver cradled against his jaw as he lit a cigarette.

They stood in a silent group. Shapiro, Harcourt and Deputy Director of Central Intelligence, James Condon. Their escort, a U.S. Marines captain, stood a few feet away. They had seen a grim-faced Secretary of Defense leave the Oval Office, and several politicians, whose faces they recognized, were waiting in another group.

Then the door to the President's office opened and a secretary walked over to them. "The President will see you now, gentlemen. An absolute time limit of seven minutes."

Langham was speaking on the telephone as they came in and he nodded to Condon and waved them to a table that had been moved in from the annex. When he had finished speaking he put down the phone and walked around to the head of the table and sat down. He slid off his wristwatch and placed it on the table in front of him and leaned forward.

"Well, gentlemen, we've got six minutes. Tell me what you want as briefly as possible."

Condon nodded at Shapiro, who sat with both hands palms down on the table as if physical equilibrium could help his reporting. Shapiro looked at Langham as he started speaking.

"The Russian diplomat, Levin, whom you already know about, has been traced to New York. The Russians are offering a hundred thousand dollars for either his death or his whereabouts. They know he is in New York, but not where he is. They've put pressure on him about a girl and he is due to phone them about midnight tonight about a deal.

"Levin was the leading figure in a KGB operation. He was chosen because his background and characteristics resemble yours, and for about eight months he has been acting as a reference point on what your reactions will be in given situations. We have solid information that he has been highly successful. We think he was not at their embassy and we think he is a possible defector. We have interrogated the KGB man who was in charge of the operation and there is no doubt that this man could be very valuable to us."

Shapiro paused and Langham waited for him to continue. When Shapiro stayed silent Langham spoke.

"What's the problem, Mr. Shapiro?"

"He's loose in New York. We don't know where he is. The Russians are hunting him and we want to get him first—alive. We have discussed a possible solution with Mr. Harcourt, who says that it has implications that make it essential to get your personal approval."

Langham turned to Harcourt. "What is it?"

"We want to use New York TV and radio stations and public announcements to make contact with him."

"So go ahead."

"The stations wouldn't give us time without your say-so."

Langham looked at his watch. "OK. Tell them it is a personal request from me and that it is a matter of national security." He looked at Condon. "Maybe he could be interviewed later to show that they've been planning this business for months."

Shapiro had his bird-dog look and Langham nodded.

"I think we need to keep him under wraps, Mr. President, until we've got more information."

"Fine. Anything else?"

And Langham stood up, looked at them for a few seconds and then pressed the bell on the table and walked back to his desk.

The secretary showed them out.

The networks had refused to grant Harcourt's request unless there was a direct Presidential approach. Langham himself, had phoned the chairmen and presidents of NBC, ABC and CBS, and there had been no problem. Murphy, Shapiro and the Director had sat in silence while the President talked to the network chiefs. Langham replaced the receiver and leaned back.

"That's fixed, gentlemen, but I think we do it in English."

He waited for comment or protest, but there was none, so he went on. "Just imagine the reactions of the public. They're looking at the ball game or a talk show and suddenly the screen goes blank and there's two lines of Russian. It would be like that darned Orson Welles radio thing that started a panic."

And at 4 p.m. exactly, after the commercials, on every TV set in use in New York City there was no sound. Just two lines of type in capitals that said, "WILL ANDREI LEVIN CONTACT WHITE HOUSE AIDE MURPHY AT 835-4106 IMMEDIATELY —COOPERATION GUARANTEED."

The Soviet office at the U.N. had phoned Saratov in Washington as soon as they saw the first announcement. Saratov had phoned Secretary of State Larsen personally.

Larsen was cool but polite. "I don't get your problem, Mr. Ambassador."

"But it is outrageous, Mr. Secretary. This man is a Soviet citizen. The matter is with us at the embassy."

"Are you sure he's a Soviet citizen?"

"Of course."

"I've got your diplomatic staff list here, for both the embassy and the United Nations. There's no Levin on either of them."

"There must be some mistake."

"Maybe. How about you sort out the mistake and let me know?"

"But, Mr. Secretary, we have cooperated in every way with the United States authorities about this man."

"That's great, Saratov. You just carry on cooperating and everything will be fine."

"May I ask what is happening to your embassy staff in Moscow, Mr. Secretary?"

"They are withdrawn, Saratov. The Soviet Prime Minister has already received a personal note from President Langham. We won't be making it public at the moment."

Levin had tried another call to the White House, but he had been referred from office to office again. He bought the *New York Times* at a newsstand and made a note of the newspaper's telephone number. He would do better, he figured, to phone and talk to Slanski first, and maybe after that he would contact a newspaper.

He had eaten at a Chock Full o' Nuts off Madison Avenue and then walked over to Fifth Avenue and into the park. There was a lake and he sat on the grassy slope trying to imagine how he could pressure the bastards in Moscow to free the girl. He wondered if a promise of his silence would be enough. He leaned back on the grass and opened the paper.

The front-page news in the *New York Times* was mainly about the situation in Berlin. World opinion went its predictable way. The Chinese denounced the Soviet actions, European governments had seen the light and there were statements from British, French and Italian politicians praising the removal of the wall. There was no official comment from Bonn or from NATO headquarters.

Levin folded the newspaper and put it on the grass beside him. He looked across the lake. There were groups of young people and families with small children and their voices came faintly across to him. There would be similar crowds in Lenin Park, strolling past the statue of the sailors and looking out to sea where the park curved out on Kronmerk Strait. He had walked there with girls himself and had stood patiently for tickets at the wide-screen Velikan cinema. He shivered involuntarily and bent his head to rest it on his knees. He would never walk girls in Lenin Park again. Today could be his last day.

In Russia he would have already been dead, and here it was just a question of time. He had heard stories of the KGB but had never absorbed the details. What would they do when they found him? But he knew that he didn't really need to wonder. The pressures on them would be enormous, and whoever killed him would sigh with relief. And the Americans. What would they do? Would they believe the assassin story put out by Saratov? The CIA reports that had gone across his desk gave him hope. They were just as suspicious and cynical as the KGB. They were killers, too, but they could possibly prefer him alive. And then as his mind ground on through the chess game he realized that there would be no reason why they should want him alive. They didn't know what he could tell them. He was just a psychopath on the run. So why risk anything by trying to contact the White House? If he could lie low for a week or two perhaps he could work out some solution. He could write a letter to the President and enclose the documents from his shoe. Perhaps. . . . And he groaned aloud. There wasn't a week left. Two days at the most. Maybe only hours. And then the mushroom clouds. The thirty-seven yellow pins on the map that had so calmly marked their impact zones. The clusters of three that took out New York, Washington, Dallas, Los Angeles, Chicago and Pittsburgh. And the single pins that picked out the nineteen prime military targets. And four hours later the ten blue targets if there was no counterstrike. If there *was* a counterstrike the 123 red pins would come out. On the cork board they had just been pretty pins that marked some impossible contingency. And he remembered the aphorism of Tertullian, "*Certum est quia impossibile est*" —it is certain because it is impossible.

He felt a terrible inertia. A need to just sit there and wait.

He remembered patients who had sat unmoving and silent, their eyes unfocused, oblivious to the world about them. The depressive psychotics.

A child's voice said, "Hello."

He looked up slowly. A small girl stood there. A four- or five-year-old, her blue eyes screwed up against the sun as she looked down at him.

"Are you tired?"

He heard his slurred voice from far away. "I think I *am*."

"I'm tired, too. We've been to the zoo."

"Did you like that?"

"Not really."

"Why not?"

"They were mostly asleep. D'you live here?"

"I'm on vacation."

The little girl turned and squinted into the distance. "I've got to go now. That's my daddy over there. The waving one." She looked back at him. "Don't go to sleep again or you might not get any supper."

She turned to look over her shoulder as she trotted off. " 'Bye." She waved.

It was just after four o'clock when Levin started to walk back through the park. He needed to find a room for the night and then maybe he would phone Slanski to see what was happening. He walked along Central Park South toward Columbus Circle and he saw a helicopter flying low, below the tops of the tall building on Central Park West, and as it approached he could hear the rasp of a loudspeaker over the clatter of its engine. It was making some sort of announcement and the people stopped and stared up as it hung overhead. He could see the pilot and co-pilot as they looked down at the streets below. It turned slowly and came even lower along the southern edge of the park. And it was then that he heard his name. ". . . Levin, who is urgently requested to contact the White House, telephone number eight-three-five-four-one-O-six. Thank you." And then the message was repeated. "This is a special message from the White House for Andrei Levin, who is . . ." He listened hard to get the number. When it came he closed his eyes and repeated it again and again.

There was a phone booth by a newsstand and he closed the door behind him to shut out the noise of the traffic. He put in a coin and dialed the number. It rang only once before it was answered.

"Murphy. White House representative. Please go ahead."

"I am answering your helicopter message. This is Levin."

Murphy tried to keep the tension from his voice. "Thanks for calling, Professor. I think I can help you to solve your problems. Can we meet?"

"I'm afraid not, Mr. Murphy. Is that all you wanted to say?"

"Professor. I know about the problem with Miss Kevan and I assure you that we can help you there. I have Slanski here with me at the place you were going to telephone. There is no longer a channel through here to Moscow. I know you must be extremely worried and suspicious, but I am authorized to give you all help possible."

"Authorized by whom?"

"By President Langham himself. I can arrange for you to meet him if you wish."

There was a long pause and Murphy closed his eyes in concentration as if he could will Levin's response.

"Mr. Murphy, I have tried several times to speak with the President by telephone. I *do* wish to speak with him. But I am an illegal alien against my will, and I suspect that you people, or the Soviet Embassy, might be glad to see me under arrest, or perhaps dead."

"What happened when you phoned the White House, Professor?"

"They passed me around like the parcel in the children's game until the music stopped. That is all."

"I'm sorry about that. Is there any way you and I can meet that would satisfy your fear of arrest?"

"I can't think of one."

"Professor, my name is Murphy. Like your girl my people are from Ireland, and I'm a Roman Catholic. Can I suggest that you meet me in St. Patrick's Cathedral? I'm not very religious, but I could not bring myself to involve my religion if I intended to deceive you. I promise you that you will not be arrested in the cathedral, and if you are not satisfied with our discussion you can walk away. I will stay there after you have gone for one hour and I will not contact anybody during that time. I can't think of anything better, I'm afraid."

Oddly enough, it was the last lame sentence that convinced Levin.

"All right, Mr. Murphy. When shall we meet and where is the cathedral?"

"You're somewhere in Manhattan, is that right?"

"I think so."

"Right. Well, ask for Fifth Avenue. St. Patrick's is the block between Fifty-first and Fiftieth. Go in the main entrance and sit in the front row of seats. I'm about six feet tall, weigh 196 pounds and I'll be wearing a lightweight suit, tan-colored, and a cream shirt. I'm forty, with black wavy hair. I've got a photograph of you, so I can recognize you. Is that OK?"

"Yes. In half an hour, then."

Levin was suddenly tired. A breeze was blowing dust along the streets. It would be like this in Leningrad in summer. He went back to Fifth Avenue, crossed over, found that he was on the corner of Fifty-ninth Street and worked out that he would need to walk south. He passed two churches; the cathedral was several blocks further. It was already on the half hour when he walked up the wide steps. The afternoon sun emphasized the twin Gothic spires and lit the big rose window over the doorway. The massive bronze doors were open, and the interior was bathed in a golden light from the setting sun that emphasized the echoing vaulted roof. An organ was playing softly as he walked slowly up the aisle.

He bowed awkwardly in ignorance, in the direction of the altar, and sat in a seat on the righthand side of the aisle. A few moments later a man walked in front of him and slid into the seat beside him. He looked quickly at the man's face. It was Murphy all right. Handsome, in a peasant sort of way. The brown eyes were smiling and friendly.

"There's a small chapel over the other side. Let's go there, it's quieter."

Without waiting for an answer Murphy stood up and walked across to the far corner of the church and Levin followed him. Murphy held aside a heavy blue curtain and Levin passed through to the small Lady Chapel. There were wooden benches with red felt covers, and Murphy patted the seat alongside him, and Levin sat down.

"Have you eaten?"

The warm casual question took Levin by surpise, and tears came to his eyes.

"Yes, I have eaten, thank you."

"I don't like talking about these things in a church, but I thought you might feel safer."

Levin looked at the tanned face. The eyes were alert and aware, and the set of the mouth spelled out determination.

"I would be prepared to go somewhere else if it would be easier."

Murphy looked at him, surprised but not off balance. "I have an apartment very near here. We can talk and eat and you can rest. It's an official CIA place. Other people will be there, but I am in charge."

Levin nodded and stood up, and Murphy led the way back down the side of the cathedral to the entrance.

Ten minutes later they stepped out of the elevator at the CIA safe house. The inner room was small but furnished with comfortable armchairs and wooden furniture.

Murphy stood, hands on hips, looking at Levin. "I'm guessing that you must be tired. How about you have a bath and a shave? We're going to be working for a long, long time."

Levin, lying in the bath, marveled at the choice of the word "working," and the "we." They implied equality, co-operation. Already he was drafted onto Murphy's team.

There was a plate of meat sandwiches and a bowl of fruit on the table, and Murphy waved him to the chair.

"Help yourself, Levin. Eat while we talk."

"Thank you."

"I know a lot about the operation in Kiev. What part did the girl play?"

Levin didn't look up as he munched a sandwich. "None. She was there for me."

"Tell me why you tried to speak to the President."

"He's making mistakes."

"Tell me."

"Have the East Germans confined your troops to their quarters yet?"

Murphy put down his drink and looked at Levin. "No. Is that what they're planning?"

"Yes."

"When?"

"Tomorrow."

"What excuse will they use?"

Levin shook his head. "They don't need an excuse. But they'll probably find one."

"What's the point, Levin?"

"They want to force you to make an aggressive response to give them an excuse to take Europe. And if you don't respond aggressively Europe will see that you're finished as a protector."

"What do you mean, 'take Europe'—actual warfare?"

"Yes."

"And what makes you think President Langham's making mistakes?"

"He hasn't reacted aggressively so far. If he had hit back right at the start the Presidium would have made the Red Army think again. They're not *all* for war. I don't think Langham will see this next incident as the touchstone it really is. The Presidium will decide which way to go next, on the United States's reaction to their troops being put under East German control."

"But you say that if we do nothing we're lost and if we react aggressively then they would start at least a local war. How do we win?"

Levin sighed. "You tell them tonight how you'll respond if they touch your troops. You get it up to U.S.-President and Soviet-Prime-Minister level. Away from the military people. Give the antiwar people something to make a case on."

Murphy stood up, wiping his mouth with the back of his hand. He walked through to the next room and picked up the red phone and asked for Shapiro. He talked for several minutes, sweeping his arm in unseen emphasis. After he had hung up he stood there for several minutes more before he walked back to the small room and Levin.

chapter
20

The limousines were lining up at the side door of the White House, and Marines were directing the drivers to the parking areas. The cars' occupants were escorted into the White House; their dress varied from tuxedos to tennis shorts and sweaters. The big table was already set out for the meeting, and the President came in as they settled down. He stubbed out his cigarette as he sat down. He was wearing a dark-blue suit and a startlingly white shirt. He looked very young, but there were younger men around the table. He leaned forward, arms on the table.

"We've got an hour to discuss a special situation, gentlemen. If we can do it in less it would be advantageous." He pointed. "That man is Shapiro. CIA. He's been controlling the surveillance of a setup in Russia. The clerks are duplicating full reports on the operation. They'll be ready in twenty minutes, but we can't wait that long. Shapiro, give them ten minutes on the operation. Then the present situation."

Langham's head thrust forward toward Shapiro to emphasize his orders. Shapiro stood up and Langham leaned back.

"No need to stand up, Shapiro."

Shapiro sat down and slid his one-page draft in front of him and glanced down. He related the essence of Operation

471 in seven minutes and twenty-two seconds. He looked to Langham, and the President looked around the table.

"Comments, gentlemen? Questions? But keep 'em short."

"How long have we known about this, Mr. President?" It was Larsen's deputy who asked the question.

"The whole operation, a matter of hours. Bits and pieces, over the last few months only."

The Chairman of the Joint Chiefs of Staff was bursting to speak and Langham nodded his release.

"General?"

"I can't see why we're wasting our time on this, Mr. President. They must be mad. It's like some crazy game."

The President gave him a long hard look. "I wouldn't mind having a man on my staff right now who had spent seven or eight months simulating Grechkov's reactions."

There were no other questions and Langham jabbed a finger at Shapiro. "Bring us up to date."

"We have made contact with the man, Andrei Levin, who has been simulating the President's reactions. He was the man who the Soviets said was running amok from the embassy—that was just a disinformation ploy by the KGB. He informs us that the Soviets intend to put our troops in Berlin under virtual arrest. The East German Army will carry out the operation and our buildings in Berlin will be under armed guard—armor, artillery, the lot. Levin says that they are determined to take Berlin and then the rest of Europe. He wants to warn the President because he thinks that we are beginning to make the wrong moves. He thinks he knows how we'll react and he thinks we'll be wrong. And he thinks this is our last chance to be right."

Langham half smiled. "Shapiro is being tactful, gentlemen. The Russian thinks my decision will be wrong. I'd like to hear your reactions."

They argued and counterargued for twenty minutes. The dossiers were brought in and distributed, but nobody even opened his copy. The meeting's proposals ranged from an immediate nuclear strike on the Soviet Union, through armed resistance, to taking no physical action but calling an emergency meeting of the UN Security Council.

Langham finally held up his hand to silence the various

protagonists. "Shapiro, what did this man Levin say I would do?"

"He said you would take no physical action but would call for a meeting of the Security Council."

"And why does he think that would be wrong? We've kept our noses clean so far."

The room was silent and everyone looked at Shapiro.

"Levin says that that would be seen as a United States surrender. No government would ever count us as an effective ally after that. They would leave it one week or two weeks for the world to get the point, and then they would ship our men to the border and that would be the end of us in Europe."

For the first time Langham's face did not conceal his anger. "And if we retaliate, defend ourselves, or go over the border and release them, we get labeled as aggressors and *they* call for a meeting of the Security Council." His voice was almost a shout.

Shapiro's face was pale and his mouth was closed tight. The Director of Central Intelligence nodded to him, and Shapiro coughed before he spoke.

"Levin has made a suggestion, Mr. President."

"What is it?"

"He suggests that you speak personally, or send a message, tonight, before they have taken the action, and tell them that we'll order our troops to open fire if any attempt is made to confine them. That we send reinforcements tonight to Berlin. He goes on to suggest that you offer a summit meeting between yourself and Grechkov and give them two hours to agree, otherwise you will convene a press conference tonight with Slanski and Levin as proof of what Russian intentions really are."

Langham looked around the silent faces at the table. "Any comments, gentlemen?"

Secretary Larsen leaned forward. "Are we sure that the two Russians would cooperate?"

Langham nodded at Shapiro.

"There's no doubt, Mr. Secretary. Levin risked his life to contact the President. Slanski is a sick man, but he will co-operate. I have no doubt on that score."

Langham looked down the table to the Chairman of the Joint Chiefs of Staff. "What's your view, David?"

"We can meet all the military requirements, Mr. President. Our men in Berlin already have standing orders to resist with force any attempt by the Soviets or East Germans to restrict their movements. But I imagine that in the present situation they might wait to contact the Pentagon, and that could be fatal. As you know, sir, the Pentagon favors a retaliatory move in Korea or Turkey. I think this is a political situation, Mr. President, and the present suggestion has the advantage of giving us back the initiative."

Two or three voices added their agreement. Langham waited a few moments for further comment and when none came he looked at his watch.

"It's seven o'clock Washington time. That means it's two o'clock tomorrow morning in Moscow. Shapiro, I want this man Levin over here soonest. General, get as many men as you can on their way to Berlin and repeat your instructions to headquarters Berlin. Warn them to be on full alert from now on. Erik, stay behind while we work out the message to Grechkov. Speak to Ambassador Forbes and see if he has any new background. But you tell him nothing of what we are doing."

When the others had left Langham took off his jacket and as he sat down he said to Larsen, "You know, Erik. That bastard was right. I *would* have taken it as one more attempt to provoke us. Those people in Moscow are going to have to come out in the open now as looking for a fight, or play ball. They'll grind *something* out of us, but with these two Russians in front of the world's press they're going to expose all this crap they've been talking about détente and peaceful intentions. But, by God, we're going to keep our powder dry from now on. What do you think—do I speak to Grechkov on the hot line or do I send him a message?"

"If you speak to him on the hot line he's going to be put on the spot. He has to react without being able to consult the Presidium. It's not easy to control a telephone conversation. You could get sidetracked. I suggest a message 'Eyes only Ambassador Forbes' and he goes straight to the Kremlin. I'll phone Gromyko to warn him that a top-security Presidential note is on its way."

"Would you let this guy Levin see it? He's going to have a view on how they'll react."

"OK."

An hour later Levin had been escorted into the Oval Office by Murphy. Larsen was already there. Langham saw the man's eyes take in the details of the room and then he said quietly, "Sit down, Mr. Levin."

The President looked at the handsome face, the alert eyes and the sensuous mouth. The ill-fitting clothes emphasized the man's position. For a second Langham was vividly aware of how lonely and disorientated this man must be. Langham moved a file to one side.

"I understand from my people that your place in Kiev was a replica of this room. Have you noticed any differences?"

Levin's face was strained and serious, as if this were some observation test.

"Yes, sir. This office is cleaner. I can smell the furniture polish."

Langham laughed, and even Larsen managed a faint smile.

"I think Mr. Murphy has told you what we are going to do." Langham's blue eyes looked at Levin's face as Levin nodded. "I want to show you the message that I am sending to Prime Minister Grechkov. I should like your comments."

Larsen handed two pages of typed text to Levin, who sat straight and silent in his chair as he read it slowly. When he had read the second page Levin started to read the typescript again. Finally he looked up at Langham.

"There are two points, Mr. President, but before I comment I should like to ask a favor."

Langham nodded.

"I should like to think about this message outside this office. I am too used to these surroundings. I must think like Grechkov, not like you. I would like to stand in your garden for a few minutes. With Mr. Murphy, of course."

Langham stood up, looking at Murphy. "Mr. Murphy, I'll

be down the hall in the press office. The Marine sergeant will take you both outside. Let me know when you are back. The white phone. Tell my secretary."

As they walked slowly down the corridor Langham half turned to Larsen. "That poor bastard must wonder who he is. You realize what we've done to him. One minute he's a respected professor at a university, then he does seven or eight months telling Moscow what he thinks I think, and now he's telling us what he thinks Grechkov thinks."

chapter
21

Murphy and Levin stood outside the Oval Office windows, the light from inside washing over the close-cropped grass. There was a faint streak of light low on the horizon, but the evening sky was clear and dark blue, and as Levin looked up it seemed a frightening fact that the same stars shone over the girl in Moscow. He shuddered and lowered his head, so that Murphy wondered if, with his eyes tight shut, he were praying. Levin found it hard to concentrate; too much had happened in the last two days, and even the smell of the new-mown grass distracted him.

A few minutes later he lifted his head and turned to Murphy. "I'm ready now."

Langham was back at his desk and Larsen sat in the chair facing Levin.

"I think there are two points, Mr. President," Levin began. "The first is a minor one. You take up the Soviet Premier on using the word 'demand' in an earlier note to you. This is a misunderstanding. There is a tendency when translating from Russian to refer to a French translation for diplomatic notes. So the word is, in French *demander*—to ask, in English, not demand. It would weaken a strong message to raise a point they would not understand.

"The second point I would raise is more important. There are members of the Politburo who will be against what they are doing. Not because they love the United States, but because they maintain that too much money is being diverted to military spending at the expense of industry and agriculture. If they could show that their way also gives benefits, then their views cannot be ignored. There are even marshals of the Soviet Union who think this way. It would be wise to give Grechkov a door to walk through. A prize. I'm thinking of technological assistance."

Langham gave no indication of agreement or disagreement. He looked at Levin's face. "What do you want to do, Mr. Levin?"

Levin shrugged. "To stay here, if you would allow that."

Murphy spoke up quickly. "I have agreed with Mr. Levin that we will arrange some deal to get Miss Kevan over here."

Langham raised his eyebrows. "You people must feel . . ." He shook his head. "Forget it. I agree." He leaned back, sighing deeply, "Good night, Mr. Levin."

Murphy took Levin back to Langley and found him a bed. He arranged for a guard to be mounted on Levin's room.

Langham signed papers for another hour and then tried to sleep in the annex. He had given orders that he was to be awakened at one o'clock.

chapter
22

At five o'clock in the morning the guards on all American-
and British-occupied buildings in Berlin had been doubled.
And instead of small arms they carried light machine guns.
Officers and men who lived out were called in, and arrangements were made for their families to assemble at Tempelhof
to be transported out when the reinforcements landed.

In Moscow it was already seven o'clock and Grechkov had
been in conference for two hours. The reply had already been
sent to the President of the United States, but there was a
reluctance for the meeting to disperse. At least two of the
earlier critics of Operation 471 were acutely aware of how
valuable Levin would have been at that moment.

Langham had sat with Larsen reading the Soviet Premier's
message.

Mr. President:

My colleagues of the Presidium and I have studied
your note with diligence. I have checked with my neigh-
bors of the German Democratic Republic. No orders
have been given to embarrass United States troops in
Berlin by them or by the Soviet Union. This is yet another example of reactionary groups in the West attempting to foment hostilities between our two countries.

However, the matter of Berlin has to be resolved immediately. The Soviet Union will not tolerate the present use of Berlin by Western troublemakers. I am willing to meet you to resolve this matter provided a satisfactory solution can be achieved in the next two months.

We look to close cooperation between our two great peoples on many fronts.

GRECHKOV

Langham pushed the sheet of paper away from him, the large type face still catching his eye. He forced himself to look away.

"What do you make of it, Erik?"

"I've got views, sir, but why not get Levin in to discuss his views?"

"OK. Shapiro's out at Langley. Get him to bring Levin in right away."

Levin had read the message carefully and had smiled as he put the paper back on the table.

Langham looked at him. "How do you read this?"

Levin went to lean back into a tutorial posture and then remembered where he was. He leaned forward. "He refers to the Presidium to give himself cover if things go wrong. That is important, Mr. President. He is not sure of the outcome yet.

"He denies that they intend to harass the U.S. troops in Berlin. So you win that point.

"He talks of cooperation on many fronts. That is what I said to you. They need, desperately, your technology. And they need your grain. And they need your neutrality vis-à-vis Peking.

"But I think you have to look seriously at Berlin. Berlin is the detonator, not the dynamite. I cannot help but say that since I was involved in this situation I have never understood why the United States clings so desperately to Berlin." He paused. "Am I allowed to speak frankly, Mr. President?"

Langham looked frosty, but he nodded.

"The Soviets genuinely see Berlin as a deliberate provocation by the Americans. I myself agree. It is a hotbed of espionage in the heart of another country. It is the equivalent of their having Soviet troops in Toronto or Montreal. You stay in Berlin because you cannot leave. And now, in this situation, it makes it even more impossible to leave. Prestige and power are involved. But you should leave. There are ways of saving face."

Larsen interrupted. "Levin, you yourself said that if we left Berlin the Soviets would have made their point. We would have no allies in the whole of Europe."

"May I make a suggestion, Mr. Secretary?"

Larsen nodded.

"Let us say that it is the United States proposal that *all* foreign troops should leave Berlin. And that the United Nations is responsible for supervising the administration of the city until an armistice for the Second World War is finally signed."

"That means you think that Berlin *was* the objective of this saber-rattling?"

"Oh no, Mr. President, the object was to either defeat the United States or humiliate it before the world. Berlin was an excuse. An excuse that all the world would have accepted as reasonable."

"You think the Soviets would agree to your suggestion?"

"They remain looking reasonable in the eyes of the world. They win nothing but a compromise. They are ahead of the United States in all arms, but they have problems. And those problems would surface like monsters when the first nuclear missiles exploded in the USSR. The Russian mind is strange for Westerners to understand. Détente is only partly bluff. They want to expand, they are imperialists, but they can afford to wait. And time is everything in politics."

Langham had looked hard and long at Levin. He opened his mouth to speak and then closed it. He stood up slowly as if he had forgotten the others, and then he said, "Thank you, Mr. Levin. You can go."

After Shapiro and Levin had left, Langham turned to the Secretary of State. "I've seen a file somewhere. A feasibility study on the benefits of leaving Berlin. Do you remember it?"

"There are three, Mr. President. One by my staff, one by the Pentagon and one by the CIA."

"Let's have a look at them."

Larsen and the President drafted the reply to Grechkov. They showed it to Levin, who said only "Yes" as he handed it back. The message was transmitted immediately, direct to the Kremlin, bypassing the U.S. ambassador in Moscow.

> DEAR MR. CHAIRMAN:
>
> The central issue in your last note to me is the future position of Berlin. The four Allied governments, including the Soviet Union, have troops in the city under the provisions of the Potsdam Agreement of 1945. This is a right for all concerned, not a concession by any government, including the German Democratic Republic.
>
> However, some of the hopes and intentions of the immediate postwar years have not been fulfilled and there is scope to review the situation. I have consulted with the governments of Great Britain and France, and with ourselves the three governments would be willing to put forward to the Security Council of the United Nations the following proposals:
>
> 1. That all troops are withdrawn from Berlin.
> 2. That this includes troops of the United States, the USSR, Great Britain, France and the German Democratic Republic.
> 3. That the United Nations should oversee this withdrawal and maintain an inspection team in Berlin for five years following the withdrawal.
> 4. That such withdrawal should take place within sixty days from our signing such an agreement.
>
> The United States Secretary of State and your Foreign Minister are both attending the inaugural session of the Scottish Parliament in Edinburgh in ten days' time, and I suggest that they discuss this proposal at that time.
>
> T. LANGHAM

Grechkov had called in Gromyko and Marshal Chuikov. The Russian and English texts of Langham's message lay on the table between them. Grechkov was smoking a cigar and his eyes were half closed from the smoke—and, perhaps, to ensure that the other two could read no hint of his reaction from his face.

"Gromyko, let's hear from you."

Gromyko had been around the top too long to need to play the courtier.

"So far as the outside world is concerned we should have achieved our point. We can get one of the Africans to raise a question in the General Assembly that will make the Security Council back off from the inspection team. The East Germans will be delighted and after this we can insist that they can sign the new constitution. Internally I can't speak. There will be some ruffled feathers, but Chuikov can deal with those."

Grechkov held up his big hand and looked at the marshal. "Can you do that, Chuikov?"

"Yes. A few promotions, a few decorations. But I think we bear one thing in mind—" he leaned back and looked hard at the other two—"this is not what we wanted. There will have to be another day. Berlin is just a snack, the Army was looking forward to a five-course meal. This is a political thing. The Red Army can walk through Europe any time you give the order."

Grechkov smiled as he tapped off the ash from his cigar. "You're right, Chuikov. There will be other days. And it must not be too far ahead. This will have alerted them. Congress will open the money bags now. Keep them uneasy, Chuikov. Turkey or Korea could play a part now."

Gromyko picked up the sheet of paper. "And the meeting in Edinburgh?"

Grechkov made a cutting motion of dismissal with his big arm. "You know how to deal with that, Andrei. Tell them we will sign next week or whenever they are ready. There is no need to make a diplomatic circus out of it."

He stood up, pushing back his chair and moving his big hands as if he were conducting an orchestra, and he said, "And warn Andropov to pass the list of CIA people in Berlin to the East Germans. Those who leave *we* can watch. Those who stay they put inside. There will be a new role for the KGB in Berlin from now on. There will be some scores to settle."

The Secretary of State had phoned Gromyko about the girl. Gromyko had feigned ignorance and said he would have to check. It took another two days to negotiate a deal. They were willing to trade, but they wanted Levin. They reluctantly settled for Velichko. A disgusted and angry Larsen left the details to Shapiro.

The three men sitting at the white table, just out of the range of the lawn sprinkler, could have been old friends discussing golf swings or the wisdom of installing computerized accountancy. But they were not.

Shapiro had done it all before, and knew the hazards. Murphy treated it as an extension of his experience, and Levin couldn't decide whether it was a dream or a nightmare.

Shapiro was looking at Levin as he talked. "For the first four months we want you to take it easy. No job. No work. Just relax. We've rented a nice little place for you in California and you can stay down there with the girl. After that we have fixed for you to work with a research team at one of the foundations. I gather the salary is somewhere around forty-five thousand a year and the usual side benefits. We have arranged citizenship for you under a new name, and Murphy will give you those documents tomorrow. Any questions?"

Levin uncrossed his legs. His voice was strained and thin. "What about the girl?"

Shapiro looked at Murphy, who finished his drink before speaking.

"She's arriving tomorrow. The Russians bring her to the mainland, and an Air Force chopper will bring her down here. You will be meeting her with us. Sometime in the middle of the morning if everything goes on schedule."

"You have doubts?"

"None whatever. But there's always the weather."

Levin looked back at Shapiro. "And we have permission to marry?"

218

"You don't need permission, Levin. It's up to you and the girl. Just tell Murphy and he'll arrange things. It's easier if he does it, because of your new identity. You'll need supporting documents."

Levin's face turned toward Murphy. "You asked her?"

Murphy smiled. "Don't worry, Andrei. She wants to marry you all right."

"Why do I need a false identity?"

The two CIA men exchanged glances, and it was Shapiro who spoke. "It's a wise precaution, Levin. The people in Moscow are always touchy about these things. Let's give them time to cool off." Shapiro stood up and held out his hand. "Have a good rest, enjoy yourselves. I'll see you before you start the new job." As Levin took his hand Shapiro said, "I forgot to mention. We've opened an account for you. Murphy'll give you the details, but there's ten thousand dollars there if you two want to buy things."

Shapiro stood watching as the two men walked across the wide lawns and ducked under the rose-covered archway to the drive.

chapter
23

The two men in white doctor's coats pushed the stretcher carefully over the rough gravel path. The man at the rear steadied it with only one hand. The other hand gripped the pistol inside the big patch pocket.

There was a pillow under Velichko's head, but the ground was so uneven that his head bounced loosely as the stretcher moved forward. The sparse strands of red hair blew in the wind, aimlessly, adding to, and emphasizing, the inertness of the big head, and the pale pasty face. The bulging eyes were closed, and a bubble of saliva at the pale lips was the only indication that Velichko was alive.

At the guard post the convoy stopped, and one of the men tucked in a loose fold of the red-lined blanket. On the far side of the pole were two Russians in uniform with two civilians and, in front of them, a captain and two NCO's of the East German Army.

A major in KGB uniform stood outside the guardroom door, talking into a telephone whose cable coiled and looped back into the wooden hut.

The white-coated man at the rear of the stretcher held a walkie-talkie radio to his ear, the aerial extended. The KGB major looked across at the two men, held up his hand and nodded. The red-and-white-painted pole swung up, and the trolley was pushed to the edge of the white line. The wind tugged at the white coats as the two men waited. It was beginning to rain.

A few minutes later the KGB major raised his hand again and the man with the radio released the pistol and raised his hand, too, and the stretcher was pushed forward. The major walked forward without hurrying. He stood alongside the stretcher looking down at Velichko's pale face. His hand slid under the blanket, pulled out Velichko's right arm and felt for his pulse. A few moments later he waved to the NCO's, and they wheeled the stretcher to the side of a green van. The major smiled, casually saluted, and the two men in white coats walked back to the American army ambulance.

Panov had dragged the camouflaged nylon sheet from the clump of trees. It was the false dawn and already some birds were tentatively singing, and wood pigeons were shifting about heavily in the lower branches of the beeches. He was wearing a dark-green army-style shirt and green slacks. He had eaten before the first signs of light, when the pale moon was still high and full in the sky.

The bunker had been raked late the previous day, and the top layer of sand was still wet from the night dew. Panov carefully brushed away the sand where he would lie, and as he stretched out on the ground it was warm to his chest and legs. He looked through the rough grass along the lip of the bunker. The two lines of the white cross that they had painted on the fairway were both visible. The distance was 926 yards exactly. He had paced it out in the darkness, and with the image-intensifier night sight the white cross was just visible.

He lay covered by the camouflage sheet, with only his head out of cover. If they were on time there would be five hours more to wait. He slid the small walkie-talkie from his shirt pocket and spooled out the flexible aerial. The embassy responded immediately, and they talked in Ukrainian. The flight was still on time and the headwinds were abating. The American air controller had given them a course, but they suspected that they would be diverted from New York to Logan International at Boston at the last minute. He switched off the radio and slid it back into his pocket.

An hour later he watched the radio unit set up its van alongside the clubhouse, and shortly before eight o'clock he heard the sirens of the police cars on Ridge Road as they started to erect the detour signs. By nine o'clock the visibility across the golf course was poor. The sun was fetching up a surface mist from the night dew. When it cleared an hour later there were three or four cars parked at the clubhouse and a TV crew was mounting a camera on a structure of scaffolding.

At ten-fifteen he saw the black embassy car sweep in front of the clubhouse, and he watched Saratov as, smiling, he shook hands with several of the waiting people. Ten minutes later the radio bleeped just once, and he switched on and held it against his ear. The plane *had* been diverted to Boston. The girl had been given documents and had been in an office for fifteen minutes. Her escort was Vassili Yevgeni, who had been joined now by a CIA man named Murphy. The helicopter had just taken off. Its ETA at Fort Dupont Park was eleven-forty approximately.

Bob Fowler sat on the clubhouse steps, the wind ruffling his hair and the notes on his clipboard. He looked out across the fairway. There were so many angles to this story. Too many angles. A Russian who had been a surrogate President in a replica White House. Who had been used by the real President of the United States. A man who had risked his life because he believed he could stop World War III. A beautiful Irish girl, with an obvious Irish name, who had been the man's lover and was now being traded, on orders from the White House, for a Russian defector. All the scenario needed now was Judy Garland and Rin-tin-tin.

Saratov had looked at him coldly and had refused curtly when Fowler had asked him for his comments. The White House staff wasn't going to say anything, and Harcourt had said that he had paid all his debts, and more, with this exclusive. Fowler looked aside to the small, neat monitor a couple of steps lower down. It showed just a rectangle of verdant green and a white cross where the chopper would touch down. All three networks were taking the program.

McMahon, the press association man in Moscow, had told

him on the phone last night that the Red Army and the Presidium were kicking the hell out of the KGB on account of Levin and Slanski. The Soviets still looked good to the rest of the world, but the Americans had come out all square. And Moscow had heard the crackle of very thin ice under their boots. He wondered what Levin would do now. It ought to be a post at one of the universities, but there was always the chance that the KGB might try to even the score. They were patient, persistent bastards, and they had all the time in the world.

Shapiro was standing alongside Saratov, away from the crowd. There was a small enclosure roped off from the rest of the people.

Both men wore lightweight headphones that were joined at a junction box on the grass. They both listened intently to the radio traffic.

"Special flight Charlie Yankee Zero Niner. . . . We are four miles northeast of Fort Dupont Park. . . . Can I have clearance please. . . ."

"Controller to pilot. . . . Hold in standard pattern at five hundred feet. . . ."

Then another voice came on with a heavy Russian accent. "Embassy to ambassador. . . . We have received confirmation from Helmstedt crossing point that transfer has been made. Codeword 'Ladybird' operating. Over."

Saratov turned and nodded to a man in civilian clothes standing by the signals van. He went up the three steps and stayed inside. A few seconds later the crackle came on again.

"Ground controller to pilot Charlie Yankee Zero Niner. Proceed and land. Over."

The word had gone through from the embassy to Panov, and the long canvas bag was already open. Without taking his eyes off the fairway he drew up the rifle, pulled down the bipod, and dug it into the lip of the bunker. The night sight was already on, and only the flash eliminator projected from under the camouflage sheet as Panov pulled it over his head and along the barrel of the rifle. It was an L39A1. Superbly accurate at long range, with a muzzle velocity of 2,800 feet per second. It could penetrate a concrete building from end to end and still have killing velocity when the bullet emerged. Ricochets would travel three-quarters of a mile.

Under the sheet it was hot and there was a stink of oil from the breech and the chamber.

Shapiro came out of the clubhouse with Levin. The Russian was wearing a tweed sports jacket and plaid trousers. On Fowler's monitor he saw that the screen showed the two men. As it lifted up to close on their faces the red light came on, and Fowler could hear the grinding clatter of the helicopter.

He started the lead-in and gave a rundown on Levin and the assistance that he had given to the White House. The Soviets, he said, were also grateful for Levin's help in achieving a peaceful solution to the problems in Berlin, and were bringing over his fiancée, a beautiful Irish girl, who was joining him in his new life in the United States.

As the chopper bounced down, the Marine escort party placed the steps in position and stood smartly to attention.

Murphy came down the steps first and then held out his hand to help the girl. She was wearing a broad-brimmed white hat and a white dress that clung to her body. She was smiling as she looked toward the crowd at the clubhouse. She was gorgeous. From the corner of his eye Fowler saw Levin move forward, and Shapiro was smiling as if he were the bride's father.

The camera was on the girl's face, and the joy displayed there was the envy of every man who watched. Her arms were wide stretched as she ran, and Levin was grinning as he loped toward her, his hair flopping like a schoolboy's. The camera picked him up and zoomed in.

The two shots were barely audible. The first one punched Levin around so that his arms flew out as if he were in water. And the TV audience and the watchers on the spot saw the second impact as Levin's skull seemed to explode like a rose-colored melon.